Magnetic Dogs

Stories

ESSENTIAL PROSE SERIES 202

ONTARIO ARTS COUNCIL
CONSEIL DES ARTS DE L'ONTARIO
an Ontario government agency
un organisme du gouvernement de l'Ontario

Canada Council   Conseil des arts
for the Arts   du Canada

Guernica Editions Inc. acknowledges the support of
the Canada Council for the Arts and the Ontario Arts Council.
The Ontario Arts Council is an agency of the Government of Ontario.
We acknowledge the financial support of the Government of Canada

Magnetic Dogs

Stories

Bruce Meyer

GUERNICA
EDITIONS

TORONTO • CHICAGO • BUFFALO • LANCASTER (U.K.)
2022

Guernica Founder: Antonio D'Alfonso

Michael Mirolla, editor
Interior and cover design: Rafael Chimicatti
Guernica Editions Inc.
287 Templemead Drive, Hamilton, ON L8W 2W4
2250 Military Road, Tonawanda, N.Y. 14150-6000 U.S.A.
www.guernicaeditions.com

Distributors:
Independent Publishers Group (IPG)
600 North Pulaski Road, Chicago IL 60624
University of Toronto Press Distribution (UTP)
5201 Dufferin Street, Toronto (ON), Canada M3H 5T8
Gazelle Book Services, White Cross Mills
High Town, Lancaster LA1 4XS U.K.

First edition.
Printed in Canada.

Legal Deposit—Third Quarter
Library of Congress Catalog Card Number: 2021949831
Library and Archives Canada Cataloguing in Publication
Title: Magnetic dogs : stories / Bruce Meyer.
Names: Meyer, Bruce, 1957- author.
Series: Essential prose series ; 202.
Description: Series statement: Essential prose series ; 202
Identifiers: Canadiana (print) 20210362413 | Canadiana (ebook)
20210362456 | ISBN 9781771837491 (softcover)
ISBN 9781771837507 (EPUB)
Classification: LCC PS8576.E93 M345 2022 | DDC C813/.54—dc23

Tell the things you can't forget
that History puts a saint in every dream.
　　　—Tom Waits, *Time*

Always know.
　　　—Thelonious Monk

CONTENTS

CANTIQUE
DE JEAN RACINE

I LOVE MUSIC FOR ITS FRAILTY. I believe every note has an afterlife, not merely silence, and that is what has brought me to the École Niedermeyer today to research the failure and triumph of sounds that last forever. The academy is tucked away in the *15th Arrondissement* where a web of streets with literary names – Rue Victor Hugo, Rue Diderot – encircle it in a harmony of cultural allusions. The new building is just as grey and formidable as the one it replaced in the Sixties; yet behind those grey walls, some of the greatest French music was created. This was the school where Gabriel Fauré triumphed over every possible obstacle that his teachers and their teachers put in his way to compose the "Cantique de Jean Racine."

The École Niedermeyer is the cradle of French music, the birthplace of almost every familiar French melody, save for "La Marseillaise" and "Frère Jacques." The interior hallway is concrete and feels military; the old school that once stood here resembled a barracks. The grey walls echo with failure. I can feel it the moment I enter because the foyer, at least, is cold, concrete, and inscrutable in its modern brutalist appearance.

The École still offers an annual competition, the Prix d'École Niedermeyer, a prize for the best new work by a student. I am here to search for the facts behind the award the year it was given to the second-best composition by a student because the judges refused to give the prize to the best. That decision may, arguably, have changed the course of French music. The prize I am researching raises many questions. How do you judge a piece of music, or any art for that matter, that is so far ahead of its time it grows in strength and beauty with each decade and needs to be heard again and again? How do you see into the future when you gaze at a musical score and say, 'Yes, that is the one people will want to hear for more than a few months. That is one that will be heard a hundred lifetimes from now.' I smile at the old desk clerk as I sit in the waiting area for the archivist to come and fetch me and take me to the stacks of boxes on the third floor where I will find the score I want to settle. Settling scores is what resides at the heart of prizes. The clerk does not smile back.

And what is the score?

Picture a young pupil of keyboard composition. He's in a competitive place. The artist needs to compete. He needs to prove he has a place in the conversation of his craft. The older students say he shouldn't be there. He's too young. His military-style uniform, mandatory for students of his time, is baggy. His family cannot afford a better-fitting outfit. Young man in a hurry, his teachers label him with damning admiration.

I have seen the picture of the boyish student in the long blue school uniform. He is leaning with a manly aura of bravado on a plinth, a score tucked under his arm, and his left hand in his pocket. He's talented and he wants to prove he's talented. He has polished his buttons. He's only nine years old when he enters the École, but he wants to begin composing. His composition teacher, M. Saint-Saëns who is, himself, only twenty-two years old, warns him about the "Mozart Factor" – the idea of becoming too much, too soon, the gluey, fallen soufflé that comes out of the oven before it is baked. He must avoid becoming the brat who places himself in the position of dismissible. No one likes a genius. Prepare yourself, everyone tells him. The future will happen, but he will have to wait a lifetime because there are others in line ahead of him who are going to get their prizes first.

When people say, "prepare yourself," to a young, precocious artist, they have two ulterior motives in mind. The first is that 'The Establishment' does not want the young man in a hurry to outshine those who have paid their dues. That's a terrible artistic dictum – the horrible term *paying your dues*. There is no such thing as dues. One either learns the art and expresses what he has learned to the best of his ability or he's second rate at what he does. Dues are another word for "not so fast, buddy, there are people with more pressing claims in line ahead of you." It means someone feels threatened by what is coming down the pike. It means that the artistic world is mean-spirited at heart and despises prodigies. That's what killed Mozart: the venom of other artists and his own prodigiousness.

The second thing that comes to mind is that the people who say, "prepare yourself," have their own favourites they are betting on. They want their favourites to win. Art is a wager. They will do anything, even break the rules of a competition, to make sure their artist and no one else wins. There is no such thing as a competition under such circumstances. There is only the pre-chosen favourite and the *fait accompli*. Case closed.

A thin woman in a tweed skirt and a mohair cardigan, the very image of an archivist, appears at the desk and is motioned toward me by the old clerk who senses her presence but does not look up from his copy of *Le Figaro* and points a boney finger in my direction. The archivist introduces herself in that clipped, rapid French that is so precise and over-pronounced yet so hard to ascertain. It is the mark of a learned Parisian. I do not catch her complete name and refer to her as Madame in my reply.

When Fauré was ready to enter the École's competition in 1863, he won but was disqualified on a technicality. The fix was in for him from the start. The École simply did not want another Mozart on their hands. They told their aspiring composer – not their best student, though, but the most aspiring one – that great music is made the same way great cognac is made: slowly.

Maybe the proverbial "powers-that-be" were putting their aspiring composer on notice for a reason. Every remark of encouragement, prizes included, is a double-edged sword. The mark of a stratified artistic milieu is the fear of original genius. That is what Gabriel Fauré was facing in 1863. He was a terrifying genius. The rules of the game, the laws of the milieu, say that a person should never tell a genius he is a genius until he is too old to care that he is.

The box of papers I want to examine might give me a clue about how genius comes down to making brilliant ideas into brilliant realities. The book I am writing is about whether prizes and awards are indicators of genius. The archivist I am following up the grand staircase reminds me of a Modigliani figure. I feel as if I am back at school as I walk several paces behind her. I look over the railing into the atrium where students, mostly twenty-somethings, pour over scores, bite the tops off their biros, or scroll through their Facebook messages looking for clues as to who is saying what about who and who the social network favours on that particular day. I explain to Madame that I am looking in the archives, letters, and correspondence for information about the Prix d'École of 1863.

The archivist stops abruptly. She turns and looks down on me two steps below her. I suspect I am about to be lectured, but instead, she says nothing. She knows what I will find. I will discover boyish letters, supplications of consideration by Fauré for his entry, a feathery yet still uncertain hand in which notes flutter on the lines of a stave like birds on the metal balustrades of the Second Empire faux balcony outside my hotel window.

Those birds stare in at me with the same penetrating look of "you aren't really serious, are you?" that the archivist gives me with her silence.

The archivist and I arrive at the top of the stairs. I look over my shoulder at the long flight I've just conquered. The prim middle-aged woman is not even slightly breathless. She does the climb several times a day. I think she deserves a prize for being in such decent shape. She seats me at a teak table and I pull the chair under me as if I am about to embark on a multi-course meal. After disappearing behind the scenes and returning with a grey box, she places the box in my hands along with a pair of white cotton gloves.

I stare at the box. It is the reason I came to Paris. I wanted to see for myself what Gabriel Fauré experienced the first time he entered a competition and won, and lost, all for the same work. Fauré entered the École Niedermeyer Composition Competition in 1863 at the age of seventeen with the idea that he had paid his dues during the years he had studied at the École, and that his score of Psalm 126, the dream psalm, was the apotheosis of his learning.

Fauré should have won his first competition, but he didn't. The people in charge saw to it that he would not win. They may have had his best interests at heart, but that's just conjecture. He wasn't cognac. He was a kid who wanted to prove himself. He knew he was good. Maybe he was cocky, and the old guard spotted that and wanted to nip that sense of social self-exaggeration in the bud. Instantaneous fame can be the worst thing that can happen to an artist.

I once heard a Canadian poet, Louis Dudek, remark that to be a poet at twenty is to be twenty, but to be a poet at forty is to be a poet. The bastard aspect in that piece of sage is that he said it to Leonard Cohen when Cohen was twenty. Put down? That's never been determined. *Ars longa, vita brevis*, as Chaucer said. A true artist must become a student of his art without any hope of graduating. Either way, success early or success late buries an artist. That's part of my thesis as well.

I put on the white gloves that could have been stolen from a street mime. The box contains the expected letters. The letter submitting the entry for the 1863 competition is polite, aulic, and addresses the judges of the École with due reverence. The next item in the box is the score. In Fauré's immature hand, the text of Psalm 126 is written out. It is the King James Version translated fairly precisely into French. It is an odd choice of psalm – a translation of a translation of a translation where all the levels of meaning compete with one another to convey their message. It reminds me of the cacophony I heard on the sidewalk as I approached the École.

The choice of the 126th Psalm as the text for his score was, on Fauré's part, a cheeky venture. The words of the 126th are about youthful hope, aspiration, the realization of dreams even when they seem impossible. It is a young man's psalm, and the choice of text suggests that perhaps Fauré knew that the fix was in, that no matter what he wrote he wouldn't win:

> When the Lord turned again the captivity of Zion, we were like them that dream. | Then was our mouth filled with laughter, and our tongue with singing: then said they among the heathen, The Lord hath done great things for them. | The Lord hath done great things for us; *whereof* we are glad. | Turn again our captivity, O Lord, as the streams in the south. | They that sow in tears shall reap in joy. | He that goeth forth weepeth, bearing precious seed, shall doubtless come again with rejoicing, and bring his sheaves *with him*.

The score for the Psalm is melodic, pastoral, and lilting. It is beautiful not only for the music Fauré devises for it, but for the powerful sense of aspiration in the words. It is not a despondent psalm but a longing paean, and in the eyes of a young, aspiring composer who aches to achieve artistic excellence, he need only look at what the Lord had done for previous winners in terms of acclaim and advancement to realize that the same could be done for him.

The next item in the box is a copy of an anonymous letter from the chief judge of the competition informing Fauré that his composition was by far the best and easily the winner, but the prize for the year would go to another student, Etienne Bernard, because Fauré had set Psalm 126 in the wrong key. The key should have been G rather than D. The flabbergasted Fauré writes in response, rather hurriedly and in shaken handwriting – he could transpose the piece if it was the best submission. I can imagine the young man standing outside the director's office, his head bowed, and his voice choked as he pleads for an alteration in the opinion, but the judges' words are final. Perhaps that angry bang I heard coming from a keyboard earlier when I waited in the foyer was the ghost of the young, broken-hearted Gabriel Fauré, thwarted, frustrated, and aware that his best, the best, was not good enough.

I ask for the box of correspondence between Bernard and the judges from 1863. "Ah, oui," says the archivist. She knows I have put two and two together and am on to something. The score for Bernard's work was, indeed, in the proper key, but its text is mundane, to say the least. He chose Leviticus 23:36-39, a passage about what one should do on the Sabbath to prepare a sacrifice to God, a meal of burnt offerings:

> These are the feasts of the Lord, which ye shall proclaim *to be* holy convocations, to offer an offering made by fire unto the Lord, a burnt offering, and a meat offering, a sacrifice, and drink offerings, every thing upon this day

I shake my head. The gastronomically correct French would shudder to listen to such a litany of charred foods: yet for all its intense listing of rules, it follows the rules. Those who follow the rules of others rarely do anything original.

Orthodoxy in religion has its equal measure in art, and especially in literature and music. If someone in charge says, "this is the way it is going to be done," then everyone who wants to be blessed in some measure must follow the same rules. This is the *trieste* of art. Epigoni abound. Bernard was only doing his duty as a conscientious student composer in a brass-button coat when he chose his Levitican setting for choir and organ: but he wasn't making art. The passage has a kind of finger-wagging quality to it. It wasn't even material for a good restaurant review. I asked the archivist if a copy of his score was available in the École's holdings. After about twenty minutes, as she rustled around in the shelves behind the large teak door, she returned with a curt "*non*."

While she was gone, I busied myself with Fauré's box of letters and records. I expected to find a letter where he expressed disappointment, perhaps even anger. There was a protest letter from Fauré's keyboard teacher, Camille Saint-Saëns, and a letter asking for the judges to reconsider their decision from a fellow student, César Franck, but they were politely worded and ineffectual. Someday, their voices would count as artillery in a debate about what French music should be, but not in 1863. They were nobodies in those days. They were not part of the ruling clique. When artistic milieus are weak or are going through a period of transition from old ways to the new, cliques always dominate the conversation. The old guard fights a rearguard action. They protect the old ways. Anger, under such circumstances, is futile. Cliques work best when they muffle any expressions of outrage.

I wanted to hear that note banged on the low keys in rage. That's what Lorca called *duende*, especially if it was a sour, minor chord. Instead, there was a polite reply by Fauré to the Director of the École stating that he would be trying again in the next competition, and he expressed his congratulations to M. Etienne Bernard. The handwriting, however, was emphatic. It was not the gentle, wispy strokes of the previous letters. Something had changed in Gabriel Fauré's character. He had ceased to be an innocent boy. He had become certain.

In the later life portraits of Fauré, his shock of white hair is the second thing one notices. The first thing is the upward tilt of his chin. Something happened to the shy and slightly awkward boy who is leaning on the plinth in the early photograph. Yes, he grew up; but growing up entails benchmarks, moments when someone is transformed by what they see or what they experience, moments from which there is no turning back. Such moments make the person who that individual becomes. Fauré became resolute in his mastery of a new idiom of musical composition that would become instantly recognizable to anyone in the world. He created the sound of French music.

In the box beneath the letter to the Director congratulating Bernard, I find Fauré's entry in the competition from the following year. 1864. The score is written in a bold, accurate, hand. Every note makes a statement on the page, and to the ear every sound is there for a purpose as if ennobled by the other notes around it. It is a composition that rises above itself. The opening bars of the piano and organ appear to be dissonant and working against each other. The organ presents a flowing repetition of melody that reminds me of a brook babbling through a forest, a steady, insistent presence that knows it will eventually build into a mighty river though it has only emerged as a spring from the earth.

I am being poetic about it, but the opening of the 1864 composition has always puzzled me. The male voices of the choir pick up the thread established by the piano and what they sing, oh what they sing is magical. The literal translation of the opening lyrics, "Word equal with the Most High …" Equal. His word. God's word. The word given by divine inspiration.

Fauré is laying down a statement. He is saying that on a level field, all things being equal, with no favourites, no predetermined scripts for the outcome of the competition, music alone will triumph. And when I examine the English lyrics, I see the composer reaching beyond himself as if to touch a distant star:

> Word of God, one with the Most High,
> In Whom alone we have our hope,
> Eternal Day of heaven and earth,
> We break the silence of the peaceful night;
> Saviour Divine, cast your eyes upon us!

The words are the work of Jean Racine, a French poet and cleric who published *Hymnes traduites du Breviare romain* in 1688. For his key, Fauré found his métier, D-flat Major, a key that years later his student, Maurice Ravel, would use for the famous *Concerto for the Left Hand*. I understand why Ravel chose that key as I examine the score for the 1864 competition. It is the key of suffering.

And therein resides the reason I sought out Fauré's composition and the story of its birth from a competition. Fauré is attempting to speak of eternal, divine love as if through a veil of human suffering. The second verse of Racine's breviary passage reads like a prayer for salvation from the fires and agonies of suffering:

> Pour on us the fire of your powerful grace,
> That all hell may flee at the sound of your voice;
> Banish the slumber of a weary soul,
> That brings forgetfulness of your laws!

Forgetfulness of rules and restrictions on art is more like it. Fauré realizes as he sets Racine's words to music that the earliest competitions were a form of agony. *Agon* is the ancient

Greek word for competitor. Each autumn, the streets of Athens would run red with the blood of slaughtered animals as they passed through the city from the high summer pastures to the low grazing grounds where winter resources had to be carefully meted out. The strong would survive. The weak would have to be culled from the herds of sheep, and especially the goats. The slaughter of the goats, their bleating cries, their screams of agony, must have been horrible to the ear. *Tragedy*. Goat song. The key of tragedy is D-Flat Major. It is the key of man wrestling with his demons. It is the key in which Ravel set his *Concerto for the Left Hand* and gave it to the Austrian concert pianist Paul Wittgenstein who had lost his right hand in the Great War. Ravel's choice of key is his homage to his teacher. Fauré had stood up for his pupil against the same forces and doltish mentality that selected the work of Etienne Bernard. When Ravel was disqualified from a similar student competition thirty years later at the Paris Conservatoire, the key of D-Flat Major was Ravel's homage to his steadfast teacher, and a way of saying to Fauré, *I know what it is like to lose a competition with the best entry in the race, and I know the whole world has lost a competition of life versus death. The world has known* agony.

As I stared at the opening choral passages of Fauré's entry for the 1864 competition, I could hear in my head the low male voices of the chorus. They were like souls of the damned crying out from the depths of Dante's hell. I knew where I had heard them recently. The voices were the ones I heard crying from a frame on a gallery wall.

A few days ago, when I was visiting the D'Orsay, I came across a small exhibition of etchings by the early twentieth-century artist André Devambez, and as I paused in front of one of Devambez's works, Fauré's composition jumped into my head, and I began to weep. Devambez, Ravel, and so many others whose works vanished into the muds at Verdun – they understood what suffering was.

The etching by Devambez that I could not pass by – I spent two hours studying it intensely – is of a group of soldiers, observed from a high vantage point. In the centre of the etching is a black dot. It is a priest. The jagged outlines around the black dot are the troops taking mass and receiving the last rites before they march out into the white void that is no-man's land. Ravel served in the French artillery, and the experience drove him to deafness so that for the remainder of his life, he clung to the memory of music rather than its reality, just as Beethoven had done a century earlier. And as I stood and stared at those figures, those men who were clustered around the black dot, searching for an inner solace and peace that offered them only fear and uncertainty, I heard the male voices that emerge from the dissonance of the opening of Fauré's 1864 composition. "We break the silence of the peaceful night … cast your eyes upon us!" Their voices are trapped in the key of mourning, and only prayer offers them a way out.

But the key of D-flat major has another meaning. It is not merely the key of suffering and despair, but of emergence, of the individual rising out of the depths of despair and defeat and finding the human soul intact, the small light that still shines after a long darkness. It is the key that says a composer has come to an epiphany, has seen something divine beyond our suffering, and something greater than ourselves rising out of our despair, and is willing to champion that small spark and set it ablaze amidst the agony and tragedy, to offer a promise of redemption. Fauré's 1864 composition, *Cantique de Jean Racine,* concludes with the lyrics:

> *O Christ, look with favour upon your faithful people*
> *Now gathered here to praise you;*
> *Receive their hymns offered to your immortal glory;*
> *May they go forth filled with your gifts.*

And with that, Fauré *was* filled with something miraculous. There was no question. To deny him the prize in the 1864 competition would have been a travesty against art. The *Cantique de Jean Racine* won the Prix d'École Niedermeyer that year. The last item in the box is Fauré's thank you letter to the Director of the École. And as I tuck it away with the other papers I have spent the morning reading, I ask myself how many people may have heard of the Prix d'École Niedermeyer as opposed to how many who have heard the *Cantique de Jean Racine*. The prize meant nothing; the work of art it generated has delivered its message of redemption to millions. Even if it had not won, I am convinced the *Cantique* would, to this day, still possess the power to move those who hear it to tears of hope and awe.

I cannot forget the first time I heard the *Cantique*. I was a student who had just missed out on a scholarship at the university. I had better marks, an elderly professor told me, but there was another student, the student who won, who they said was more deserving. "These things are all political." I sorely wanted that scholarship. It would have assured me a place in graduate school the next year. The other student, the one who got the prize, got the spot at grad school, and promptly failed out.

The sad aspect of competitions is that one always wonders afterwards what might have been. What would have happened to *Finnegan's Wake* if *Ulysses* had established Joyce's reputation to the degree where he and not Pearl S. Buck won the Nobel? Reason dictates that prizes do not mean much other than the pat on the back they convey to the winner. They are indicators of the moment when preference, choice, politics, unseen circumstances, favouritism, artistic stupidity, and even bad luck play into the process of deciding the outcome of agonized competitors.

Hearing the *Cantique de Jean Racine* at a concert the night I received the news about the scholarship changed me and the way I look at the world. I had never heard a piece of music so beautiful. Then I learned of the story of its birth and I came to believe, yes believe, what the philosopher Boethius argued in his *Consolation of Philosophy*, namely that all fame is rumour, that what is real lasts, and what is too distant to see is never far away from us, and what is painful is true. Boethius calls it heaven. And to hear Fauré's *Cantique* is to acquire some inkling of what heaven might be like for those who choose to believe it exists.

Ars longa, vita brevis.

One hundred and fifty years after it was composed, I hold in my hand the original score for the *Cantique de Jean Racine*, and the music is even more beautiful today because it has endured the test of time. I return the box to the archivist's desk. She must have gone for lunch because I cannot find her when I peer through the tall teak door. I decide it is also time I lunched.

As I reach the bottom step on the grand staircase, I catch sight of an old friend crossing the mezzanine. Paul Rouger is the Conductor of Les Solistes Français, a brilliant ensemble that performs frequently during the summer months in Sainte Chapelle. In the embrace of the soaring Medieval stained glass, Rouger's treatment of classics such as Vivaldi's *Four Seasons* and Vitali's *Chaconne for Violin* creates a reverence in the moment that has moved me to trembling more than once.

I got to know Paul the summer my daughter was ten and I brought her to Paris. We had front-row seats. During Fauré's *Nocturne,* one of the horsehairs on Paul's bow came loose and without missing a beat, he plucked it and tossed it to the stage. When the concert finished, my daughter ran up and grabbed the strand as a souvenir. When he asked her what she thought of the concert, she replied: "I thought I was in heaven." That is how our friendship began.

We pause for a moment. I don't want to keep him. He says he has to get across town for a rehearsal for a concert that evening. I ask him what the group will be playing.

"Fauré's *Cantique de Jean Racine*," he said.

You are justified in thinking that this is a convenient moment of *deus ex machina*, but it is not. He really is performing the *Cantique* with Les Solistes and the Choir of Saint Sulpice. There are moments in one's life of tremendous serendipity and this is one of them. He rummages in his pocket and holds out two tickets. "Just one," I say. "I'm on research here alone. I've been researching the *Cantique*." He smiles, pats me on the shoulder. "Let's talk about it after this evening's concert. *A bientôt*."

Entering Sainte Chapelle is an experience akin to dying and being reborn. Through the courtyard of the Palais de Justice, one enters a dark, tomb-like portal. Over the door is a Medieval frieze of Christ releasing the souls of the righteous from the jaws of Hell. They are the virtuous ones, *born sub Julio*, as Dante describes it, who wait in Hell for the coming of Christ and a redemption they anticipate will happen someday. I wonder if that was how Gabriel Fauré felt when he received news that his setting of the 126th was denied the prize. Waiting and longing, uncertain if redemption will ever come, staying strong, patient, and believing, he picks up his pen. He hears the low, male voices intoning. He finds the notes that explain the human heart. Patience is the hardest part of life for an artist who is certain of his art.

It is 7 p.m. on a June evening as I take my seat in the front row, just down from where my daughter and I sat a decade before. Sainte Chapelle always brings me to the verge of wordlessness. It was built by Louis IX of France to house the Crown of Thorns. The word *agony* runs through my mind. The darkness of agony … and then transcendent beauty. I am part of a moment and place, and I am at that convergence when two works of art meet and time stands still. The choir files in, followed by Les Solistes, and then Rouger. The orchestra tunes, the singers clear their throats and come to attention. The audience falls silent. The light of the solstice sunbeams through the north wall on which the prophets and the singers of Psalms are depicted in the fire of ancient glass. And as I look up at the jewel-toned image of David playing his harp, the light begins to sing.

BALCONY SCENE

O UR TOWN IS LAID OUT LIKE A CHESSBOARD. Two powerful families who dominated the place for almost two centuries, the Cassavoys and the Farradays, have fought for control.
First they fought over lumber rights. Then it was land. Then the
battleground shifted to public opinion. Each had a newspaper
of different political stripes. Each had a radio station playing
different kinds of music.

The young men from the two opposing sides challenged
each other to street races in the night and many died as a result.
The Adagio River ran between the two sides of town and the
two factions and when the government ordered a bridge across
the flow to connect the two business districts, the two families
fought over who would build it and nothing was done until
the Army Corps of Engineers stepped in and did it themselves.

The common ground, the meeting place, was an island
in the river known as Paris Land. Even after the government
stepped in and constructed the bridge, there were always issues about who owed loyalty to which family. The Main Street
consisted of the business district joined by halves of the Adagio
span that drew us together more than either family could, a
street where we found our necessities — shops, banks, the hospital, a library, a cinema that kept changing hands and was

shuttered every other year, and the short-order restaurants where we would sit, read the newspapers from both sides of the river, and gossip among ourselves. It was important for us to keep up with the comings and goings of the Cassavoys and the Farradays. They were our soap opera, and we were waiting, almost with bated breath, to witness the spectacle of a tragedy in our own backyards.

But despite our best efforts to start our own businesses and live as if there was no divide, our history told the story of two houses, equally opposed, brought together by love and grief. We all knew there were four places where, no matter who anyone was or which family we sided with everyone had to pass through: the hospital where we were born; the home for the elderly, Montalet House, where we went to await our inevitable ends; the funeral home; and the town burial grounds. We lived the majority of our lives in a no-man's-land between the Cassavoys and the Farradays.

The widow, Julia Cassavoy, went willingly to Montalet. Her cousin, Ty, was already there, paralyzed in his right arm from a stroke. On the night of her sixteenth month in Montalet House, Julia decided to hold a masked ball for the residents – even the non-ambulatory ones. She had told her nurse and the others on the organizing committee that the worst thing for someone of advanced years was to hear others having fun without being able to participate. The tables in the dining hall were stacked and set to one side. The periphery of the room was lined with the dining chairs so those who grew tired could simply sit, watch, and enjoy the music. The lights would be dimmed.

On the day of the dance, Ron Farraday arrived as the newest resident at Montalet House. His family decided it was the best thing for him – they wanted him out of the way. He had been fine up until three months prior to his admission to Montalet House. His wife, Rosamund, had been a much-beloved figure on her side of the river. She died in a car accident. Ron had been at the wheel. He had also been drinking. He injured his leg, had to use a cane, and had trouble caring for himself. His family told him that Montalet House was his only option.

Just prior to the dimming of the lights for the dance, Julia handed out costume masks, the men's black with sequins around the edges and the women's pink with small feathers framing the disguise. The theme for the evening would be *commedia dell'arte*. The men were Arlequino. The women were Columbina.

Ron Farraday had arrived that afternoon at Montalet House but the few pieces of furniture he brought with him didn't arrive until supper time. He did not feel up to attending a masked ball but the sound of music filtered through the corridors of the home and drew him to the second-floor lounge. He watched the dance from a juliet balcony above the dining hall. Some of the residents were dancing with their walkers. Some watched from the sidelines. Although it was hard to see in the dim purple light – the glow ball made matters worse – Ron fixed his gaze on a woman dancing with passion and joy, absorbed in the rhythm of the music.

Ron thought of his Rosamund. He remembered how beautiful she was that summer afternoon when she pulled up beside him in the downtown in her pale blue Mustang. They had gone joyriding in the convertible. Ron had come to believe that those who age never really see themselves as they are: they perceive themselves as who they were and wish to remain.

Ron took the elevator to the lower floor and at the door he was handed a *commedia* mask: *Il Capitano*, the dashing hero. He laid his cane on one of the side chairs, fearing that he might be turned down by the spritely lady if she thought he couldn't keep up with her moves. He walked up to Julia, though he did not know who she was, and asked if he could have the next dance. As he held her in his arms, he could feel the warmth of her skin through her blouse, her heart beating and radiating a life he never thought he would feel again after he buried Rosamund. "I'd like to see your face," he whispered in Julia's ear.

Julia smiled, cocked her head, and after a moment replied, "You will have to earn that with more than your dancing. I don't believe I have seen you here before."

"I'm the new boy in town," Ron said, leaning into her ear. "Just rode into Dodge tonight. Someone said this is your dance. You've done a splendid job."

"Why thank you," Julia said, smiling. "You're a good dancer."

"Limp and all, eh? Have to keep up with the other inmates. I've heard some of these boys can really cut the rug."

Julia laughed. "I shouldn't tell you this, but some of them have trouble cutting their food."

"I hope you don't mind me saying this, but even with a mask on you are a stunning-looking woman."

"Widow," Julia said. "It has been five years now. My family says I need to be here to be looked after, but truth is I am quite capable of looking after myself. I have a nurse, and she flitters around me with this pill and that, but for all the good she does I might as well be taking my own medicine."

"Isn't it strange," Ron said as he looked in Julia's eyes through her mask, "that after spending our lives looking after so many people, so many who needed us and trusted us, we reach the end and no one wants to trust us? That saddens me. Accumulated wisdom ought to count for something."

"Here, here. I spent my life wanting for nothing, but even now, when my family says I should want for nothing, the one thing I want is my freedom. I want to be able to walk out under the stars whenever I want, to look up, to follow a shooting star and try to say my entire name before it burns out. In the Philippines, they believe a person who can say their entire name in the length of time it takes for a falling star to burn away, will be the luckiest person alive."

"The lucky ones are those who have short names, I guess. My name is…"

Julia cut him off. "Don't tell me. I want to know you as my mystery man. I want to know you as the handsome dancer who has come to whisk me away from aches and pains of the present. I want to dance with you and believe that I am young again, and maybe young forever."

"If that's what you want. I'm a man who has given everyone I've known and loved what they have wanted, so I might as well grant you that. Let us be young forever."

They danced together for the next ten songs, then Julia held him at arms-length, and looked at him. "Thank you, good sir. You have given me an evening of magic. I need to be about my business now. Duty calls. I must conduct the draw. I am supposed to oversee this event."

"May I meet you for breakfast in the morning," Ron asked?

"You'll have to wear your mask or I won't know you. Thank you again for a gracious evening. I would love to see you again, and I probably will."

The lights went up in the hall. The glow ball stopped spinning. Some of the revellers shielded their eyes from the bright lights. Julia climbed up the steps of the stage, and Ron returned to his chair where he had laid his cane before taking to the floor.

"Ladies and gentlemen," Julia said, raising the microphone to her lips. "It is time for the draw but before we do that, it is time to remove our masks so everyone can see who they were dancing with. Our revels now are ended!" With that everyone reached up and pulled the masks above their eyes, everyone except Ron. He did not want to remove his mask. For him, the mask was magic. For the hour that he had danced with Julia, he had been young again.

Julia's cousin, Ty, had been eyeing Ron for at least half an hour. He studied Ron though he could not tell for certain he was in the presence of a Farraday. Ty decided it was worth testing to see if the masked man was, indeed, Ron Farraday. He remembered the old taunts shouted across the stone bridge over the Adagio. A Cassavoy never walked away from a fight. If it weren't Ron, he would apologize. If it were, he would show him a thing or two with his fists. A Farraday in what Ty considered to be Cassavoy territory was an invitation to settle old scores.

"You bastard!" Ty shouted. "Who told you to barge in here and dance with Julia all evening?" Ron had just picked up his cane from the seat and gripped it. A cane was a symbol of infirmity, and at that moment he felt strong enough not to need it.

Ty grabbed Ron by the shoulder and spun him around. Ron lost his balance and fell. Julia sucked in her breath as Ron's cane bounced off the parquet floor. An old friend of Ron's, Mark, ran to the fallen Farraday, but instead of pushing Ty away, he picked up Ron's cane. Then in a fit of anger at the attack, Mark turned and struck Ty across the side of the head with it. Ty gasped and sank to his knees. A trickle of blood flowed from his nose, and then his right ear. He choked, and fell over, fighting for breath through his blood. Ron struggled to his feet and tried to grab for the cane, but an orderly snatched it from him as another attendant bent over Ty then looked up and spoke.

"He's dead," the orderly said to Mark. "You've killed him."

Mark staggered back, shaking his head in denial at what he had done, and ran from the hall. He ran through the corridors and onto the driveway before the attendants could catct him. He ran as hard as he could then clutched at his chest and sank to his knees.

"Calm!" Julia pleaded. "Everyone stay calm!"

Mark got as far as the gate of Montalet House. There his heart had burst. The evening ended with the flash of blue lights from two ambulances. Ron was taken to his room away from the gathering where he gave a statement to the police.

Everyone else who had been to the dance dispersed. The lights in the corridors were dimmed, and within a half an hour, the home was silent.

The nurse came into Julia's room. Julia was weeping.

"There, there, my dear. Yes, go ahead and weep. Get it all out. Ty was your cousin. He was your family here. Ty was good to you." Julia sobbed and turned her face to the pillow.

"Why, why did it have to happen?"

"Ah, Mrs. Cassavoy, no one really knows. The universe is a terrible and strange place. Here, let me give you something to help you sleep."

"No, that won't be necessary." Julia paused. "It was going so well. It was a beautiful evening, and then the old feud found its way inside these walls. Why can't the world just let us be?"

"You're right. You are in your golden years. This is a time for peace when all the passions of the world, love and hate, should be left behind."

Julia sat up, wiped her tears.

"And what is life, Nurse? What is it? Is it the silence and the stillness before dawn when I know for certain death is taking its practice aim at all of us? I've heard that silence. I've heard it speak in its darkness and tell me I am at the end. But I won't accept that. Why should I go gently? Why should I just lie back and let time run out on me? Why should any of us do that? You weren't there, but tonight I danced with a beautiful man. I thought I had known him all my life. When we spoke together it was as if he was reading my mind and I his. I've never known such a connection with someone yet I felt he'd always been part of my life, a character in the wings waiting to make his entrance on my stage. And he did. Something has touched me. I can't explain it. Something miraculous I always wanted to feel and was denied me. Tonight, I held a certainty in my arms as we danced. Maybe it's age, but age teaches one what to trust and what not to."

Ron stood at the window of his room. The night was darker than any he could recall. The moon was hidden. The emptiness of the early hour reached into him and he felt helpless and alone for the first time in his life. Maybe it was the death of Mark. Maybe it was the way Mark had died after stepping in to defend him. The gesture was noble but pointless. Ron could not contain his grief. Everyone was being taken from him.

Heartbroken, Ron slipped out of his room with his mask in the pocket of his dressing gown. The nursing station was unattended. He limped down the stairs and entered the dining hall where the police had just taken down the yellow tape and the final investigators were shuffling out. The tables and chairs had been relocated to their regular places for breakfast. The glow-ball was gone. The dining hall had lost its magic.

In the darkness, Ron heard someone sigh and he turned and looked up. Julia was standing at the second-floor balcony. She was clutching her mask in her hand and weeping. She sighed again and Ron donned his mask and moved along the wall beneath the balcony so she would not see him.

"Why?" she said almost silently though Ron could hear her. "Why is my dance ending? I have danced my life away, yet I thought the dance would never end. I would be dancing still, with you my masked man, my hero. And now, they will never let us dance again. Where are you?"

"It need not be," Ron replied, moving from the wall and its shadows to stand among the tables. "It need not be. I am here. Please, please dance with me."

Julia looked down, startled that someone had replied to her out of the darkness, "Is it you?" she asked.

"Yes. I am sorry about your cousin. So very sorry. I have no idea why he wanted to attack me."

"I know," she whispered. "You're Ron Farraday and I'm Julia Cassavoy. Our town, our pasts, our families, have dictated we could never dance together. We must occupy opposite banks of the same river, drink the same water, breathe the same air, and yet be separate."

"But we are two human beings. We're two people aging and facing that moment when we'll run out of time and our lives will have been thwarted not by who we are as individuals but by who we are as townsfolk of this place we call home. We're more than just bodies waiting for our time in this world to end. We're alive, and we need to embrace life with every moment."

"If the orderlies find you here, they'll confine you to your room for a week."

"Then let them find me," Ron declared. "Let them tear me away from a vision of life I glimpsed with you this night. They can lock me up. They can medicate me out of my mind, but they cannot take from me the magic I felt when I cast my cane aside and danced the night with you. I was young again."

"And I, also."

"Julia, Julia Cassavoy, for I know that is your name – and a name means nothing if it is not meant worn as a badge of life: I am a Farraday. Why must we be prisoners of the world others have made for us when we have the right to choose our destinies?"

"I know. I know, Ron. But our families will not permit it."

"Tomorrow, tomorrow they are letting us go for an outing with a member of our family. I have a plan. Tell your son or daughter or whoever is picking you up, that you want to go to the mall. I'll tell my daughter-in-law the same thing. At eleven, tell your chaperone you need to use the washroom in the food court. I'll tell my daughter-in-law the same. Meet me behind the loading entrance. There's a corridor between the fries stand and the Thai place. Meet me there, and we'll slip away."

Julia paused for a moment, then nodded though Ron could not see the gesture. "Yes," she said. "Eleven tomorrow. And Ron?"

"Yes?"

"Bring your meds with you. Adieu."

The next morning Ron and Julia slipped away from their escorts and met at the door behind the loading entrance. Both were scared. Both knew they were breaking the rules of Montalet house, as well as betraying the trust of their families. But they had to seize the moment. They saw each other without the masks from the night before when the mayhem of the dance's end left a kinsman dead from each of the two houses. They stood for a moment, hands joined, then kissed.

Ron had a taxi waiting. "Where to?" the driver asked.

"Anywhere," Julia answered. "Wait, I have an idea. Have you ever been to the Basilica – the monastery is out in the country, far, far away from town?" Ron nodded. "It is beautiful there and no one will find us."

The taxi drove to Main Street and followed it over the stone bridge where the road branched off toward the Basilica.

"Do you know Father Larry there?" Julia asked. "He has been a comfort to me over the years. He listens. Ron, I think there's more happening between us than we can admit right now. We've just walked away from all the comforts, all the coddling, and all the rules that have surrounded us for years. And in spite of what happened last night, in spite of the decades we have put between us, I feel there is more to come for us."

Ron squeezed her hand as they left the taxi, entered the church, and stood under the dome of the main aisle. Father Larry appeared. He looked surprised to see them – "Ron, a Farraday, with Julia, a Cassavoy!" he exclaimed. He ushered the couple into his study behind the altar and asked them to take a seat on a leather couch. "This is, indeed, a rare day. The elders from two families. Is there peace at last between everyone?"

Ron spoke first. "Father Larry, we've come for your help. Julia and I just met. Last night at Montalet House. It was during a masked ball she organized. Last night we discovered the world has stood between us, and we want to be together."

Julia squeezed Ron's hand and he intertwined his fingers with hers.

The priest looked at their hands and then in their eyes – and he saw such sincerity and ardour in them.

"I know," Ron said, "we're too old to be married and our families wouldn't permit it, but would you at least bless our love?"

"Ron and Julia, love is a mystery. It is a divine gift. People like to say it conquers all and heals all wounds. If it can bind the Farradays and the Cassavoys even for a spark of an instant, then the saying is true. Let me ask you a particularly important question. I know you do not want to marry. So be it. But what purpose do you see this union serving?"

Julia spoke up. "Only to say what we have discovered in each other is real, and perhaps worthy of being called holy. We should not have to bear old wounds. We both realized on our way here today that hatred and foolishness kept us from a life of happiness together. We married, and I think I speak for Ron as well when I say our lives were not without happiness or purpose, but they would have been much different had the old hostilities not stood between us."

"Are you sure this is not merely infatuation? Infatuation strikes hard and fast and it can deceive."

"No," said Ron. "I believe, with all my heart, this is real. We have so little time remaining. I want Julia to know I feel a bond to her I have never felt before. I don't know if that is love, but I know there is something beyond mere words that binds us." Ron gazed into Julia's eyes, and she returned the look with tears welling in hers as she smiled. "Father, if this is love it moves in the strangest of ways. Two days ago, we could have been enemies staring across the river at each other, and I would have died an old and bitter man, living with fear, feeling abandoned and lost in the world. Now, she is here with me, and I don't feel alone."

"Please, Father," Julia said, "please don't leave us to wither and fade away, not now, not at this point in our lives. We need what little happiness we can give each other."

The priest reached for their hands and drew them together. "I cannot marry you. You need to think this over longer. But I will bless you. I see no sin in such a bond if what you feel for each other is all you have. May God bless and keep you, and may He deliver to you the beauty of the love he shares with all things."

When they left Father Larry's office, Ron suggested they stroll through the grounds of the Basilica. There were woods skirting the seminary buildings and with warm spring days just beginning to open buds on the trees, the moment grew more perfect for Ron and Julia.

"I even brought my birder's glasses," Ron said pulling a small pair of binoculars from his coat pocket.

"I'd no idea you were into birding. That's been my passion for years. I belonged to the Audubon Society."

"Me? The Ornithological Association. That's probably why we never knew we shared a love of birds. Even the two birding societies refuse to share the same ground on the same day – as if the birds really cared."

They paused on the forest path and she let go of Ron's hand. "Look," Julia whispered, "Spring is really here." They stood in silence and listened to a birdsong. Flecks of yellow darted through the high branches.

"Are those wild canaries?" Ron asked.

"Maybe they are goldfinches."

"I'd prefer they were wild canaries," he whispered back. "Why?"

"Because canaries are a sign that spring is here to stay. The goldfinches arrive earlier but they are just passing through. The canaries tell us life is in full bloom. The summer is almost upon us and soon the days will grow shorter. There is a sadness to the canaries. They tell us that life is beginning again but the days will become darker and we are running out of time."

"But I do love goldfinches even if they are here only briefly," Julia said.

"Then let them be goldfinches," Ron replied, handing Julia the binoculars. "Let them be the birds of a briefer season. We'll make the best of it no matter how short our time together may be. Let them sing and wake us each morning to a new life."

"So be it," Julia said.

"Let's make a pledge, Julia. Let's pledge we will love each other all our remaining days. Here," Ron said, taking his fountain pen from his vest pocket. "I'll write my name on your hand in banker's ink, and you'll write your name on mine, so even if we are separated we'll still carry with us more than the eight letters of our last names. We will wear the eight letters that are the sum of our first names, Ron and Julia." She held out her palm and he wrote Ron on her hand. He held out his, and she wrote Julia with the letters flowing along his heart line.

By the time they returned to the Basilica, the police had arrived. The families had tracked the couple through the taxi company. Julia's son and Ron's daughter-in-law were shouting at each other across the driveway. The old feud had not abated though, for one blessed afternoon, Ron and Julia had walked in the woods and found a way to leave the world behind. Both were whisked away in separate vehicles and were taken to the hospital at the far end of the Main street.

Julia's family insisted she had lost her mind, and demanded she be admitted to the Psych ward where she was to be put under immediate sedation. Julia's son shouted at her, "Those goddamned Farradays want to sink their claws into our holdings! You can't trust them. You can't. You're a foolish old woman with delusions, dangerous delusions!"

Hearing the harangue of his daughter-in-law, Ron clutched at his left arm. He felt weak and dizzy and was immediately put into a private room in the cardiac unit. He asked to keep his clothes and his fountain pen. His daughter-in-law saw Julia's name on his hand and was incensed.

"What were you two thinking?" she hollered at Ron. "Especially after Mark's death and the terrible news that he killed Julia's cousin. Are you insane? Have you totally lost your mind? Those Cassavoys could sue us. Or worse, they could manipulate a merger. Just like that! They'd take over our paper and our media company and put us in the poor house. I have half a notion, old man, to make sure they shackle you in your bed both here and back at the home where you are going and where you are going to stay! Running away like that! That's madness, a certain sign of dementia. And do you know what that woman is trying to do? Do you? She's using you as a pawn for her family. A merger of our publishing houses would ruin us, not them! We'd be the losers! And if you think I'm daft, I heard Mrs. Cassavoy's son saying the same thing to his brother. I'm getting the lawyer tomorrow to make sure you no longer control your assets. Power of attorney, old man! Power of attorney! You're not going to ruin what the Farradays have taken a century to build, especially with that Cassavoy woman whispering in your ear. They'd like nothing better than to witness the downfall of our paper and our house."

Ron kept silent. He did not get into a hospital gown and did not even take off his raincoat or his tweed fedora. He sat on the edge of the hospital bed and stared at the frosted glass window of his hospital room. All he could think about was Julia. When a nurse came in to check on him, he asked about Mrs. Cassavoy.

"Where has she gone? Is she all right?"

The nurse turned on her heel and headed toward the door. He called after her.

"I want to see my priest. I need to talk to my priest. Not the hospital chaplain, but Father Larry at the Basilica."

The nurse, turned, looked at him, and left the room.

Julia had been taken to the terrible Seventh floor. The Seventh floor had been a common joke when Ron and Julia were younger. If someone said or did something stupid around town, the response was "You're headed to the Seventh floor." Rumour had it that those who were incarcerated on the Seventh floor rarely came out with their minds intact, and if they did they referred to it as the Seventh level of Hell. Ron had to find Julia. He had to get away from the madness of the hospital and the town.

When Ron and Julia had been taken away, Father Larry followed their ambulances. He read the anger in the eyes of the younger generation who hurried the lovers away from the Basilica. Father Larry was not young himself yet he understood that there was a real though sudden attraction between Ron and Julia. He saw the way they looked at each other as they had sat on the couch in his office. Was it a miracle? He knew that look. It was a look two souls give each other when they are in love.

The priest arrived on Ron's floor and overheard the conversation between the nurses as he stood at the nurse's station.

"That old man is inquiring about the woman who came in at the same time with her family, and he is asking to see his priest. I don't think there's anything wrong with him. His EKG looks fine, too, and the blood work just came back and it looked normal," one nurse told the other.

"You've got to wonder what they are hiding from or being hidden from," the other nurse said. "Mr. Farraday's daughter-in-law left strict instructions that he was to have no visitors. That seems kind of cruel. It is like they're locking him up."

Father Larry interrupted. "Did I hear you speak of Mr. Farraday? I'm his priest. I was here visiting another patient. I've been hearing Mr. Farraday's confession for years – a sort of spiritual counsellor and golf buddy, depending, of course, on the weather of the day."

The nurses laughed.

He continued, "It would be grand to see him, if only to say hello and wish him well, if it isn't any trouble."

"His daughter said he's not to have any visitors."

"Ah, I see. Well, let me know if he asks for me."

"Father," the nurse who had been in Ron's room said, "he did ask for you. Hospital policy permits pastoral visits if the patient specifically requests them. Mr. Farraday said he wanted to see Father Larry from the Basilica."

"How fortunate! I am Father Larry. Isn't it wonderful how coincidence borders on miracles?"

One nurse looked at the other, and the two women nodded together. "Alright," one said. She showed the priest into Ron's room. Ron stood up as the nurse left.

"You look like you're about to go somewhere, Ron."

"Father, you have to help me find Julia and get out of here. I don't know where she is."

"I do," said the priest. "She's locked up on the Seventh floor. I have no idea what they are doing to her up there."

"Why are they doing this to us? Don't we have a right to lead our own lives? They say we are old. Yes, we have many years of life behind us and, perhaps not as many ahead of us. But love is not measured in time. When a man and a woman love each other, no matter what age, they will hold on to each other. My love for Julia, fresh as it is, is no less than if I fell in love with her when we were twenty. Perhaps it's greater because we bring to that love an understanding that comes from having stood up to the world and time and all the wrongs we have done and have been done to us. I see nothing in that to prevent us from saying in the face of twilight that we are human beings who are worthy of our humanity."

"Brave words, Ron," Father Larry said, "but you are preaching to one who is already on your side."

"Father, Julia and I have so little time together. Every second is precious. Every second is a second lost if we are not together. I have watched my friends cradle their dying lovers. Their love did not diminish. When their spouses passed away, they did not stop loving them. They reached out, aching, for them, but even in their pain, their love was strong because love is a form of bravery, and only cowards would say it is foolish at any age."

"I know," Father Larry said.

Both men fell silent and stared at the frosted white glass window of the room as if it were the horizon of a mystery they could not solve.

Father Larry looked at Ron and put his hand on the man's shoulder.

"I think I have a plan. I know where the nurses keep the medication tray, and I am aware there are a number of people on this floor who are prescribed sleeping medications. They have told me so themselves. I've often followed the nurses on their rounds when I've been here to tend to the sick and the dying."

Ron shook his head.

"Now, don't get ahead of me," Father Larry said. "What I am about to suggest is unethical and dangerous, but I see it as the only way to get you two out of here. I think I can find enough pills, just enough and not too much, to make you appear to be dead, at least with a pulse low enough to trick an orderly. I will tell them you have been pronounced dead. He will wheel you down to the morgue. I will try to find Julia and bring her down there, somehow, if I can manage to free her from the Seventh floor. Then I can bring you around, and you can leave together through the entrance where the hearses pull up to take the bodies away. It is risky. Are you with me on this?"

Ron nodded. Father Larry squeezed his hand and left the room. A few minutes later, the priest returned with several paper cups.

"They're not paying attention at that nursing station. I could have taken the crown jewels. Now, wait for me to call your room and then take the pills. There's enough there for pleasant dreams but not enough to kill you. I'm sure of it. I'm on the same stuff myself."

"Are you certain this plan will work?"

"It's the best I can do. What's the extension number on the phone there," the priest said pointing to the nightstand. Ron didn't have his glasses on.

"Eight, zero, eight."

"Good. Wait for my call, Ron. Now to Julia."

When the priest got to the Seventh Floor to ask for Julia Cassavoy, there was a commotion at the nursing station. A security guard was talking with the nurses. Father Larry drew into the conversation. Mrs. Cassavoy had gone missing. They were certain she was somewhere in the hospital, but where was she hiding?

In the emergency room on the first floor, Julia found an empty gurney and a white sheet. She lay down and pulled the sheet over her head. Several minutes later, an orderly came and wheeled the gurney with Julia in her winding sheet to the elevator. Beneath the sheet, she lay still. She felt cold with anxiety. Her hands became as icy as if she were dead. She heard the bell of the elevator and felt the descent to the basement.

The room where the orderly took her was cold and had the sour scent of antiseptic. "Be still," she thought to herself.

Someone pulled the sheet back for an instant, looked at her face, and then picked up her wrist and read her wrist band. A voice said, "I guess the paperwork is coming down on this one." Then the sheet was replaced. A moment later, she heard a door open, and felt a darkness surround her as two sets of hands lifted her onto a metal slab. She lay motionless, making sure as she breathed her chest and stomach did not rise and fall and give her away.

"Is death a cold, silent darkness?" Julia wondered as she lay in her crypt.

Upstairs, Ron waited. The minutes passed. Each one weighed on him as if it was an hour. Father Larry had not called. Had he not found Julia? He peered around the door of his room. The nurses were wheeling the medication wagon from patient to patient.

"We'll be right with you, Mr. Farraday." And noticing he still was wearing his fedora one of them called, "Hey, take off your hat and stay a while."

Ron realized that if the nurses found the pills Father Larry had stolen for him, everyone would think Ron had pilfered them to end his life. Ron lifted the top of the tray table beside his bed and poured the pills inside. He set the empty paper cup on top then removed his fedora and tweed jacket and laid them on the bed.

As he passed the bathroom door, he turned on the washroom light, set the handle to lock, and pulled the door shut with all his strength to make the nurses believe he had settled in and was busy in the bathroom. When the nurses were in a room two doors down, fighting with a patient who was refusing medication, Ron slipped down the hall and took the elevator to the basement. He had still not received Father Larry's call to proceed with the plan.

He wandered through the stark, beige corridors until he saw sign for the morgue.

"Is death a labyrinth?" Ron thought to himself.

At the door of the morgue, a gaunt man whose cheeks had sunken in around protruding cheek bones was sitting at a grey metal desk. The attendant was wearing grey hospital scrubs. The man stared. Ron smiled at him.

"Can I help you?" the attendant asked.

"Yes. Has a woman come in here recently, an older woman, grey hair, elegant-looking?"

The attendant stared. After a moment, he asked "Are you Mr. Cassavoy?"

"What do you mean?"

"They just brought in a Mrs. Cassavoy."

Ron staggered against the doorframe.

"Hey, you'd better sit down. Are you Mr. Cassavoy?" Ron nodded. "Were you with your wife when she passed?" Ron shook his head. "Would you like to see her?" Ron nodded yes.

The attendant took Ron by the arm and raised him up.

"Are you sure, sir, you are ready for this? I can leave you alone for a few minutes if you wish."

He led Ron into the cold room. There, the attendant opened a door and slid out the slab where Julia lay.

As she came out of the darkness, Julia was again afraid she would be discovered. She lay still, her eyes closed as the attendant drew back the sheet and left the room. Ron stood over her silently. Then, he reached into his trousers pocket where he had been carrying his meds all day. He opened the steel vial where he kept the nitro pills for his heart condition, and holding up the container whispered, "Here's to my love!" and swallowed the contents.

At the sound of his voice, Julia sat up, looked into Ron's eyes and whispered, "No! No!"

Ron sank to the floor. He reached out to hold her hand, her name still written on his palm, and collapsed before their fingers could touch.

Julia raised her hand to her mouth. She heard the attendant's chair squeak on the floor in the next room and fearing she would be taken from Ron again, ran to the door and bolted it. Then she kneeled beside Ron Farraday, cradling his head in her lap, as he smiled up at her and whispered, "My heart is breaking." He closed his eyes.

She stroked his forehead, and as her hand passed to the back of his head, she saw his name where he had written it that morning, printed in neat letters across her heart line.

"Ron, my love, what has the world done to us? Why should we feel the weight of the stars and all the darkness around them? Why should it all come crashing down upon us when we thought we both had a chance at the happiness we'd been denied? Oh, Ron. Had we not been separated by a river and our families, had we come to know each other in our youth and not at the last gasp of our lives, we could have been so happy." Tears poured down her cheeks and her voice broke.

The orderly was banging on the door. She heard Father Larry's voice from the other side calling to her, pleading with her to open the door. She could not rise to her feet. She lay on the cold grey linoleum floor beside the body of Ron Farraday, and reaching into his shirt pocket, drew out his fountain pen and unscrewed the cap. She held it to her neck. "O dagger of love make your mortal sting. Be true and write the ending to our story!" she said in a clear, strong voice, then plunged the pen into her neck.

When the door was finally opened, when the lock was finally undone, Father Larry stood with the security guards and nurses over the two bodies. The two lovers had gone missing from their wards, and their families had been summoned. The Farradays and the Cassavoys intermingled shoulder to shoulder, staring silently at the spectacle of Julia embracing Ron, both motionless. No one could look away, and none of them could comprehend what they were seeing.

"Stand aside," a man in a black suit said. "I am the Chief of Staff in this hospital." He bent and held each wrist, checking for a pulse. Neither had one. He read the names written on each palm.

"How could this have happened? Two leading citizens dead in this way. This is a place where people come to be healed. Not this."

"They were in love, and their families kept them apart," Father Larry said. "They were trying to get away. I am so very sorry. I am responsible. I tried to call him in his room. He told me the extension was eight, zero, eight but I couldn't get through to stop him in time from leaving his room and going in search of her."

A nurse from Ron's floor spoke up. "I believe the extension in that room is three, zero, three."

Father Larry began to weep. "I failed them. God forgive what should not be forgiven. I failed them!"

The Chief of Staff stood and looked down on the bodies.

"The old wounds have been open too long. Look at what they have bled. There are no longer two houses. There is only one town and all its pointless rage and grief. A shame on both your houses. Were you so incapable of putting aside the old wrongs that two people, regardless of age or family or which side of the river they came from could simply love each other? A shame on both your houses."

No one said a word but everyone bowed their heads, some to pray and most in shame. The town fell silent that night. The youths from the two sides of the river did not challenge each other to races. The shops shuttered and remained closed for three days. United in grief, the Cassavoys and the Farradays met on the bridge. The talked together for several hours and when they parted they embraced each other and promised they would do everything they could to set aside the past. The Adagio flowed between the two sides of the town and the sun rose and set several minutes later each day until the season changed and darkness settled on both sides of the river as winter arrived.

COMMERCE

Architecture aims at eternity.
—Christopher Wren

N UMBERS TELL ONLY PART of the story of 25 King Street
West. Behind every number there is a person who can
attest to what the number means and what strength and skill
men must possess to animate dust and stone into a breathing
work of art. Such men are numbers. Commerce is a number.
The building contains endless numbers: numbers of the past,
numbers of the present, and numbers of the future. Commerce
was made from numbers, a cipher of numerical palindromes
spun backwards and forwards. The corner stone was laid on
October 29, 1929. The tower opened on January 13, 1931.
Backwards or forwards, the marvel of the age added up to
thirty-four stories, each one bought at a price no one bothered
to count. It is accounted among the iron workers of New York
who raised the Empire State Building – many of whom came
north to build the Commerce – that every storey a skyscraper
climbed cost three lives. But no one kept record of how many
men fell or were crushed, or simply came and went through

the portals of the site as unrecorded numbers working toward an enormous sum.

When the tower finally opened, what was known were the hard numbers on which a person could put a calculable price – after all, what price can be put on a man's life? And what could be measured is staggering:

476 feet high.
9,300 tons of steel.
190,000 cubic feet of stone.
27,000 square feet of linoleum.
6,633 square yards of marble and tile.
817 days labour.

A memorial over the south portal to 258 bank employees killed in World War One.

When Commerce was finished, 3,000 men and women went to work in the building each day, rising to their desks and offices in mahogany elevators that climbed at a rate of 800 feet per minute, faster than if they were taking off in an airplane.

When they sat at their desks, they were connected by 600 telephones to twenty-five switch boards, that were interlaced by more than 346 miles of cable.

Those 3,000 men and women would eat their lunches, supplied by the bank, in a cafeteria that served over 6,000 meals per day, have their hair trimmed to slick perfection in a barber shop that cut 275 heads per day, and carefully snipped over 87 moustaches before closing time each evening. Each day men in the basement would open and close a 52-ton vault door that was the entrance to a safe with top, bottom, and sides of steel thirty inches thick and reinforced with concrete. No one, except the chosen few at the top of the bank, knew how much money was held in the vaults.

Numbers.

Numbers meant everything to the bank's supervisor of buildings, Colonel Duncan Donald, a Scottish veteran of the Western Front who demanded respect and discipline on the site from the day they broke sod where an old Methodist church once stood to the day he turned in his keys in 1955 and retired from service to the hills of his native Scotland. Donald, so he claimed, had hand-picked every man who worked to construct the tower. To him, they were the soldiers he had commanded in the muds of Flanders – rag-a-muffins who could transform an impossible situation into the reality of victory. And the 3,000 men under his command inched the steel and stone higher through the summer heat, ripping winds of spring, the cutting air of autumn, and the gales of winter. They climbed at a rate of two stories per week; men walking girders with fiery rivets clutched in St. Dunstan tongs; men who had lives, pasts, and families; men whose names are not remembered in the way that the 258 bank employees who made the supreme sacrifice were remembered and venerated on the south door.

No one kept track. Such a number demanded a face, and if the number had a face, it had to have a story. Stories take time. They slow construction. They take the mind off grandeur. Tom Baker, however, who wanted this story to be told, had a face. He passed away quietly from old age in a city-endowed retirement home in Hamilton in 1998. You can see Tom Baker in three of the photographs from the construction of the Commerce. He is the black man with a woollen peaked cap pushed back on his head. His dark eyes are always looking into the camera's lens whether the photographer intended it or not. He says, "Yep, I'm here, and if you want to know the story, just ask me. I won't be hard to find."

Tom Baker had a friend who was Italian. He had been christened with the names of great artists in a small farming village south of Pisa – Tom couldn't remember the name of the place or who he would write to testify about the man he named as a brother in the sky – but he could not forget his friend's name: Giotto Verrocchio.

Joe, as Giotto was called by the other workers, does not appear in any of the extant photographs of Commerce. He was always just a little out of the frame, always just a little behind the photographer, steadying him on a beam as the wind picked up, or down in the ground making sure that the official eye of the grand work would not come to grief over any debris left in the way. Giotto Verrocchio went by the name Joe Verdy because it was, as Joe said, easier for everyone to remember.

Joe told Tom how his mother had had a vision of great men looking down on him as he sketched. Perhaps they were the heads that eventually crowned the building. She had taken him to the village priest.

"Who was a great artist before Verrocchio?" she asked, and the priest has replied "Giotto" because somewhere in his studies he had read Vasari and the *Lives of the Artists* and knew that Giotto was the morning star of the great age of Italian *virtu*.

Joe had been through some rough experiences on the Tyrol front where men had clung for their lives to the heights of mountains, not knowing whether it was better to die by falling or take an Austrian bullet. Joe found himself hanging by his fingertips to a rock face, as a regiment of Tyrolean Austrians poured fire upon his brigade. Joe looked down. A voice in him told him he should not be afraid of falling. Falling was only a matter of approaching the earth faster than usual. The earth was hard, yes, but not as hard a life if he survived the fall. It was better to fall and know that the rest would be harder.

He imagined a picture he had seen in a gallery in Firenze, a painting by Giotto, where angels hovered above a saint in all his holy majestic gold leaf. The saint's hands were attached to heaven as if he was a puppet on God's strings.

So Joe let go.

He fell, but he said that as he fell he felt himself floating, almost as if he had sprouted wings.

As Joe fell in that nameless battle for perpendicular gain, something caught him. Tom wanted to put it down to a tall tale workers tell each other when they are killing time and earning money for it, but Joe looked at him, sincerity written all over his face, and added "if you don't believe, you don't understand."

Joe had promised his mother he would go to Rome and become an artist. The same priest who baptised him, now a doddering old man who mistook Joe's scribblings of figures huddled with their rifles on purgatorial perches for the masterworks of a great *cognoscenti*, wrote to the *professore* in charge of a small art school that had established itself in the former of house of Claude Lorrain on the Via del Babuino in Rome and commended Joe to the maestro.

It was not a grand academy. It was a second-rate art school that aspired to maintain the virtues of mannerist style. Joe kidded me that you could do better with one of those art schools you find on matchbooks. On his arrival at the Via del Babuino, he presented his work to the *professore*, who dismissed him as a scribbler, and sent him off. With nowhere to go but enough money raised from his soldier's pay and his brothers and sisters, Joe made his way to Naples and caught a steerage passage to New York.

New York, in the early 1920s, belonged to the Irish, or at least work belonged to the Irish. "The Italians," he explained, "they were just too new. No one liked them. But Toronto? That's an Italian name, or sounds like it, and there weren't many Italians there yet, at least not enough to make the Irish fear for the potatoes on their plates."

After his first day of hacking his way through the brown glacial till on which the city had been laid ever so delicately, Giotto Verrocchio ceased to exist. A new man was born from the earth of a place with an Italian-sounding name. He emerged from a sewer trench one hot afternoon as Joe Verdy, worker 547 in the city trench brigade. Until construction commenced on the Commerce, Joe had always told his friends that he could stand to be a number in Toronto because nothing seemed to add up.

Joe had worked at Mount Pleasant Cemetery one winter. While digging graves, Joe watched the wealthy citizens of the city come to grips with their grief, their black motor cars trailing after black hearses, some horse-drawn, some motorized. The wealthy ones need someone to open the doors for their mausoleums, their palaces of the dead, and the poorer ones (though not much poorer) required that the ground be opened as it would for any mortal. For a few weeks until the debate was settled, Joe was the boatman to the high and the mighty on their final journey. He would have preferred to stay and do the cemetery work, but someone in charge had a brother who had lost an arm in the war and wanted Joe's job, so he returned to the tunnels beneath the earth, laughing all the way – who would have heard of a one-armed gravedigger? – and thinking to himself that the next trench he dug might cave in and be his own grave.

Joe told Tom the day they met that the new building troubled him. A November rain was falling. A steam shovel bit into the earth and pulled up a headstone. The next gulp in the steel jaws raised a coffin. The headstone was only partially intact. The only thing they could read on it was the name "Sarah." Sarah's casket broke open as it dropped from the steel jaws and hit the mud. She was still wearing a long, blue dress with tarnished lace around the sleeves. She had been in the ground a long time and her body was reduced to fleshless bones. But as she came to rest, her right arm came up from her body, and a boney finger pointed at the sky. Joe wanted to hold back, but he and Tom were motioned forward by the foreman.

"Get that thing outta here," he hollered at them. "I don't care where you put it, but don't let the Colonel see it or he'll have ten fits!"

Tom said he was sick to his stomach at the sight of the corpse, but Joe simply nodded and said, "C'mon, I have hauled a lot of bodies in my time," and he nailed together what was left of the coffin, gathered the body as best he could, and told Tom to take the head end. Tom remembered how there seemed to be such focus and patience as Joe spent the day hammering new boards around the old coffin wood. When he had completed the lid and fitted it into place, he carved the name Sarah on it with his pocket knife.

They waited until darkness. A policeman stopped and asked: "What's in the crate," and Tom answered: "Tools. We've just started here and I didn't know what to bring."

"Who is Sarah?"

"Ah, officer, she's my girl," he said, patting the letters on the lid. He planted a kiss on the end of his right hand and slapped it down on the wood. "I love to think of her when I'm busy building things. I'm building her a dream house one of these days."

Joe borrowed a wagon from a fruit stand man he knew, Parfetta, the banana king, and they loaded the coffin on the wagon and took it down to where River Street crossed the Don River. They lugged it up the slippery slope of the hillside into the Necropolis.

They dug down about four feet, not as deep as they should have, Tom recalled, and laid Sarah to rest among the famous early Victorians of the city.

As they were about to walk away, Joe turned and whispered over his shoulder, "Be good to us, Sarah. Remember those who remember you." That said, Tom could not get the picture out of his mind of the dead hand pointing to a stormy sky where they would be aiming every sinew and fibre of their strength.

That night as Tom lay awake in his boarding house room in Cabbagetown, he listened to the rain nattering on the window pane as cats loved and scrapped in the alley beneath him. He had caught his first glimpse of Commerce that morning when a bank employee stood huddled with Donald and Pearson in a heated discussion in the Anglin-Norcross office.

Tom had read about the Tower of Babel – not merely the Biblical one in Genesis that God confounded, but an ancient structure that had been unearthed by archaeologists in the remains of the Turkish empire that had crumbled in the Euphrates valley. The British had marched in to the valley to seek the oil that lay beneath antiquity. He'd seen a picture of a pyramid-like structure, a ziggurat, stacked like a decorated cake, one smaller layer atop the last, until the confection stood precariously tall. He'd seen the same image in another book during his New York days. Tom had haunted the New York Public Library and had seen a painting of Babel – or was it Mount Purgatory in a book by Dante … he wasn't sure – that bore an uncanny likeness to the Commerce he and the other men were going to raise in the small patch of ground between King and Melinda Streets. The Mountain that rose up in Dante's purgatory had been called Mount Hope.

The lot on which they were going to work seemed too tiny to hold such a building – an old churchyard, large enough for a Victorian meeting house the demolition men had hauled down, but not spacious enough to fit a skyscraper. And the word skyscraper went round and round in his head as he fell asleep with the picture in his mind of a needle of steel tearing open the dome and letting the stars pour through and pave Toronto in gold. That is what the future would look like. Skyscrapers. Stars rolling down Yonge Street toward the bay. He would have to tell Joe about his dream if he remembered it in the morning.

Building a skyscraper, Tom would say, was not an art but a science disguised as art. Maybe that is what attracted Joe, the failed artist, to work on Commerce. The building would be a work of art, inside and out. Every door handle, every light fixture, every detail of stone frieze-work and carved wooden trim had been designed with a grace and precision overseen personally by Commerce's architect, John Pearson.

Pearson had remade the center block of Parliament after the disastrous fire of 1916. He had cobbled his design for the Peace Tower together from the spires of Westminster Abbey and Lincoln Cathedral to create a singular, cyclopic vision of time's eye to watch over the nation, *ad mare usque ad mare*. Pearson had put his stamp on Toronto by designing the new Trinity College on Harbord Street. Parliament and the college had both been Gothic structures, buildings that spoke of faith, vision, and the fusion of beliefs with reality. "Our man the Daedalus," Joe would say, laughing. Commerce, however, would be Pearson's testament to might and empire. It would refer to all the great realms that had asserted themselves through ancient history, but with one difference: this new statement of power and command would rise up rather than spread. A temple of money, it would reach up and touch heaven.

If the sky was the limit, the skyscraper would press the frontiers of the next empire, the unshakeable rule of commerce, beyond the bounds of anyone's wildest dream. But no matter how great the achievement, few people realize art is won at a great cost, a human cost. The artist labours to learn his craft and practice it, and the cost is his life. A tower, a magnificent and lasting work of art, unshakable from its foundations to its pinnacle, rises in a battle where men struggle to defy nature.

And so the rise began, paradoxically, by going down into the earth. Commerce, for such a large building, would stand on a seemingly miniscule plot of land, 149 x 168 feet. For its day, it would be one of the slenderest skyscrapers in the world. Tom realized that he and the other men would be constructing an impossibility.

On the morning of November 3, 1929, Donald stood beside Pearson on a wooden crate just inside the site fence and addressed the men.

"Today," he exhorted in a commanding voice, "we begin the task of creating something grander than anything this city or this empire has ever known. Gentlemen, let us reach for the clouds!" By the end of the week, five steam tractors hauled the giant shovel out from forty-five feet below street level, and the last of four hundred and sixteen trucks hauled away the debris. They were about to celebrate when the men hit bedrock – the Lorraine clay shale on which the mud of an old lake bed sits, and on which the downtown of Toronto had been built.

"Feet of clay, the whole place," Tom would say. The clay was not so much an obstacle but a reminder: the entire city, brick by red brick, was made of the shale the Taylor family had dug out of the side of the Don Valley at Todmorden Mills. Joe had joked that he could build a neighbourhood from the clay they hacked out with pick axes over the next month. Joe revelled in the irony that what rose above the earth was a reminder of what lay beneath it. Toronto was, for all intents and purposes, a city living its life inside out.

And just when the shale was about to become the butt of a joke, a seam of natural gas appeared out of the layers, and the men fell ill without explanation. Natural gas, as it is in homes, contains a sulphurous additive that alerts anyone that the air bearing the gas is poisonous; but when it comes directly out of the earth, as it did one Friday morning, men dropped without explanation until an engineer on the site determined the source of the problem. Joe came up from the pit choking and vomiting.

"It is like a war down there," he said, clutching at Tom's shoulders.

The gas problem was put to rest by the time the Monday morning shift came to the site. Joe and Tom went down into the earth and shovelled like stokers on an ocean liner. The gas, however, made the men aware the work site would provide more than its share of surprises.

Having vanquished the bedrock, the next task was to underpin the side of the Bank of Nova Scotia building to the west. The Commerce crew had dug so deep there was the fear the Nova Scotia might collapse. When the hole was stabilized, they dug down further, hacking with pick axes through the cold November days as the snow fell. When Donald blew the whistle one night, they shook hands and wished each other a Merry Christmas.

As the new year began, even though it was freezing, Donald ordered in the cement trucks to pour the floors of the sub-basement. Joe and Tom thought they would freeze to death as they stood in rubber boots with the others pushing the grey mass into the corners of the foundation. When it came time to pour the walls, the Anglin-Norcross man in charge was certain the forms would hold. Tom and Joe had gotten to know a man named Keith – Tom was never sure if it was his first name or his last name – and he lived out across the Don in a small house with a wife and four children. He was the first victim. The form burst. The concrete came flooding over him. Frantically, the team dug and dug, sinking up to their waists to find their buried friend, but when they found him, the mass of quick dry mix had almost set around him.

That was when Colonel Donald had the reporters banned from the site. Instead of having the press on hand to report the developments, Donald found a stenographer who had a flair for writing, and he would issue daily progress reports about how many cubic tons of concrete had been poured that day, how fast it was drying, and what the next stage would be in the building of Commerce. And when the walls and floor finally set, a huge tarpaulin was pulled over the site, and work lights were set up in the darkness below ground. The lowering of the vault would be the next task at hand.

Pearson positioned cranes around the centre of the basement walls to lower first the 300-ton vault and then the 200-ton vault. The respective doors, forty tons and fifty-two tons, would be brought in separately and pinioned into place. There is a picture of Tom in the archives, one of the few of the men at work, and he is looking over his shoulder at the camera as Pearson explains the process of setting the heart of the bank into its eternal resting place. For Joe, the idea of a vault reminded him of the crypts at Mount Pleasant. "They will lock up failed branch managers in there," he said laughing.

The crane on the south side started to buckle under the weight of the heavier vault, the way a man's knees bend out under him when he is about to faint. The stress of inserting the lighter one first had caused metal fatigue. A wind out of nowhere swept into the pit, lifting the peeled-back edge of the tarpaulin into an unfurled flag, and slamming the steel structure against one of the foundation walls before the entire crew rushed to push it, as if they could, back onto its predestined path. That cost two men, new guys who had just joined the crew that morning. Neither Tom nor Joe knew their names. If they had known them, they would have gone to see the men's families that evening to offer their condolences. As the concrete was poured around the walls of the vault to make it everlasting, Joe crossed himself and said a silent prayer for Keith and the two new men. As the bodies of the two nameless compatriots were carried out, the men stood in line in quiet respect, caps off, for their fallen comrades. Joe leaned over to Tom and whispered, "We are soldiers in the war of art against nature." Work continued.

By the beginning of March, the walls of the lower concourse were in place except for the decorative stone facing of scrollwork and art deco gargoyles that were being carved in Montreal. The arduous task of replicating the Baths of Caracalla as the main banking hall began in earnest. Colonel

Donald, speaking on behalf of the trustees of the bank, had declared that "the edifice must have dignity."

The hall has that air to it, yet to stand in the great hall is to feel dwarfed. The three enormous "electroliers," massive bronze and gilt chandeliers with over eight hundred lights in each, presented more weight than a rounded, vaulted ceiling could hold. Pearson came up with an ingenious idea of hoisting electric engines into the space behind the decorative octagonal niches and the interlace of stone that connects them. Joe, who was used to crawling in small places during his sewer work, volunteered for the hoist crew. Looking down from the one-hundred-foot-high ceiling to the floor where the marble tiles were standing in clusters of crates awaiting their fitting, he felt as if he was back on the mountain side again. "It's too near to fall to, and not high enough to grow wings on the way down," he said to Tom who worked the cable crew to steady the three-ton fixtures.

One of the men in the ceiling crew knocked a wrench from edge of the opening and it fell upon a man below, splitting his head. Tom always said that hard hats were one of the tools they could have used. A wool cap or a worn fedora was no match for a wrench. The man was carried away on a stretcher. No one knew whether he lived or died. But once the hoists and their engines had been installed, the electroliers rose above the hall, and each month, a maintenance man still makes the difficult climb into the dark recesses between the ceiling and the floor above it, to flip a small black switch, and raise the fixtures a half inch against the gravity that would pull them earthward. And with the completion of the structural work on the great hall, the marble and gilt men on their scaffolds filled the space, and the Baths of Caracalla, in all their Roman elegance, took shape in the heart of the financial district.

The wrench falling, Joe said, was a premonition of problems ahead. Tom said Joe was superstitious. Joe wore a tiny gold cross around his neck and a leather scapula that had been blessed by the art historian priest who had christened him. He crossed himself earnestly each time a body was carried from the site, and when the other workmen broke their ranks and dispersed after an accident, Joe would stare at the place where the man's body had fallen – stare at it as if he was studying a sacred object. But despite the omens and the signs the men kept to themselves, the central tower began its ascent, floor by floor, as Colonel Donald ordered them forward with the fire of a Scottish warrior.

As the city settled into the clear mornings of summer, Tom and Joe would stop and watch the view growing more and more expansive with every storey added to their quest of the sky. And with each storey, there were the fallen. Two, sometimes three, never four, but often five as Tom remembered it, were counted with every floor of steel and cables. A beam being raised might suddenly twist in the wind as a man reached out to receive it. He might grasp it and have it pull him off his narrow perch, or it might swing into another man, farther along the floor, someone minding their own business, doing a completely separate task, and knock the life out of him. To work high beam steel was to be aware that life required eyes in the back of one's head, eyes that no man had.

In the famous picture of men eating their lunch while seated on a beam thirty stories up on the Empire State Building, a photograph that has been called the icon of immigrant America, the iron workers are relaxed and jovial. They are smiling. One is reading a newspaper, another is smoking a cigar, and the viewer of the photograph just knows that the man will flick his ashes over the edge where they will be caught by the wind because they do not possess the weight of a body that will be drawn by extreme gravity to the ground below.

Tom and Joe, especially Joe, knew that circumstance was always waiting just an eye's blink beyond a man's vision; yet for all the circumstance of fate that surrounded them, the two friends would pause on a summer morning and stare over the rooftops of the city, talk about what they saw on the horizon, and marvel at the blue of the lake reaching to the far American shore.

When they had attained the twenty-storey mark, Joe asked Tom one August morning what the strange white cloud was on the southern lip of Lake Ontario. They stared for a few minutes together, turning every now and then to see if the floor foreman might catch them at ease, and then returned their focus to the peculiar white plume.

"That's gotta be Niagara Falls," Tom told him. "We oughta go there one Sunday before the summer is done. I've always wanted to see the Falls." Joe nodded. He had never seen Niagara Falls, though the woman who ran the boarding house had a Scene-in-Action lamp of the seventh wonder of the world in her dining room, and on special occasions such as a boarder's birthday, she would switch it on. The heat from the bulb inside spun a celluloid fan inside the glass chimney, and the celluloid was painted with a picture of water tumbling over the brink of the cataract on the American side.

"Yeah," he said, "that would be good."

The next Sunday morning they boarded a train at Union Station and by eleven a.m. they were walking along the Gorge, looking down at the swirling water where men were working the weekend shift to complete a new hydro generator.

"They say that new plant will light Toronto," Tom said with pride.

"There's a dark side to everything," Joe replied. "Do you think we ever get enough light? I mean we're up there in the clouds, literally, like the one that blew through the other day when it was foggy, and I reached out and caught a handful of fog. And you know what?" he said opening his closed palm and showing it to Tom. "Poof. Nothing. That's darkness at its best, in the middle of the day. Nothing to show for it either."

Tom stopped and pointed toward the Falls. The white plume was rising in a mist, and from the surging cascade a rainbow formed in the sky above them as the sun caught the tiny droplets of water.

"Maybe we're rainbow catchers," he said trying to cheer Joe out of one of the dark moods that often overtook him. "We're the first to see the world from that high up. We're visionaries."

The next day when they broke for lunch, Tom found Joe sketching the horizon of the southern side of Toronto, the harbour stretching before him, and the lake glistening. He was drawing the glistening. Tom had never seen anything like it.

"Death and beauty stand beside a man when he is working where no one, not birds or angels, has ever dared to go," Tom said, his voice falling to a whisper as he recalled watching Joe sketch.

That was the last time Tom saw Joe at his art. Maybe one of the Anglin-Norcross men caught him with a sketch book hanging out of his pocket, or maybe Colonel Donald had seen him and accused him of being a cowardly lay-about as he did when he shouted at the men during his daily inspections. Or perhaps Joe's artwork had been a violation of the strict "no photography" rule that was ironclad on the site. Tom always wondered what happened to Joe's notebook. When he asked Joe's landlady the following February if it was with Joe's things, she had no idea of what Tom was talking about. The pictures, however, not just what Joe had drawn but the scenes themselves, were burned into Tom's mind, and he carried them with him for the rest of his life and tried to describe them to anyone who would listen, even when he grew old and words failed him.

The crew was nearing their final storey, the observation deck on top of which Commerce's revolutionary heating and air conditioning system would be installed along with a special system for ionizing the interior atmosphere. A doctor who sat on the Board of Trustees was convinced that work efficiency would increase thirty per cent if the air the clerks and accountants breathed was ionized.

Pearson erected the last of his cranes in the centre of the building to distribute the force and weight it would have to bear. The spot where the crane stood, would, in several months' time, become the fabled boardroom where the fates of men and their enterprises would be decided by the policy minds of the bank.

The boardroom structure, almost separate from the business of girders and floors, was ready to install. It would be modelled on a dining room from a Restoration era Great House Pearson had seen in England. The floors would be laid with Killybeg carpets imported from Ireland, each costing $35,000, in a regal red oriental hue where no animal in the pattern was repeated. The rug on which the board room table sat spread over a space the size of a small house lot in the east end, and the table weighing over two tons would have to be raised with the stone Sinaitici heads and inserted in the room before the exterior facing of Indiana limestone sealed everything in as if it was a crypt entered only by a private elevator from the director's office.

The sixteen stone heads arrived from Montreal in crates the size of houses, and with them their sculptor, Eduardo Andolino, who had been conveyed by special limousine from Montreal to Toronto because of his fear of trains. The Sinaitici arrived on September 20, 1930, just as the leaves were dropping from the trees that spread a green carpet across the city. The winds were picking up. Raising the enormous heads would be a challenge.

It took over three hours for each head to be hoisted. On the first day, there was a snag in the cables on the south face – the Melinda Street side of Commerce. The rain fell, and a man named Micky tried to repel down the wall with a crowbar to see if he could solve the Gordian knot that suspended the ancient king in midair. The wind caught him, slammed him against a window, and he fell from the harness, bleeding, and presumably unconscious because no one heard him make a sound until he hit the boards of the hooded construction walk. The crowbar clanged off the roof of a truck. Joe and Tom watched it happen. There was nothing they could do.

Joe turned to the foreman. "I'll go next," he said. "Give me a crowbar. I was in a mountain regiment in the last war."

"Where?" the foreman asked. "We didn't have mountains in Flanders … just mud and trenches and ridges."

"The Alps. The Tyrol. I was on your side, so don't worry about me gobbing the job. Lower me down."

The men eased Joe down. He could see the crowd below gathered around the fallen man. But instead of pushing off from the south face, Joe clung to the smooth stone, his arms spread, as he stopped at every window sill to grab hold. He reached the tangle. The cables had twisted round each other a dozen feet above the top of the enormous head. Joe realized that he would have to go down to the head, stand on its brow, and spin the inscrutable block of stone until the tangle unwound. He anchored himself on the forehead and pushed with all his might off the wall. The head clanged against the stonework like a bell clapper.

Pearson and Donald were screaming at him through a megaphone from below not to put an enormous hole in the side of Commerce, and Andolini called down through a piece of pipe from above not to put a crack in his "Courage."

An absurd thought ran through Joe's mind: if this head had been Foresight, none of this would have happened. As the head swung away and returned to the side of the building, Joe held on to the cable and began to run, pressing his feet as hard as he could before the head pulled them off the wall. The block swung, and Joe held on for dear life as it snapped free of its knot and the cable came undone. The head began to rise again.

Tom had held his breath the entire time. When Joe reached the thirty-second floor where the bust would be laid before its final installation, there was the artist, standing atop it, doffing his cap and bowing as if he had performed a circus trick of superhuman strength.

Andolini and the men, Tom among them, gathered round to help Joe off the block.

"How did you do that?!" Andolini screamed at him. "You have the strength of Hercules."

"I'm Italian, like you," Joe said, smiling. "We're all spiders at heart."

As Joe sat down and a fellow workman handed him a cup of black coffee from a thermos, Tom bent down. "No, really, how did you do it?"

"I figured out which way the wind was blowing and let it do all the work. I was simply steering it. And remember," he called after as Tom began to walk away and return to his job, "some ancestor of mine taught Leonardo everything he knew. Hey! Leonardo was a genius! An Italian genius! There's nothing we can't do."

The shift ended a few minutes later. The Fensome men had installed the elevators, minus the fancy panelling that would be trimmed in before the building's grand opening set for January. There were reporters at the back entrance on Melinda, so the workmen were ushered out the grand front door where an ambulance was idling, and the driver and stretcher bearer were smoking before taking the body of the fallen man to the morgue. A caduceus was painted on the white side of the vehicle. Joe stopped Tom. He pointed to the symbol for Mercury on the van, and then to the caduceus carved in Andolini's frieze work above the front entrance to Commerce. Mercury's winged rod was the symbol of the bank. "Do you think they have all ends covered?" he asked Tom. Tom was exhausted and just shook his head. On the long walk east, Joe could not stop talking.

"You know, it was the same up there as it was in the battle when I fell to my death but didn't die. I thought I had wings."

"Don't joke about that," Tom replied without looking up from his footsteps. "Don't joke about that."

"And why are you looking at the sidewalk?"

"Superstition. I don't want to step on a crack. Some people say it is bad luck."

"Phah, bad luck. When your time comes, your time comes. That's all."

"Look, Joe. We've made it this far. We're almost at the top. They've started to move in to the lower floors already, desks and chairs and stuff. They're putting up partitions and doors. We've almost finished. Don't ya think I want to make it to the next job where I can be just as terrified?"

"Terrified? You, Tom? You ain't said nothing about that all this time. Hey, we've even looked over Niagara Falls and into the abyss together. You don't think a few rooftops are going to put us off course, do you?"

But Tom said nothing the rest of the way, stopping only at Joe's door to nod goodnight.

The following week, it was the turn of the last Sinaiticus to rise to its vigil in the sky. An October wind was blowing down on them. Shovels, lumber, anything not tied down, was moving across the area that would soon become the observation deck with guides and free telephone calls to anywhere in North America so tourists could call home and tell everyone there they were on top of the world. They would, for the princely sum of twenty-five cents, reach the top of the world, the highest building except for the Empire State. It had taken Joe and Tom almost two years, and back-breaking work to reach that place in the sky where Sarah had pointed. Tom arrived early and huddled near the elevator to keep warm.

"Where's Joe?" the foreman asked.

"He'll be along. He's coming. I know him. He'll be here."
As he spoke, the elevator doors opened and Joe stepped out.
He breathed into his hands, his shoulders hunched and tense.
He was feeling the cold even through his work jacket, scarf,
and gloves. Joe saw Tom and turned to him.

"You were right. I shouldn't have joked about this stuff,"
his eyes looking toward the rise of land to the north that
marked the St. Clair Avenue hill. The bitterness of the day had
set the furnaces of Toronto alight, and columns of grey-white
coal smoke curled from every chimney and swirled in the air.

"Tommy, let's get this head out of the way and find something else to do with our lives."

"What happened, Joe?"

"In the war, we had a pact that we wouldn't talk about
what we saw ahead."

"But this ain't the war. C'mon, you can share it with me.
After all, we've been through this thing from bedrock to high
heaven. And here we are. C'mon."

"Okay." Joe paused and huffed into his hands. "Okay.
Gimme a second. I had a dream last night. I was falling, just
like in the war. I was trying to grab on to something. Truth is,
when I fell off that rock face in the battle, I didn't grow wings.
I reached out and my sleeve snagged a piccolo of a tree branch.
Small. It shouldn't even have been there. I should have dropped
to my death like all the others. But there I stopped, my feet
dangling beneath me, the branch biting into my arm like a
snake, biting me and saying, 'yes I have you and now you will
bleed for me until you grow wings.' I reached up but instead
of catching the branch I felt a hand protruding, and I swear
to God it was a piece of rock that had the imprint of a man's
hand on it, a hand curled in a half grip, and I grasped it. And
then another, and another, until I found a ledge that was shelter
from the line of fire, and a cleft in the rock that was dark and

tunnelling into the mountain. Like Dante. Ever read Dante? He is frightened by three beasts as he makes his way on his life's journey, and he takes refuge in the rock."

"Like the hymn Rock of Ages I used to sing in church when I was a boy."

"Maybe like that. I don't know what you sing. I just waited in that crack. I watched the rain pour down. I watched my comrades fall past me with looks of despair and helplessness in their eyes. I watched bodies of the dead and wounded bounce and spin. And there I was. And there I was again last night. It doesn't go away. You joke about it. You joke to keep the darkness out. But it doesn't go away, and I realized when I woke that I don't have wings any more. I'm just a fool afraid of what he cannot hold in the thin air."

Tom stood dumbstruck for a moment. "Okay, let's get on with it then. We're soldiers of the sky, aren't we? We've got our marching orders. Let's go forward together."

The workmen gathered around the last open side of the observation deck. The crane swung out over the building and the cable was lowered to the street. After a few minutes of hooking and securing the great weight, the block rose into the air. Andolini was not there to see it. He was asleep in the King Edward and had forgot to ask to be awakened. The wind slapped at the men's faces, reddening their cheeks, as if to insult them, to say they were little, and the works of man were little no matter how opulent their arts might be, or how ancient or how defiant of death their declarations were.

And as the final head reached level with observation deck, the head of enterprise, the god of commerce, Joe Verdy reached out to be the first to grab the cable, and the wind with a gust pushed the head away from him, only a matter of inches, and before Tom could reach for him, he was gone.

Some said that Joe reached out and tried to grasp for passing window sills as he fell silently. Others swore he had reached out like Leonardo's Vitruvian man and spread his arms so that his reach was equal to his height. Whatever the case, Tom could not look down for his friend, and instead fell to his knees and searched for him among the swift grey clouds that ran toward the lake like frightened horses.

When the windows of Commerce were cleaned for the first time in 1954, one of the cleaners was puzzled, suspended three hundred feet above the street, to find a small piece of paper wedged in the stone facing of the east side. He said it had caught the morning light or he wouldn't have noticed it. Tucked between the seams of Indiana limestone, was a drawing of the view from the twenty-third floor. It was a depiction of the lake. The waters were sparkling. In an ornate, European hand, the artist had written the words "The Lord is my Shepherd. The view from number twenty-three on the day we set off for twenty-four."

And as the new foreman of the full-time window cleaning staff walked along King Street and tried to relate the strange finding of the drawing to a *Toronto Star* reporter who recorded the first brightening of the glass since Commerce had risen into the sky bringing the gods of money closer to the stars, he was asked how much rope was being used for the window-washing project.

"Exactly?" he said, pushing his fedora back on his head. "Well, to be precise, four hundred and thirty-two miles and forty-seven yards of it give or take an inch. It's all in the numbers. Numbers boggle the mind but you need them if you're going to do a project like the Commerce. They pay me to keep track of all the numbers. They may not seem human but I can tell you there is a human element behind every last digit. It's the things they didn't count that bother me sometimes. I wonder, how in the heck did they get all that material up there? They couldn't build it from the top down. It was bottom to top or it wasn't going to happen. Sure, you can say it was all a trick of some accountant who ended up with a desk, third row from the door on the sixteenth floor with a big black adding machine on his desk that he cranks when he wants to tally a long string of numbers. But those figures alone don't tell the whole story and I doubt anyone will ever make the whole thing add up in blood and sweat, though that's what gets the jobs done. And never forget," the window foreman said taking the yellow pencil from behind his ear and tapping the reporter on the chest, "someone's got to remember the numbers."

"You talk as if you built the place yourself," the reporter said.

"Maybe I did," the foreman replied.

"What did you say your name was?" the newsman asked.

The foreman smiled and looked up as the observation deck tore a hole in a cloud and the inscrutable eyes of the enormous stone heads, barely visible from the street level, stared into the mist.

DRAGON BLOOD

"THAT'S HOW THOSE CREATURES sharpen their claws," the cobbler said.

The other men nodded. They looked to him as a source of knowledge. In fact, he knew nothing at all about monsters. His rank in the community was based on the fact he was the king of skittles and a champion at bowls.

What would happen if the monster reached the saffron fields and trampled the delicate flowers to the ground? The crocuses were just past their bloom. The stamens had been gathered. What would become of next year's harvest?

Those who thought they saw it described a large snake with eight legs. Did it breathe fire? Would it pounce on them and tear them to shreds? Some said there were no such things, that dragons were vanquished long ago. St. George was real. He was the angel who guarded the nation. No one would craft a lie about that. But what if they had been real? Did they still lurk in chambers at the bottoms of lakes and terrify mankind as they had once done? What if the apparition was a dragon?

As the fog burned off, the hunters found evidence of scorched earth. Dragons breathe fire. They found the bones of three roasted sheep. If a dragon hungered for a lamb, why not a man? And there were markings on the trees nearby, scratches carved in the tree trunks. Each claw mark was filled with a red sticky paste.

"Blood of the lamb," the cobbler whispered. "As in the Bible. A plague is on our land."

The others nodded.

Aside from the fears of losing their livestock, the eight-legged creature awoke ancient horror. They could picture the beast trampling their precious walled field. The name of the town depended on that patch.

Saffron Walden. A field of crocuses.

What had awakened the beast of legend? Should they consult the Book of Thel or the Book of Daniel? Was this a portent of how the world would end? A dragon was a precursor of a land plagued with pestilence and sores. Where was the saint who would stand up against it? Who, among them, would be their St. George? Were they the lambs being led to the slaughter?

* * *

Admiral Qi dropped anchor off the eastern shore. Most days his ship was hidden by fog. It was springtime in this place of rain. Qi lowered his bamboo sails. The shift of the tide moved his ship in a circle. Though his vessel was named *Sun Shining on Waves*, he needed the fog to be his cloak.

He had fired on fishermen who came too close. They dropped their nets and rowed away.

He was desperate to replenish the crew's food and fresh water. Their last landfall had been Beī Zhŏu, not the near coast but the far side where he witnessed people with dark skins shackled and loaded onto ships. He could do nothing to help them. He was outgunned.

At the land of rain, Qi sent a landing party ashore. Han were not welcomed in the Xī waters. He knew their chance of survival was slim but he chose his second in command to lead the landing party. Zheng was the bravest among the ship's company. If they were to have any chance at success they would have to venture in disguise.

People, Zheng said, were afraid of two things: well-armed intruders who they would stand and fight and creatures they would run from without a fight. It made good sense. Disguise would create fear. The landing party was instructed to move to the west, heading toward Xī where the sun always set. They were to mark their route by carving numbers in trees and each number would be inscribed with red ink. If they became lost they could retrace their steps by following their markings until they reached the sea.

But just as Zheng's men put ashore, Admiral Qi's ship came under fire. The attacking ship had a swan on its prow and was likely a warship that outgunned and outmanned *Sun Shining on Waves*. Rather than risk his ship and his crew, Qi withdrew into a fog and his shallow draught took him close to shore where the larger, deeper enemy could not follow.

Zheng ordered his landing party to don the disguise, a mask that was certain to frighten the pale ones.

"Ghosts always run from the bravery we wear," Zheng said. "We shall wear the dragon on our shoulders and in our hearts."

Qi had prepared for the voyage by commissioning a dragon so, if along the way, they encountered people who were friendly to the Han, they would entertain their hosts with a dragon dance.

To survive the dampness and the hardships of the voyage, the dragon would have to have leather for skin. It would be red, for courage and joy so even if *Sun Shining on Waves* vanished into a springtime fog, Zheng and his party would carry the dragon's strength on their shoulders and know it was never far from them. Qi's ship wore dragons on its sails.

"You, Zheng, and your dragon men are the bravest of the brave. You have come farther than any Han has travelled. We are in a dark place now, a land of constant rain and fog. But do not fear. We are a small force, and though outnumbered, you shall wear the skin of the dragon on your shoulders and the fire of its strength in your hearts."

Qi trusted the courage of his men. He believed all men possessed courage even if they struggled to find it.

He had risen in the ranks because he led by example. He instilled in his sailors a clear-minded thinking to do their duty whatever obstacles they faced.

After defeating a fleet of pirates from Taohuagang that were laying siege to the fishing city of Ningbo, Admiral Qi was ordered to explore the Xī (western) Ocean beyond which little was known of its realms. A scribe in the Palace of Eternal Water unrolled an ancient map and pointed with a stylus at the empty seas far beyond India.

The scribe said that this land was where the foreigners lived. Their ships were sturdy. When they came to trade among the Han, they endured great hardships and travelled tremendous distances. There was profit in their ventures.

The map depicted the outline of eastern Africa, but beyond that lay the sea which the ghosts called home. Qi was told, if the foreigners could brave such seas, a man of his courage would triumph over the waves. He was given a single ship, *Sun Shining on Waves*, and told to select the best men he could find for his crew.

Within months, having put the emptiness of the Xī Ocean behind him, Qi turned his bow toward the běi (north) waters. The sea before him was vast and friends would be difficult to find there.

At first, the waters were cold and stormy and grew even colder as they hugged the coast of what he knew was the far side of Feī Zhōu, or what the Portuguese traders called Africa. The Han, though, had never ventured that far north. Why should they? When traders came to them, there was no reason to follow them home. Reason dictated that the Han should let the wealth of foreigners come to them. The seas were rough. Han ships that had ventured so far from home seldom returned. But the cold ocean suddenly became warmer as the current pushed them toward Ôu Zhōu, a land the outsiders called Europe. Then the winds died. *Sun Shining on Waves* was becalmed. The sun beat down upon the crew. The men grew thirsty.

The currents were the least of Qi's troubles. The weather in the year of Qi's voyage was unusual. Reports from everywhere Han ships sailed said that odd storms arose. The winds were not as anyone anticipated.

Though Qi had no way of knowing it, meteorological accounts of the spring of 1686 describe the season as one of the rainiest on record for England. When the horizon was not curtained in rain, a veil of fog overran the waters. Qi's men collected rainwater as it fell.

Sixteen-eighty-six was also the year the fields of eastern England turned to mud. Nothing grew. Those who augured the skies said that mischief was afoot in the world.

In the constant downpour, unable to find shelter, hungry, foraging for what they could find or take from the fields, the men under Zheng's command soon lost their way. Their markings in Dragon Red, the numbers they painted so carefully as they began their trek inland, did not dry. Dragon Red, a hue of ink produced in India and favoured by scribes in the vast bureaucracy of the Middle Kingdom would only set in a warm room. Outdoors, painted on trees, the numbers ran in the rain or became a sticky ooze in each wound Zheng's men carved to mark their nocturnal march inland in search of provisions. And when Zheng tried to find the sun, he found its light glowing in all directions behind the low, grey clouds.

* * *

The cobbler, whose name was Isaiah Corbett, boasted he had killed the dragon. He insisted to all who would listen at his shop door that the same skilled eye that had made him a champion at bowls and skittles enabled him to slay the dreaded beast. At first, the townsfolk of Saffron Walden were grateful and acclaimed Corbett as their very own Saint George, though he would have had an even better claim to fame if he had stepped forward with a pike and in the manner of the legendary saint who had slain the beast with his lance and brought the dragon's head with him to the village as a trophy from his combat. If he didn't use a lance, one woman questioned, how did Corbett kill the monster? Corbett refused to answer.

The rain began to let up. The fields started to dry though it was almost too late in the season for them to plant a decent crop. The crocuses were drowned. The townsfolk said: "Take us to the body of the beast. We want to see it for ourselves. We can sell parts of it to offset our losses from the saffron."

Corbett said it was dark, and early morning, when the combat in the forest had taken place. The air was thick with fog, so thick he could not recall the precise location in which he felled the dragon. He had used a pike but left it in the belly of the beast. Why had he abandoned the other men? Was he mad or simply foolish? Alone, he made the perfect target for the dragon. He had been a fool. And could the word of a fool be trusted? An old woman, the widow of a baker who had died the previous winter, confronted Corbett to provide proof that his story was true.

"If you were there once you can go there again and we will follow you."

Then someone raised the possibility that the dragon might not be dead at all. It might be merely wounded, and "A wounded dragon would be looking to avenge its suffering even if the gashes Corbett inflicted proved to be mortal wounds."

Corbett had no choice but to lead a tour into the syca-more copse and produce the body. One man said he thought he smelled rotting flesh and noted, "Dragons leave a terrible stink." They found nothing and, while a dragon could not be captured, it did feed fears enough to make a good tale. The creature soon became a topic of conversation.

The story of the dragon of Saffron Walden spread to Lon-don. Men of reason scoffed at the idea but the curious were drawn to the spectacle a dead dragon might present. Roads to the village were crammed with the curious. Merchants in the town raised their prices and the village became a carnival.

Among those who came up from London to say they had been there when the dragon, dead or alive, was revealed to the world was the painter Godfrey Kneller, a rising portrait artist who, although talented, was still seeking his first noteworthy commission. Kneller knew he had to capture the spirit of some-one who possessed a future – a man of science – and despite rebuffs he pursued a young mathematician who had already explained why the Earth attracted falling bodies.

Kneller knew the mathematician was interested in two things: numbers and colours. Perhaps the number of scales on a dragon's back, a meeting of zoology and arithmetic in a pattern that presented or defied the Fibonacci sequence, would interest Kneller's sitter. Perhaps even a scale from the monster's back, iridescent as a hummingbird's feathers, would incite the man of science's curiosity enough to arrange a sitting for a portrait. And if the dragon was real, the science of zoology would be altered with relics from ancient folklore.

Early on the morning of June 5, as the sun rose in a low mist on the fields and the dewed tufts of grass sparkled like fairy crowns, a tour of a hundred souls with Corbett at the front walked toward the woods. Kneller, along with many oth-ers in the procession, stopped at the edge of the forest.

Corbett explained that, if his memory served him, he and his group of yeomen had ventured into the heart of the forest from that point, armed only with a pistol and the weapons one might either take from a barn or whittle to a fine point the night before their search for the dreaded dragon. Some on the tour were bored by the commentary. Others were eager to see the dragon got underway. They were warned not to stray too far from the procession in case the beast was merely wounded and lurked behind the trees for an opportunity to avenge the wrongs done to it.

"You do not know what perils await you," Corbett called after them in a flare of showmanship.

Within a hundred yards from the clearing, the crowd had spread out, most looking for souvenirs of the fearsome creature. One little girl shouted that she had found a tooth from the monster, but on close inspection, it was only the tusk of a wild boar. A woman was certain she had found a scale clutching the roots of a tree but the object was nothing more than a toadstool. No matter how hard the crowd searched, not a trace of the dragon was found. Most began to wander back to the village, angry that they had wasted their time searching for a fiction concocted by someone's imagination.

Kneller, however, was one of the last to leave the forest. He had gotten a twig inside his shoe and leaned against a tree to empty it. When he pulled his hand from the trunk of a sycamore, the eastern side of the tree was carved with a strange set of parallel sticks, one short one above a longer one, both slightly slanted. They had been carved not as a lover's knot or even a symbol or a vagrant's warning but as a form of writing. The lines had been painted with a gummy red substance that would not wipe clean from Kneller's palm.

He stared at it. He was certain he had seen the odd configuration of lines before. He walked due east to the other side of the forest and found another carving on another sycamore

– this one composed of three horizontal lines. These were no mere dragon scratches. They were meant to mark someone's way, signposts for a path out of the woods, made perhaps by a person who was lost and left as markers so they would not retrace their steps and wander in circles. He took out his artist's sketch pad and pressed his palm to the paper and in doing so printed the image on the page.

On his return to London two days later, he consulted a sea captain who had made numerous voyages to the Far East for cargoes of blue and white porcelain he sold to wealthy London merchant families as decorations for their houses. The sea captain stood in the light of his greeting room window and examined the page from Kneller's notebook.

"These, sir, are Chinese numbers. I know them from pottery merchants in the East. They would show me their account books to make me believe they were doing an honest business. Little did they know, I had learned to read their columns of figures. I did very well on those voyages. This is the number three."

The Van Gelder paper in the notebook held the dark red marks. Kneller sent one sample, the number two, to Isaac Newton, requesting that the man of science study the odd deep red for the virtues and character of its hue. The mathematician agreed to admit him for an audience.

Newton was fascinated by the colour. The red was not bright but a deeper tone, more like dried blood than any red he had seen in artists' studios. But the semblance of blood about it made Newton uneasy. Who on earth would favour such a tone? Red was meant to be a lively colour, the shade of vitality but not morbidity, and this red was beyond any red his experiments with colour had revealed to him. The red on the Van Gelder paper was troubling, mysterious, and full of secrets. He and Kneller agreed that they could live without it. It was, indeed, the colour of dried blood. The red was splattered on a plank of driftwood and when it dried it had unnerved Kneller because the dragon blood was not from a dragon. It was the blood of murdered men.

Kneller admitted he had witnessed the dragon's slaughter on the beach near Maldon. There had, indeed, been a dragon. It contained unarmed men. Their death had been a spectacle. The unarmed men emerged from the body of the mythic serpent and were felled by musket balls as they tried to flee. Were they pirates? He could not say for sure; but the image of their pain, their twisted faces, and their hands reaching out to a ship off-shore haunted his nightmares. The images would not let him be.

"Those men were slaughtered without trial or question. They were shot on the beach and in the shallows by a patrol of the King's Own Men."

"Tell no one," Newton said. "Do not speak of what you witnessed. What you saw was the felling of the last of all the English dragons. What you saw was St. George in combat. And if you speak of it, no one will believe you. No one believes in dragons anymore."

Newton leaned forward toward the fire in his hearth, holding the sample of the colour in his hand. "May I?" he asked, and Kneller nodded. The paper flared. "You saw nothing," he said, wiping his hand on the front of his waistcoat. "For your own future, and perhaps for mine, the colour you found does not exist."

In the first portrait Kneller painted of the author *Philosophæ Naturalis Principia Mathematica*, there is not a single brushstroke of red, an omission both men agreed to in advance of the sitting.

* * *

The sun was not an ally for an admiral attempting to hide his ship. *Sun Shining on Waves* was unlike any vessel on the seas to the Xī of Ôu Zhŏu, the North Atlantic. Its square bamboo sails were designed to capture the maximum amount of wind, but the hull of the ship was designed for stability in typhoons and rough seas and not for speed. Qi knew if he took *Sun Shining on Waves* into the shallows, he might come under cannon fire from the land and if he sailed into deeper waters, the ships from the land of rain would surround him and outgun him and show him no mercy.

On the fifth of June, Qi decided he would draw the enemy to him. Everything he knew about warfare advised him to taunt but not to touch his opponent's superior forces. His knowledge of the complexities of Ôu Zhōu told him Europe was not a unified place, not like Zhōngguó where the entire world of the Han was governed by the power of Heaven. He decided to draw the enemy out and then do the unexpected: circle back and retrieve Zheng's landing party – if they were still alive – and then sail toward another kingdom. If he was lucky he could create a confrontation between enemies while Sun on Shining Waves slipped away.

But the boat used by Zheng to put ashore had been discovered in the dunes where his men had buried it. News reached London that Chinese characters had been read on trees near Saffron Walden, and a dory that fit no known description of a fishing boat had been located on a beach near Maldon. The Royal Navy *Swan* had exchanged fire with a vessel that could only be described as Asiatic in origin. The outsiders had to be repulsed. Trade with China would remain at arm's length.

* * *

Zheng and the landing party made it to the beach where they had put ashore a month before. They had failed to acquire the Admiral's supplies and had spent their return trek to the coast running for their lives, pursued by men in red. He would feel shame to return empty-handed. He prayed that *Sun Shining on Waves* was still safe and had not been sunk by the strange people of the land of rain. He would return the Admiral's dragon intact in the hope that somewhere they would be greeted with kindness.

As Zheng's party emerged from the low trees that led to the dune where they had buried their dory, he realized the spot had been disturbed. Behind them, and well within hearing, a column of men in red coats and pointed black hats was approaching. It would be foolish for anyone to search for the dory. Zheng had to assume it was gone.

He was about to despair his men would be caught between the sea and the soldiers when *Sun Shining on Waves* appeared around a headland and weighed anchor a hundred yards offshore.

One of the red soldiers, a man with a sword, was yelling commands at Zheng and his men. Granted, Zheng's men had lived off the land. They had stolen sheep to survive. What was a crime in Zhanggou was most likely a crime in the land of rain.

In one final act of defiance, he ordered his men to become the dragon. They would not fight. They would dance for their enemy. They would snake their way across the beach and from there those who could swim would make their way to their ship. If they died they would die with the courage of dragons. They would rear their heads and beat their drum. The idea seemed absurd to Zheng but, exhausted and haggard along with his , he felt he had no other option.

The dragon leaped from the undergrowth.

It spun, snarled, and roared red glory, turning, and shaking its head at the soldiers, some of whom were standing, others kneeling, as they raised their muskets and aimed at the creature.

Zheng's men danced to the edge of the waves when the man with the sword shouted a single word and musket balls tore through the dragon's flesh. Three men dropped. But the dance continued. The dragon danced into the water, its tail rising and falling in the arms of those who held it and shook its head.

Another volley.

Zheng saw two more of his men collapse. He felt a firebolt tear through his shoulder. He let go of the head and saw it for an instant bobbing beside him in the waves. The water turned red with dragon blood.

He could see his ship was drawing closer as a ball struck him in the back of his head and his memories of Zhanggou and the dragon-toothed shores where his brothers were sitting and mending their nets faded to a dream of eternal night.

Admiral Qi ordered his men to make full sail as three ships rounded the headland, cutting off their passage to the open sea. Desperate not to be defeated easily now that victory or escape was hopeless, Qi ordered his pilot to steer a new course.

"Aim for the biggest ship!" he shouted. "Prepare yourselves to fight to the end."

He sent five men below to spill every ounce of oil they were carrying and set *Sun Shining on Waves* ablaze.

"Prepare the barrels of gun powder forward!"

They would ram the enemy and fight to the death.

The bow of Qi's ship was about to collide with the side of the largest enemy ship when his opponent's heavy guns breathed a shout of fire. Those who survived the cannonade did not survive the combat. *Sun Shining on Waves* exploded, far enough from the enemy to do no damage. The bamboo sail, burning, collapsed, and the hull of Qi's ship hissed in the waves leaving shards of tiny floating flames that shone like broken fragments of sun.

The battle was of little consequence. A note about the skirmish was slipped into the back of a logbook at the Admiralty Records in Greenwich, but at some point in time, the note disappeared. The three British ships, with no men lost, sailed south toward the mouth of the Thames where the largest ship, the *Royal Venture*, was quickly repainted to erase signs of combat.

No one in diplomatic circles in London was any the wiser for what had happened, and ships from England plied their trade routes to China around the Cape of Good Hope. They came first for spices and pottery, then for the tea, the most precious commodity the Empire had known. And when tea wasn't enough for English tastes, the next commodity was opium.

The Captain of the *Royal Venture* was summoned to St. James Palace by the newly crowned monarch, James II. As a token of thanks and a purchase of silence, the Captain was given a small blue and white jar containing a new drink that was popular at court. The sweet-smelling, dried green leaves became a beverage when added to hot water. The jar that held them was porcelain painted with dragons on both sides.

* * *

When writing an official explanation of the disappearance of Admiral Qi and his ship, *Sun Shining on Waves*, along with its entire crew, a scribe in the Palace of Eternal Waters rose early one morning and bathed his body in a bowl of cold water. He wanted to be sure the narrative he would write would be about more than a ship being lost, sucked under by a wave in the vast empty Xī between Zhanggou and Feī Zhōu. The Admiral whom he noted he had met twice was an elegant man who had a natural air of seamanship and gallantry about him.

The scribe began by grinding red berries into a paste that had been brought from India by Buddhist monks. The paste was cut with liquefied pig's fat and made fluid with some drops of expensive plum wine. He stared into the bowl of red ink, saw his reflection, and set to work.

The aroma of the plum wine made him wonder how dragon blood ink might taste but the fact the other scribes never consumed it made him think twice about putting some on his tongue. He had heard stories of monks far away, who lived a long time ago on an island in the cold. Their lives were surrounded by the northern sea where they copied their texts onto scraped skins of deer. If anything, the story was something to scoff at, yet there was a sense of wonder to it. It was said the monks shovelled the words from their mouths and to do so wetted the tips of their brushes between their lips to make the ink more pliable. It sounded ridiculous.

For a moment, though, he considered the puzzling idea of writing on deerskin and thought it a waste of such a beautiful animal, and tried to imagine the taste of deer meat, though most dishes that came to the Palace of Eternal Waters were served first to the Emperror or his chief appointee. What the men above him did not want was passed down the chain of command, and one time he was lucky to have been given a dish of venison cured in cinnamon and spiced with cloves. It was delicious on top of his ration of rice. He wished he could have asked for more but a man in his position was not permitted to ask for anything other than what he was given.

On paper, better than deerskin for the ink, the story of the bravery of Admiral Qi needed no embellishment and was given the reverence the admiral deserved. Instead of wasting the ink on his tongue, he dipped his brush in the deep red liquid and began to write of an endless voyage to where the sun never set, even on rainy days when the downpour would not stop. And he was pleased as the fine brush tip wrote the characters. The Admiral would be honoured if he was there to see it.

Dragon Blood was the ink reserved for the most important stories. When it dried, the scribe rolled up the lengths of precious rice cloth paper, some sheets illustrated with pictures of *Sun Shining on Waves*, and placed them in a bamboo tube covered in fine gold leaf. He set it on a shelf in the Palace of Eternal Waters where he was sure it would remain forever, and its deep, perfect red, the colour of honour, would glow brighter than the drowning sun after it sets in the western waves.

MAGNETIC DOGS

———

THIS IS A STORY OF TWO DOGS.
   One is black. The other is white.
   One is called Ink and the other Paper.
   They are supposed to belong together because they have magnets attached to their feet.
   The magnets help them stand up, and when they are turned over on their sides the magnets stick to each other and won't let go.
   If they are placed on a table-top, one behind the other, they chase each other around. If Ink chases the white one through plates and cutlery while waiting for a coke to arrive, Paper will spin around suddenly and face Ink, because that's the way magnets work, especially with magnetic dogs.
   They are made of plastic, but they supposedly came from the same litter of Scotty dogs. That's a story that was made up about them.
   They are short and hairy. Their ears are pricked for listening, and their faces have beards like sages.
   Litter is an odd word. It implies something that isn't wanted and is tossed away. It is a word that says a person is breaking the law by littering, by throwing something away. Anything. People

litter because they stop wanting something. Sometimes they stop loving something or someone. That's litter, too.

Once you have something you have to keep wanting it. That's the idea behind having something. You need to keep it. If you don't want something you at least have to have forgiveness – both the kind you use to forgive others and the kind you use to forgive yourself.

There was a woman who was my mother and she could not forgive my father. That's what she said.

She went away and took my sister with her when I was seven. I have forgiven her, but I know she hasn't found forgiveness because she hasn't found me.

That is where the magnetic dogs come into the story.

They are always ready to forgive each other.

One is always ready to turn around and see what has been left behind.

That is why I have to find my sister. She has Ink and I have Paper. We have a story we need to finish.

When I was young, my family lived in our car. My Dad was looking for work and couldn't find any, or at least he couldn't find what he wanted.

We drove when we could. We sang songs together. Sometimes we sang "Row, Row, Row Your Boat," and Mom would throw in an extra line at the end by saying, "Marilyn Monroe." Other days the round was "The Blue Bells of Scotland." That one was about history.

If we ran out of gas, Dad would have to work. People didn't want to employ him because he had long hair and a beard. Long hair and beards were considered bad back then.

Sometimes people threw rocks at us as we drove away. They'd scream about how we were ruining society, and that my sister and I should be taken away because Hippies weren't fit parents.

Mom would have to work too. For a while she made beds in a hotel we couldn't afford to stay in. It was the kind of hotel where you could park your car in front of your room's door and watch it in case anyone tried any funny business. Mom would keep the door open as she was working and my sister and I slipped in and had baths.

One day, my family stopped long enough to stretch their legs and feel the evening cool on the New York Thruway.

When we stopped the car on a pull over, I loved to hear the trucks pass. They cried all the way to their destinations. As they drove farther and farther away, the cry turned into a sad, trailing song that always ended the same way.

We had enough money for gas the evening we pulled into the Savarin to use the washrooms. In the yellow-tiled wash-room, the stink of men in the cubicles made me sick to my stomach, but not wanting to lose the last meal of the day and go hungry yet another night, I sucked in my gut like my father told me and just held it down. Some men spat gum or hork into the urinals. That was gross. They'd look down and hit the rubber mat in the urinal – I could barely reach it when I stood on my tip-toes – and gob an assortment of cigarette butts, pink mangled bodies of chewing gum, and hork.

I usually had to pee upwards. I felt grown up when I stood with all the other men, some of them looking down and some looking up as if they were searching for the answer to something important on the ceiling above them. There was a strange attraction about peeing with men, a kind of magnetism that wasn't love but more a sense of belonging, more a sense of being one of them.

One day an old, fat man stood to the right of me for a long time, fumbling in his pants for his dick and when he found it, he sighed loudly as if he had just found paradise, but his thing wasn't pointing the right way and his pee shot out sideways and hit the man to his right. I stood there laughing until the man who got wet and the fat man told me they'd bugger me if I didn't get the hell out. They were going to settle things "man to man," and that made me feel kiddy and menial again. I didn't know the word bugger, but I had the feeling it was one the things I'd been warned about when I went into the washroom on my own. My mother had told me not to linger because there might be men in such places that would make off with me. These must have been the guys she had in mind.

After that day, I tried not to dream of them at night. My fear was the men would look in the car window and snatch me or my sister as we slept.

I wanted to protect my sister even though we had to share the same backseat day and night.

In every town we stopped at, her one treat was a dime – his last dime father always told her – to buy a daily paper, and she would read it out loud to us about the horrors of the world.

Sometimes we played the car game churches and cemeteries on highways that featured only fences, trees, and the occasional industrial building. My sister was two years older and always beat me at the game. She tore out the comic sections and kept them in an empty Kleenex box under the seat. That was her special area. 'Peanuts' was her favourite.

We would come along-side a convoy of army guys in green trucks. The trucks were full of soldiers, but the closer we looked the more they seemed to have the faces of boys. We'd flash the peace sign at them, and if their sergeant or lieutenant wasn't following behind in a Jeep they'd flash the peace sign back. My Dad would shake his head and recite some song lyrics about going to Viet Nam and "Oh me, oh my, we're going to die."

I had seen boys their age hanging around the edges of gas stations in the small towns where we stopped to see if my dad could find work. They'd be leaning against the gas station's plate glass window or white stucco walls and they were all chewing gum and squinting at us if we drove in out of the sun.

Sometimes one of them would lean in the window and tell my Dad they didn't pump Hippies at that station, and my Dad would say nothing and drive away. If the boys had long hair, they'd saunter up when we drove over the pneumatic bell and say things like "Peace, brother," and slap my Dad's palm which was called "laying some skin."

One gang of boys who Mom called hoodlums peered in the car window when we lay sleeping in the parking lot of a K-Mart or a Bradlees'. My sister woke and screamed. Then the boys saw my father roll over from one thigh to the other in the front seat and he rolled the window down just enough to tell them to fuck off and that he had a gun in the glove compartment, which he didn't have but threatened to use to scare off problem people.

One of the kids yelled: "Let's scram."

But those army guys or boys like them were dressed in green fatigues and ammo belts and held rifles between their knees. Mom said they were fated. My father said they'd be fine. There were palm trees where they were going, and that was what I thought heaven might be like when I was young. A warm place to die with palm trees.

I loved palm trees, even little ones. There was one just inside the door of every Savarin on the New York Thruway. The Savarins had exotic Arabic style script fastened to the stone towers that served no other purpose than to rise above the thruway and create a landmark and give drivers the idea of an oasis.

When a person entered, there was a gift shop on the left, a sit-down restaurant with pies my mother said were fly bait in a glass case, and the washrooms were straight ahead, women on the right where my Mom and sister disappeared and men on the left.

I was never permitted to buy anything in the gift shop or the restaurant. What I wanted more than anything was in a coin-operated vending machine – a pair of magnetic Scottie dogs. Every Savarin had a machine and in every machine were cellophane packages with two dogs locked feet to feet. I'd seen a girl playing with a pair at a rest stop where there were only picnic tables, but as she got up to leave she slipped the dogs in her pocket and skipped back to her car.

Near Rochester we stopped and, because my Dad was taking a long time in the washroom, I wandered into the gift shop to "browse," as I told the clerk on my way in. Someone had put money in the machine and then forgotten to turn the handle. I turned the handle. The coins fell inside the machine and chished against the others. I pressed the button for the dogs to see what would happen. The lady behind the counter looked over at me. I picked up the cellophane envelope with the dogs, held it up, and beamed at her. She nodded in approval.

All the way back to the car I worried about what I would tell my parents.

They were having an argument again.

My mother said she was tired of constantly driving from town to town and looking for work. She screamed at my dad that she was going back to Charlesburgh, a little town in the south where my grandparents still lived. My dad shouted back "Fine," and "Go ahead." Then they didn't speak. The night was falling, and we had to find a place to park where the cops wouldn't hassle us.

Syracuse. My parents didn't want to go into the center of the city. They were afraid the police might chase them off if they lingered around the suburbs, and the downtown was dangerous. We'd been robbed there once. They took the ten dollars my dad needed for gas and food.

I woke up first.

The car in the morning always smelled as if something had died in it early in the night. We had to sleep with the windows almost up, and four people breathing the same air can make a small space pretty awful.

Dew had formed on the windshield.

My sister was curled on the floor of the backseat.

I took the cellophane wrapper out of my jeans pocket and bit through the package.

The dogs rolled into my hand. They were held together at their feet, and I pulled them apart and set them on the shelf of the rear window. I drew the white one close to the black one, and the black one spun around. As I lifted whitey, the other Scottie jumped up and snapped itself to the base.

My sister woke and looked at me.

"What are you doing?"

"I found these dogs at the Savarin."

"Did you steal them?"

"No, they were in the machine. Someone had paid for them and left them behind. I don't steal."

"I want one."

"They're a pair," I said. "You can't split them up."

"What are their names?" she asked.

"Dunno. What's black and white and goes together forever?"

We thought for a moment. My sister looked out the window. "Dunno," she said.

"I do. Ink and Paper."

We spent an hour as the sun came up over a field of Black-eyed Susans, playing with the dogs. We had to be careful when we said woof because we didn't want to wake our folks. I put the black one in my pants pocket and my sister tucked the white one in her box of comics.

Mom opened a carton of crackers for breakfast and the last tin of apple juice.

Dad said we'd be going into Syracuse because he heard there might be a job there for Mom.

We parked in a back alley, and Mom took my sister with her because, she said: "If they see the kid they might hire me."

My sister had the Kleenex box under her arm and waved to me with her free hand before Mom grabbed it tightly.

Dad went away to see what he could scrounge. I waited in the car by myself. The front windows were partially down, but as the morning wore on the interior grew hotter and hotter.

That was the last I saw of my mother and sister.

Dad returned later in the afternoon.

He smelled of beer. I didn't know where he had found the money.

As the sun went down, it was clear my mother and sister weren't coming back.

Dad sighed. "Get in the front with me. I don't think your mom and sister are riding anymore."

"Where did they go?"

He turned and looked out the window, not wanting to look at me in the front seat. "Buddy, I think we're going to head home to Canada. Your mom flashed some bills at me last night and said she and Frannie were going to catch the first bus south."

"What about me? What about you?"

"She said we should go our own way. I don't think she wants us anymore."

I didn't know what to say.

Tears rolled down my cheeks.

We headed north up the Ninety-five.

There are no Savarins on that highway.

We came to the border. The man in a uniform asked how long we had been gone. My dad said he didn't know, but he couldn't find work in the States and he was heading north, back to the mine. The border guard asked who I was and my birth date. I told him, and he waved us through. If he had asked if I had anything to declare I would have told him that my mother didn't love me enough to take me with her.

This story should have a different ending. In a typical story, my mother or perhaps my sister would find me. My sister would appear at the airport. She would throw her arms around me and realize how much we were alike while acknowledging how much we had changed over the years.

I would tell her that I am a businessman with a small company in the near north, that I am doing well, that my wife and children are looking forward to meeting her.

We would walk together to the car in the airport garage, me carrying her bag, she rooting around in her purse for Paper, the white magnetic dog while I held Ink in my hand to show her.

Before the drive north, before I would tell her about Dad's last years and how he never remarried because he always thought Mom might be out there waiting to reconnect with him.

I'd tell her how he stopped wandering, how he settled down and made a life for me that she should have been part of.

She would hold out the white dog, place it in the palm of my hand, and see if they would connect again as if they had never been separated, though they were worlds, poles, apart. But Ink has never found its Paper, and this story without a proper end awaits a resolution that will never come. The world is made of stories, and most of them are imperfect, unfinished business.

Mom?

I often think about her but only in an abstract way. I can't remember her face. She had a nice smile, but that's what people have told me. I don't know what became of her.

Charlesburghs appear in five southern states. They are like the Fayettevilles that proliferate on maps of twenty-eight states in the labyrinth that is America.

In the States, people are restless. They move from town to town and city to city, unlike people on this side of the border who settle in one place and refuse to budge from their homes unless they get the bug to go looking for something, which isn't often. They dig into the rock and look for what will feed them.

When a place can no longer sustain a population, or when there is no one to pass on a home to after a long, hard life, people simply walk away and leave their pasts to the hands of nature. That is the legacy of my father's north. I have nowhere to go back to now, and if my Mom or my sister sought us out, there would be no one there to find.

Dad often said that it was Mom's idea to go in search of America. She'd read the restless writings of Steinbeck and Kerouac, the literature of perpetual motion. She used to turn from the front seat and tell us she was a living compass, that she always knew what direction we were headed in even if our father didn't. My father knew where north was. It was where he belonged, and he pointed the car there with me and him in it and stayed true to it. He was the real compass.

For me, the magnetic dogs were not merely a childhood novelty: They were symbols of a past I wanted to cling to. In some ways, they repelled and chased each other. In other ways they clung to each other tenaciously.

I will never know if the magnetic dogs had more power to attract than repel. I only have one, and when I spin it, the black dog's nose always points north.

The rocks and trees and small gnarled lakes that were familiar to my father bored my mother. She was the one who had to keep moving. She was like a sheet of loose paper that gets blown by the wind. Maybe my sister was paper, too.

When we were a family together, Mom often asked my Dad why Northern Ontario was a magnet for him.

He didn't know.

I often find nickels stuck to Ink when I carry him in my pocket.

Maybe the earth is magnetic in the place father called home.

The ore he dug certainly was. He never wore a wristwatch.

"Magnets," he said, "stop time in its tracks." He grew more and more quiet as we moved from town to town through the years of hard work, and he died a peaceful man with nothing to say, perhaps because of the throat cancer or because he didn't have anything more to say, a man alone with his silences, and so many questions unanswered.

I don't want to be litter. I keep asking the questions though I never get any answers.

Maybe my Mother didn't have enough money. For months after we had gone our separate ways, I kept hoping she would call or write. I thought my sister would look at her magnetic dog and remember it was called Paper and that would jog her mind to send me a letter or a postcard.

Perhaps she would find me in the rented rooms of Sudbury or the small hard rock, hard luck towns where my father went down into the bedrock each day and emerged tired and stinking from his shift in the underworld. He worked in hell, both literally and figuratively, lived in purgatory, and dreamed of heaven, but he told me one night after we'd had a few beers at the kitchen table that he always looked over his shoulder as he emerged from the underworld just in case Mom was following him to the surface. The poet in him kept me inspired, and the practical man kept me fed and clothed and in school.

I kept the black dog beside my bed each night knowing that its mate is living somewhere called Charlesburgh. The black dog would stick to a metal lamp or a doorknob, but Paper will probably never be found. You need ink and paper to make a story.

My pen is ready but there is nothing to write on, and there isn't anything more to say.

The magnetic black dog is beside me as I type my thoughts on an imaginary white page of my computer screen and wonder how I will forgive my mother. The page is a kind of blindness, but I see what I am saying, and I can't. The past, once it is set down, remains the past. Ink has dried.

TILTING

THEY OUGHT TO MAKE A MOVIE ABOUT TERRY. I could retire and go live someplace on the earnings if I wrote the script. For the time being, I raise chickens. I've always raised chickens. My father and my grandfather before him were, to put it politely, in the poultry and exotic fertilizer business. Eggs, legs, and fertilizer. I've learned a lot over the years from those birds. Chickens don't care about anything. People say they are stupid, but they are focussed. They chime in with their own opinions if you understand that opinions are just clucking. They do what they do. They lay their eggs. They know when you are going to push the cage through the rows of pullets and pick out the ones that seem fatter than the others. They are brave but they suffereth long and are kind. Terry's family never got around to raising chickens. Chickens might have saved him from the windmills. Terry hated wind turbines.

Sometimes, parts of Terry's nemeses would fall off and go flying through the sky as if they were launched. Apparently, when the windmills rose out of the landscape, the company that made them hadn't laminated the blades properly. Terry and I stood for several hours one day watching a workman repel from the top down to the edge of the huge knives in the air so they could be glued back together again. We took turns saying

"he's gunna fall, that fucker's gunna fall right about NOW! …
nope. In five minutes? Betcha five minutes."

Anyone who met Terry knew those forty-foot blades sliced
the air inside his head as much as they cut through a good
mid-winter wind. The whirr of the turbine hummed a constant
B flat like a song stuck in the brain. Terry told us about the
music one winter day down at the gas station where we used
to gather to gab about stuff.

"That's the way Schumann went mad," I told him because
I read that somewhere and wanted him to think I am musical.
"And A Flat kept playing over and over in his brain. The song
had nowhere to go. It just kept turning."

I'd look out my kitchen window across the way and see
Terry. He'd stand out where his yard met the field, lean on
his fence, and by the hour look up at the flickering between
himself and the sky. After a storm, big chunks of ice would go
flying through the air and he'd wait to see where they'd land
and write it down in a little notebook he carried in his work
shirt pocket. In spring and again in the fall, birds would drop
into his hands as he stood beneath the spinning blades. Their
blood rained from the sky. Heaven was crying, he told us.
Heaven was bleeding. He caught their broken bodies and you'd
see him disappear behind his dilapidated smoke shed and bury
them with dogs and barn cats he'd loved.

Within weeks after the windmills went up, Terry's cows
stopped giving milk. The incessantly spinning arms caught the
sun and strobed and flashed into his bedroom as each day
began. His cows ambled to the far end of his outer field one afternoon and pressed their bodies against the barbed wire fence
until their skin split open as the razors gave way beneath the
weight of their black and white Holstein bodies. They headed
down the Eighth Concession and disappeared over the hill. The
police asked him if they were his as he stood beside an over-
turned transport on the main highway and stared at the bodies

down the road and in the fields to either side where they had been knocked dead. "Yes," he said, "these were my milkers."

"No, no, no, a thousand times no, a million times no," Terry had insisted for years at meetings and deputations, but the local Corporation was not interested in his protests. We should have had the courage to speak up more, maybe do a protest or something, but we had enough problems of our own without taking on the government. Yet the more he said the word 'no,' the more it blended with the rhythms of the hammering metal workers and the engine of the crane as the white tower rose in the middle of the next farm on our line, a place that had been in the Jessup family for generations.

Jessup needed the money. Terry met Til Jessup one day at the gas station and the neighbour said that his wife's headaches had driven her to try and hang herself in the cellar, so they were moving away, walking away leaving everything behind them, and going to live with their daughter in the nearest town fifteen miles away. He blamed the wind turbine that had been set up too close to his house. The whirr was something a person didn't hear if they listened to it long enough, but his wife kept trying to hear it because she played the piano for local weddings and when we got together for parties. The music in her drove her over the edge.

The neighbour had an old horse named Mary. "Come by and pick her up. I don't have the heart to have her butchered and I don't have the bullet to do it myself."

Terry and that horse got on well. Sometimes old horses are assholes. They arrive at your farm and when you put them out to pasture they go home even if they no longer have a home to go to. But Mary knew that Terry was her best shot at a longer life. He brushed her and tied ribbons in her mane. One day he rode her bareback past our farm and my wife and I just stood where our old front porch used to be with our hands across our foreheads to shade out the sun and watched him saunter by. He probably thought we were saluting. We couldn't hear what he was saying, but he seemed to be talking to her and she was nodding her head.

My wife had remarked several weeks before that Terry didn't have enough to do now he was out of the dairy business, so I went to the shed and hauled out a box of books left over from the church rummage sale and left them on Terry's kitchen stoop. Old crap. Long stuff. The kind of stuff no one wants to read even if they have the time. The day he rode by our farm he had a book in his hand, so he must have been reading to the horse. I liked that. My wife thought it was daft, but she knows I talk to my chickens, so what's the difference with a horse?

Winter came too early to Terry Thurm's farm. Snow danced like a runaway bride as it crossed the open fields, some of it piling up against the side of his barn where it could not run any farther. Every time he looked out his front window Terr, like the rest of us, saw lovely straight ribbons of snow cross the open road. They blew in lines as if they were off to tie someone down to the place they'd always been.

Down at the gas station, Terr would read aloud copies of the letters he had sent to the corporation. "My cows wouldn't milk and ran away. My neighbours ran away. I have an old horse. It is sick, and I can't afford the vet because my cows are dead and even before they died they wouldn't milk. No, no, no, I say to the wind turbine. Have mercy on me. God have mercy on me. Stop the goddamned arms now." We'd all nod because we understood what he was going through. The Corporation had stopped answering once the machine had turned on and the arms spun. "I am still paying in pain and suffering for my hydro," he wrote. "Fucking well paying for the electricity that has ruined my life."

The Corporation loved to tell us that the turbines gener-ated enough power to light the entire town even though the town was nowhere near any of us. Our rates would go down, they said. No such luck. We paid and paid. Some of the fellas down the road couldn't pay any more so they just upped and left. They left their great grandfathers buried in the corner lot at the crossroads of the Ninth Line and the Fifth Concession where someone had meant to build a church a hundred years ago and couldn't find enough faith hereabouts to gather a flock.

As far as the eye could see on the horizon south of my farm and Terry's, the turbines rose out of the landscape. Their arms waved in the sky as if they were beckoning us to come closer and embrace them. Come! Follow us! We know the way. But up close they were more enigmatic. Each tower had a set of steps and a small steel porch as if they were homes to thin Methodist needle creatures. An oval-shaped door ten feet off the ground led to a circular staircase that corkscrewed through the hollow interior. I know because I pried one open the day I was out chasing a deer across my property.

The deer thought she would run for the thicket that lay a hundred yards away from the base, but the corporation had cleared all the scrub so there was no place to hide and someone who had probably come the week before to do maintenance had failed to lock the gate around the barbed-wire frost fence that kept the tower enclosed. I had the doe trapped. She ran back and forth looking for a way out but I stood at the entrance to the pen. Her front hooves beat against the fence as she frantically tried to get away. I raised my rifle.

And what did she do? She turned and stared at me. She stared like one of those female heroes standing before a firing squad in a war movie. 'No blindfold for me. No sir. I want to look into the eyes of the men who are going to shoot me.' I slowly lowered my weapon. The buzz of the arms through the winter air and the groan of the turbines, lower now because we were directly beneath it, ate into my soul.

"Get outta here," I said to her. Rather than high tail it out with her white flag flashing behind her, she sauntered through the gate, her head held high as she walked so close to me I could have thrown my arms around her. As I left the enclosure, I shot the lock off the open gate, and fired two more shots into the hinges so that trap would never close again, at least not until the next time a repairman came around.

The weather remained January even when it must have been February. Goddamned awful winter. Sometimes I couldn't see across the fields, but one day a circle of sun appeared above our farm and even through the clouds of snow I could see someone down by the turbine. It was Terry. He was mounted on his horse and had a long piece of what looked like a length of round doweling under his arm. Something that looked like a rusty screwdriver was tied to the end of it. The rod drooped and pointed down. The horse was shifting from leg to leg. I got on my jacket and walked out through the stubbled heads and almost snow-bare fields to the base of the tower I had left open. Terry was shouting now, not at the horse, but at the turbine. Mary was rearing up and snarling because she was as into what he was doing as he was.

"Hey, Terr, what's up?"

"I am about to remove a monster from the world."

"Okay. Say Terr, how?"

"How what?" he shouted to me as he started to back Mary up and then gradually turned her in a tight arc until they were facing the tower again.

"How you gonna remove it?"

"Rosamunde and I shall do battle."

"Shit, Terr, you're not Don Quixote."

"No, I am Sir Terrance, knight of the sorrowful concession, and I yield no more to these beasts."

"You're shitting me, right?"

With that he dug his heels into Mary's side, or should I say Rosamunde's sides, and the horse and rider charged the tower. I tried to stop them at the entrance to the gate but they galloped past me, the snow flying in the wake of every hoof print. Together, horse, lance, and rider, they slammed into the tower. Terry went face first over the horse's head. The horse tried to veer off at the last second but the rod hit the metal wall and snapped. The screwdriver end flew up in the air as Terry bounced off the steel porch. The rod and Robertson came down squarely into the centre of the horse's head and the animal toddled sideways, struggled for its footing, before kneeling before the victor. The creature shook its head in disbelief and fell over on its side.

"Holy fuck, Terry!"

He lay there stunned. He had broken some of his teeth. His shoulder was still part of his body but in a different way, and a meander of blood tried to find its way from his forehead to his feet. I dragged him home to my house. My wife was out. She would have shit herself if she'd seen him. She would have been all over me for not stopping him if she'd come home early. But what was I supposed to do? The guy went idiot. Right there. Full idiot. Can't say I blame him, though, but full idiot though.

I sat Terry down at the kitchen table and gave him a glass of Johnny Walker, but he said it hurt his teeth so I drank it even though some of his blood had dropped into it. I grabbed my rifle and went back to do the right thing for the old horse, but by the time I got there the Lord had done his work, so I just put a bullet into the door of the tower and went home. By the time I returned, Terry had wandered back to his place. I knew he'd gone home because he'd left a dribbling trail of his blood in the thin dusting of snow from the bottom of my stoop all the way down to the end of my lane.

That night I borrowed Jeff Tyne's four-wheeler and I dragged the dead horse into the bush beyond The Corporation's clearing. I felt sad for the horse. I'd never seen something die in a pointless cavalry charge like that. Granted, it was a sick horse. It probably would have keeled over in Terry's barn before spring arrived, but my heart ached, nonetheless. A person gets used to the life and death of animals on a farm. That's the way it is. But not like that.

I didn't see Terry for a week until I heard an axe early one morning. It wasn't the pock, pock of someone having a go at a tree. It was a ding, ding of someone striking an empty oil drum or breaking apart an old tractor. My wife sat up in bed. I got up and looked out the window. It was Terry. He was having a go at the tower again. This time he had an axe. Ding, Ding. He'd cuss and continue the work.

"Aren't you going to go out and stop him?" my wife asked as she bent down and peered out the window with me. "He's gone bonkers."

"I can tell you more, but not right now …" I hollered. She stood up puzzled and pulled her flannel nightgown tighter around her throat.

I hated going out before I had my coffee, but I also hated to see a friend in trouble.

"Hey Terr, whatcha up to?"

"I'm going to chop down this huge tree and haul it off with an ox."

"Where'ya gonna get an ox?"

"I found one. It was just standing out in a field five farms the other side of your place."

I glanced to the side of the tower. There stood an ox chewing on some scrub that was poking up through the snow. "You mean Frank Jatther's ox?"

"It isn't his anymore."

"I dunno. Didja ask Frank?"

"He wasn't home."

Terry had put some good dents in the side of the tower. The blows had taken the white paint off the surface so that the scars were silver. He hacked and hacked, huffing, his face turning redder and redder with each blow as he shouted, "Fall you bastard," through his broken teeth that were turning brown already along their fractures. Then the axe snapped. Terry fell to his knees and wept.

"C'mon, Terr, let's go to my place and get some coffee." He was weeping and shaking as I put my arm around him and led him off. I wished I knew what to do with the ox because I didn't have anything to tie it up with to the fence. I looked at the ox and it looked back at me. "Stay!" I shouted.

I wished I hadn't ruined the gate. It was an open invitation for Terry to take out his frustrations on the Corporation. After an hour or two, Terry seemed to be okay. My wife's bacon and eggs settled him, and he warmed up. But he had gotten a far away look on his face. It was the look of a man who was seeing into the future and did not know what he saw there.

Thank God the winter wasn't a long one. The ground hog was right, and spring came just around the corner. The ribbons of snow turned into ribbons of dust because we hadn't had enough snowfall to wet the soil and keep it down. As I passed by Terry's farm one day to check on him and kept going along the concession, I saw signs of life at the abandoned Jessup place. A young guy and his wife were moving in, so I turned up the lane and went to say hello because I figured it was the neighbourly thing to do.

The new guy was about twenty-five or thereabouts, his wife was pregnant. She was wearing a black parka with a big hood that hid her face, and he was in an open plaid shirt that had quilted lining. A green toque sat perched on his head like a tea cozy. He'd grown what we call a grandfather all over his lower face because even though most of us don't shave every day around here, we do manage to shave on Sundays when we don't go to church just because we gotta respect the Lord in some little way. The new guy had a canvas mailman's bag slung over his shoulder and heavy suspenders holding up his jeans like the kind my pappy used to wear when he got old. The guy came up as I got outta my pick-up and extended his hand.

"McCuddy, Buddy McCuddy, and this is my wife Tiffany. We've come to help redevelop the local economy. We're going to grow lavender and make bees-wax candles."

A bit of a wind was picking up as I said my name, and I knew he didn't catch it because it got blown away, and he probably didn't care. The pregnant woman turned her face from me because the dirt had devilled up and was getting in her eyes. I chatted this and that with Buddy. I told him who lived where and what they tried to farm. He told me he was going to grow lavender to dry and sell in the city and that he didn't mind the windmill turning on his land just near the edge of his back forty because it was "eco-friendly, man, and everyone has to like get into the earth." I just nodded, called "welcome" over my shoulder, and drove away. Then, I thought to myself, "Who the hell eats lavender?" I mean, I guess you could, but everyone around always thought of themselves as useful in a humble sort of way. We raised things a person could eat. People always need to be fed.

I had to go into the gas station because the package people had dropped off a part I needed for one of my ventilation fans. When I got to the cross-roads the provincial police were there and the guys were standing around a broken window at the back and shaking their heads. Jeff Tyne was shaking his head as we all stared silently as the glass on the floor and the table of tools strewn haphazardly more than they usually were on the work bench.

"Someone broke in last night."

"Kids?"

"Dunno. They stole the acetylene torch, some gloves, the goggles, the torch cart, a couple of crow-bars ... cuttin' stuff."

My first thought was that someone was going to plan a bank heist and cut their way into a vault if they drove all the way to town. There wasn't much worth stealing in our local bank though. Then the wildest thought hit me.

"Holy shit!" I ran out of the gas station and jumped in my truck. I broke some land speed records to get to Terry's farm. I opened the door and shouted hello, then shouted his name. He wasn't in the barn. He wasn't in the shed. His truck was still there, but that was nothing new because most people knew he didn't have the money for gas anymore. I went out and stood in the wind at the edge of his yard, and that's when I saw him. He was over at the turbines on the McCuddy's land, so I drove over lickety-split to the hydro access lane.

"Hey Terr, how's it going? Whatcha up to?"

"Won't be long," he hollered back as he stopped, and pushed his black goggles up on his forehead so he looked like an aviator.

"Just working on this one. Then I'll get to the next and clear the land just like my great grandfather, and then, as they say, after a long time the cows will come home." He laughed and repeated "the cows will come home."

He pushed the goggles down and snapped the sparker and the nozzle came to light again with its pinpoint blue flame. Terry had been making good head way. The acetylene hissed and snapped as a snake-shaped black line traced its way from one side of the tower and was almost ready to meet the far side.

"Tough job, eh Terr?" I shouted.

It was hard to talk, and Terry just nodded.

"Wind is coming up. There's going to be one helluva storm." I tried to converse, but the sound of the torch and the whirr of the blades drowned me out. I went up to him and he shut the torch off again.

"What the fuck do you want now?" he said, annoyed at being interrupted.

"Hey Terr, why don't you finish that later," I said, hoping to use some psychology on him and persuade him to come back to my place for a drink. He just smiled at me as if he thought I was daft. His front teeth were now black, and his shoulder drooped as if it didn't want any part of him. "You know, you don't want to be beneath one of these things in a spring storm."

Lightning was flashing to the north and the storm was headed our way. "See that bolt? That could hit us right here, right where we're standing. C'mon back to our place and we'll have a Johnny and wait for it to pass, and then you can get back to work." I was hoping the provincials would follow me to my place or at least to Terry's and put two and two together. They hadn't.

Terry made the final cut in the windmill's skin. "I also cut the spiral staircase inside," he said with a proud smile on his face. "Take you up on that dram now!"

We sat at my kitchen table. I sat Terry with his back to the window, so I could face looking out at the tower. My wife muttered something about us drinking during the day and went upstairs. "Call the police," I whispered to her. I sat there waiting. No police. Where the fuck were they? Terry was into his fifth tall Johnny.

The storm came faster than I had anticipated. The sky grew dark over our little no place in the middle of the world, and the wind became so fierce and the clouds began to turn a yellow grey. I wondered if a tornado was going to touch down. The rain fell and fell so I could barely see the tower.

Then I heard a sound as if a monster was having its body ripped apart. It was a sound of metal groaning and shrieking, a loud "EEECH!" but in a high note, and as a curtain of rain passed away to the south I could see the tower leaning and leaning as if it was dying in tremendous pain. The blades were spinning, faster and faster as the storm caught it at its odd angle, and then a tremendous crack broke over fields in an explosion. The turbine hit the ground, and its head came off the neck. But as the blades hit the ground they continued to spin. They walked on three legs across the open space the Corporation had cleared. They stepped over the fence between the lots the way a giant or a monster in a Japanese B movie strides over buildings. I stood at the window, and dropped my glass in disbelief and Terry turned, raising his glass, and shouting in victory as if he had just won a championship.

One of the blades smashed through the McCuddy's house, right dead centre, and jammed in the foundations, before the other two, their arms up, dropped their hands like a pair of scissors, and cut the dwelling in two. I ran out of my house as fast as I could, leaving Terry laughing and stomping his foot on the kitchen floor, and my wife almost falling down the stairs screaming, "Christ-ee, Christ-ee, Jes-Us, holy Jesus!" in panic.

I arrived at the McCuddy place. The husband and wife staggered from the remains of their house, and I stopped in shock to look at them, splinters and plaster covering their heads, and bits of plaster and lathing stuck in his beard. They fell to their knees and tried to hug each other, and all I could smell in the soft rain was the scent of lavender, and for a moment I thought it was beautiful – the perfume, the newly rearranged beams and walls, and the white blades reaching up to the sky. Then a bolt of lightning came out of nowhere, raced down the blade to the foundations of the Buddy McCuddy house, and struck the furnace's oil tank. The explosion knocked me to my knees, and it was the explosion that finally brought the police around, bless 'em.

The ambulance was a long time coming because it is a long way from somewhere to nowhere. The McCuddys were fine. They were homeless but fine. The quantities of lavender seeds they had stored inside their home in lieu of furniture went up like incense, and I thought of the holiness of what I had seen, the power of God who speaks in odd ways and appears in angry clouds and threads of lightning just when you think the storm has passed. And back at my place, with my wife hiding in our basement, Terry was dancing with the almost empty bottle of Johnny Walker, his legs kicking high in the air and his arms raised like some Judith who celebrated the drowning of an army. The police took the bottle from his hands, wrestled him to the ground, and cuffed him. One of the officers read him his rights as they lowered his head into the back of the cruiser.

About five months passed before the Corporation and the hydro folks figured out what to do with the remains of the tower. It did not fall down completely. It tilted to the east but in such a way that through the long summer months when the sun was slow to set, its shadow, like a tower of Pisa, passed over the fields of the abandoned McCuddy farm and my back forty. The shadow crept over the hydro right of way lane and counted the hours over Terry's empty place just before the sun went down.

The guys at the gas station would sit around as we waited for someone to find they were short on fuel, and we'd fill the hours between my morning egg collection and cleaning of the white shells, and my evening return to the cluck of my brood, and they would ask me to tell the same story I told my hens. My wife had heard it a million times, and the more I told it the less she believed it had happened right before her eyes. I'd end my version of the story for her with, "You know, it was probably those books you made me leave him to pass the time – that's where he got his ideas. You're culpable, sweetheart, culpable."

The local people believed in Terry the more I told the story, for they too had shouted no and no one had listened. Now, they had something to believe in. They had a hero and they had his legend. There was even talk down at the gas station of building an enormous, twenty-foot high statue of Terry with an acetylene torch in his hand and a pair of black goggles over his eyes just like the Paul Bunyan statue tourists flock to see somewhere in Minnesota. Nothing came of it, though.

But when the next election rolled round, we all voted out the bastards on our local council and wrote letters to the government to say we weren't going to pay our taxes until we were compensated for the damage the windmills had done to our way of life. No one answered us, of course, though to have a voice felt good. Gotta shout at something. But the windmills kept on turning, either right before our eyes or in our dreams as if they were hands of a clock trying to time the length of our remaining days, and the power they made flowed through us and beyond us and became someone else's light.

When I told Terry's story, I always ended with the bit about how my days with Terry ended. I could hear the police radio on the dashboard, the voice asking and asking for a reply from the officers on the scene.

"Come in 942. Someone cut down a what? A house was chopped in half with scissors? The baby was full term but delivered on the way by the husband? Repeat, 942. Repeat, 942. Come in."

Before the officer pushed me away, I was able to get close to the cruiser. Terry was shouting out the thin opening between the no-draft and the glass as he swivelled round in the back seat so he could see me.

"Hey, Terr, what are you saying? What in God's name did you do?"

"I'm a goddamned legend now! And forever and forever, whenever people in these parts stand in the middle of nowhere and wonder where they are you can tell them Terry Thurm made this place. You can tell them this is where I killed a monster. You gotta admit the world is a better place now. Yes sirree, a goddamned, fucking good place."

LEIPSZTHOU

I ALWAYS WONDERED WHY my grandfather had ordered the workmen to leave a portion of the balustrade missing from the balcony of his tower office. The drop from the tower, down the cliff-side to the ground, is about five hundred feet. To look over the edge, to let go of the railing, was one of the most frightening things I could imagine. I did not understand the meaning of the gap, or the name of my family mansion, until I received the telegram earlier today.

"Things are about to change," I said to my assistant, Godfrey, as he stood behind me with the message in his hands. I had asked him to read me the news three times until the meaning sank in.

On nights such as this, beautiful summer nights of cool lake breezes that gently sway the docked air trains in their moorings along the shoreline, Godfrey and I would stand at the open doors of the balcony and admire the peacefulness of the star-rise to the east. In such moments, I believed the peace would last forever.

The view from Leipszthou had always seemed to me the view into eternity, and if not eternity then into a place where time, at least, stood still. Beneath the tower of Leipszthou, I could see the lights of Grimsby, the orchards and vineyards stretching along the south shore of Lake Ontario, and the lights of the factories and houses in the lush greenery of Toronto across the lake.

I never knew my grandfather except by his philosophical writings and his other works. I also barely knew my father. Each of them married late in life, and each of them clung to the idea that change was only necessary when it would benefit humankind. The Harmon Washing Machine was but the first step in a march that was propelled by standing as still as possible for as long as possible. If a shirt needed starch, then why not time itself? "Board-stiff," my grandfather would remark. "That's the best way for the world to be."

My grandfather purchased Leipszthou from a Bavarian prince around 1905. He moved it block by block to the top of the Niagara Escarpment, and it was finished shortly before his death in the late 1950s. Well over one hundred years old, he stood one night on this spot, looking upon this same view, and collapsed by these balcony doors. What he left to my father, and eventually to me, was a clean world. "Cleanliness is next to Godliness," my grandfather always said. He had dreamed of a thousand years of peace. My time, two hundred years after the Battle of Waterloo, was but a fraction of that dream.

Peace, cleanliness, and good living. Those words were enshrined in the constitutions of governments the world over. He had written those constitutions when his money and his power had brought the world together in an unforeseen harmony. Mankind not only celebrated the Lord's Day on Sundays, but also Wash Day on Mondays.

Growing up in Missouri following the Civil War, my grandfather's life had been dirty and miserable. His father had founded a hardscrabble farm and worked it until the flesh on his hands was worn to the bone. When droughts came and the farm blew away, there was never enough water for the horses or the crops, let alone for laundry. My grandfather went out into the boney fields one day to bring his father a dust-filled bag of bread and cheese. He found him dead, face caked with the blowing soil, his hands reaching into the air to grasp at particles of his vanishing farm that just whispered through his fingers. In that moment of weeping, when the world of his childhood choked in his throat, and his voice sank in his chest, my grandfather had a vision: the steam-powered washing machine.

In Chicago, he sought to patent that vision, though no one would back him. "Women have tubs and washboards," potential backers would scowl when they declined to fund his enterprise. "The next thing you know, women will want the vote." But my grandfather was undaunted. With what little money he had earned from shovelling livery stables, he boarded a train that brought him to Toronto where he found a banker who considered cleanliness a Christian virtue. That is when the Harmon Washing Machine Company was born.

I have an original Harmon in my study. It is a large oak barrel with polished brass fittings, chrome-plated screws, gleaming polished steel casings for the motor, and a steam-fired engine that exhausts through a handsome black pipe. Within a few years of the company's founding in 1878, the Harmon and its succeeding variations, the Harmony, and the smaller, more compact Harmonium, became a standard feature in every Canadian home. Women loved the idea that they could pour a small amount of flaked soap into the barrel, fire up the engine, and their clothes would become clean. On stepping down as Prime Minister, Sir Charles Tupper became the first statesman in the world to endorse a Harmon product, exclaiming from newspaper ads and posters, "I am worth my starch in a Harmonized shirt!" The old war-horse of Cumberland made a small fortune by putting in his good word for the machine.

"Everything depends on clean clothes," my father told me the first time he showed me around the tower. I was not permitted to go out on the balcony, "Because," he said, "it is yet to be completed."

On my father's desk were three books. One was a Gutenberg Bible. Another was Shakespeare's *First Folio*, and the third was the *Libra Veritas* of the artist Claude Lorrain.

"Did you know," he said, touching the right-hand edge of the *First Folio*, "that laundry is responsible for the great works of literature? During the Renaissance when papermaking was a new art, the sheets on which these books were printed were made in Holland by a family called Van Gelder. They gathered soiled shirts, used table and bed linens, and even used personal clothes of good quality, brought the rags to their factories, and turned them into paper. The idea of airing one's dirty laundry in public was absurd. The idea of turning it into paper, on which great ideas could remain beyond the reach of time, was remarkable." Every day, my father's assistant would turn the page of each book, even if no one had paused to read the words on the previous day. I made sure Godfrey kept up the same ritual for me.

My grandfather always tried to outdo himself. He invented a steam-powered wringer to squeeze the excess water from shirts and bed-clothes, a steam-heated drying machine, and a shirt-press that added starch to shirts and took the wrinkles out of sheets simply by laying them on a padded, heated surface. The young Canadian nation beamed with clean apparel. Men could own as many shirts as they wanted because they were so easy to launder. My grandfather used the profits from the Harmon line of machines and purchased clothing factories in Quebec and the United States, soap-rendering companies, beef packing plants to supply the tallow for the soap, grain farms to feed the cattle, and so on, until he owned the network of businesses that fed the washing machine its insatiable supply of dirty clothes.

Then, he expanded his operations, first to England. It was my grandfather who earned the catchphrase "You could sell soap to the English," because of his pioneering efforts there. The English loved to look tidy. Next the Germans bought into the idea. They were fastidious about cleanliness. Health conditions improved in both countries, inspiring my grandfather to diversify into the hospital business, under the belief that healthy people did more laundry and needed more clothing. The French were the last ones in Europe to hold out. They held to the old belief of "parfum," but eventually the Harmon tide overran the République. Africa, India, China, Australia, South America—all these places were transformed by the miraculous power of clean clothes. Thus, the Harmon empire grew to rule the world.

With such an empire, it is understandable that my grandfather was literally printing his own money. It was at this time that he found the castle of Leipszthou. It was situated atop a mountain in Bavaria—no place to run a business. The winds and the snows often brought down the telegraph lines running in and out of the castle, so my grandfather solved the problem by choosing the lip of the Niagara Escarpment on which Leipszthou now sits. It was conveniently close to both the United States and the major cities of Canada. The Transatlantic Cable provided reliable communication with England and Europe, though he eventually installed his own, and his air train docks jutted proudly onto Lake Ontario.

The air train was my grandfather's next great vision. Getting around and managing his affairs in New York and London was a small problem to solve. Helium-filled balloons with lightweight inner frames, made of a wood his explorers discovered in the Amazon jungle, were tethered together to create buoyant, massive, floating vehicles. A single train could cast an eclipse over a small town.

Powered by steam engines and propelled by large turning blades, an air train could travel over thirty-five knots per hour even in a headwind. From each balloon, he suspended railway cars that in total could seat over a hundred people. The beauty of steam engines was that, as they propelled the air train, the excess steam filtered into a secondary balloon system, so that the vented hot exhaust gave the entire air train more buoyancy. Toronto to New York? Ten hours. New York to London? Thirty-eight hours. The world became a smaller place. As my personal air train made its return journey home, I could always see the spray rising from Niagara Falls and the white towers of Leipszthou on the horizon.

My grandfather's world was a place where steam was the supreme ruler, and he was the ruler of steam. Others had unsuccessfully tried to come up with such inventions.

A man named Ford, and some of his ilk, such as Buick and McLaughlin, aspired to run a horseless carriage on petroleum. My grandfather had an intense dislike of a thin-faced little man from New Jersey who wanted to exploit what he called "oil." So, within a week, my grandfather put an end to the horseless carriage and the oil business, and bought out John Rockefeller, Henry Ford, Sam McLaughlin, and Charles Buick. He took their patents, rolled them up in tubes, and stored them in the vault adjacent to his office in Leipszthou.

Steam engines did have to burn something, and my grandfather decided that the best thing to burn would be an invention of his called Splatt, a mixture of cow dung, left over from the beef and tallow side of the business, and soapy wash-water collected from homes that owned Harmon machines, which was then reduced to a syrup. Controlling this mixture of carbon by-products meant that my grandfather commanded the entire circle of life, "from birth to death, and how to get there," as he liked to quip.

Steam, the one thing permitted to escape into the atmosphere, changed the climates of the great cities. Trees grew lush. Drought was confined to a memory. It rained every day, but only at three o'clock, and the white puffy clouds against a blue sky were considered by everyone to be things of beauty. Cloud readers popped up in all the cities, replacing fortune tellers, auguring a person's future by reading the shape of the clouds directly above them. Life was beautiful.

With such wealth and power, the crowned heads of Europe fell in line with my grandfather's wishes. After all, he could buy them several times over if he felt like it. The greatest danger my grandfather perceived was war. He remembered the dirty bushwhackers riding through his family's farm, demanding food and water at gunpoint. When his father left for several months to Kansas City to seek work, a vagabond, still in a tattered grey uniform, kicked in the door and grabbed my great grandmother. My grandfather picked up his father's shotgun, and when the renegade tried to draw on him, after throwing my great grandmother to the floor, my grandfather blew the man's head off.

Killing was not what upset my grandfather. The dirt of the man, though, sickened him, and as he shovelled dust onto the body, he threw up all over the bushwhacker's corpse. "Filth," he said, over and over. "Dirty, rotten filth." For my grandfather, filth and violence were the most deplorable conditions a human being could stoop to. War was violent and filthy. The instruments of war, as opposed to washing machines, ruined clean shirts. Those wounded and dying soiled perfectly good white bed clothes. In his book of "Pronouncements," his one supreme principle was that "the destiny of mankind is to be clean and to remain clean, and nothing, no human drive or heartless disposition, must separate the human race from its destiny to meet God in a state of cleanliness." Those words are carved over the door of his mausoleum. The crowned heads and leaders of the world agreed with my grandfather. Though my grandfather kept a very low profile, his actions and philosophies brought about his portion of the two hundred years of peace, the end of which is now thrust upon me.

The massive defeat of the French army at Sedan had sent a huge message to the world: wars could be won by the power of technology. The Prussian needle gun, the Union Army's Gatling gun, and Nobel's invention of TNT—all these things made the world a dangerous place. When men went to war, they did not do laundry. Laundry was what made the world a peaceful place, and being the prime stakeholder in that peace, my grandfather endeavoured to make sure that military technology would progress, but slowly and under his absolute control.

On his advice, the nations of the world transformed their armies into public safety brigades. Instead of marching out to do battle with instruments of destruction, they answered the call of need whenever and wherever it arose. The shovel was mightier against a flood or an earthquake than a pistol. Peace meant that everyone had a far higher standard of living. Peace was the time when people bought washing machines. A man knew that if he left his house in the morning, he would come home to it in the evening with a clean white tablecloth on which his dinner would be served, clean sheets on which to sleep, and a fresh, bright shirt for the following morning, in which he could greet the day.

The time the Harmon saved was a gift for men and women. Not only could a man do his own laundry, but the free time afforded both sexes advanced cuisine, arts, and literature. Education was possible for all men and women who wanted it. Women were given the right to vote and equal pay. There were soon as many female doctors as there were male. Disease was almost eradicated because the universities, virtually overflowing with equal numbers of male and female scientists, found medicines to prolong life, thanks to my grandfather's funding. Indeed, longer life, my grandfather argued, meant more laundry, more peace, and more wealth. He had made the perfect circle.

That circle started to come undone about a month ago. On the eleventh of April this year, the heir to the Austro-Hungarian Empire, Karl Frederick, and his wife, Maria, were visiting the small city of Sarajevo in the Balkans. A man in a dirty brown shirt, which obviously had not been laundered in months, stepped out in front of their horse-drawn landau and fired into the couple's carriage, killing them both. Emperor Herman immediately blamed the Russians because the assassin had been born in Kiev. He called out his safety brigade, armed them with needle guns, mounted Gatling guns on the backs of wagons, and proceeded to march north through the small portion of his frontier that bordered Russian territory.

I cabled both of them immediately and told them to stand down. I caught the first air train from Grimsby to London, but during my crossing the situation worsened. The French Prime Minister, Monsieur Dedalier, mobilized his safety brigade in support of Russia. I begged Czar Ivan to stand down, that nothing good would come of this desire to despoil the beauty of Europe and stain the hands and bodies of his men. The telegram was intercepted by Kaiser Victor of Germany and, within hours, his troops were poised and ready to strike. I asked that a peace conference be held in Stockholm. Shouting and accusations opened the meeting, but I soon had them calmed down.

"I will not let any of you destroy the world as we know it. We have held the evils of war in abeyance since Waterloo, and now that it is 2015, there is no reason for us to unleash the horrors of a dirty world upon the masses. The *Pax Victoriana* was our chance to dream, and imagine, and invent. The *Pax Harmonia* has been our cornucopia. We will all lose, and I can predict that every one of you will topple from your thrones by the end of it. This is not the end of days. This is merely a moment in the great unfolding of time. We will be blessed by God in His heaven and by the children of the Earth if we simply let life proceed and provide a world for everyone where cleanliness is next to Godliness."

When the meeting broke, and when all the leaders, kings, czars, kaisers, and emperrors had shaken hands and embraced and agreed to let the great peace continue, I thought I had solved the problem. I thought the armies had stood down. I was wrong.

Earlier today, while I was working at my desk and eating a bowl of beautiful green grapes from the vineyard below Leipszthou, Godfrey appeared from the telegraph room with the first of several messages in his hands and an ashen look on his face.

"Mr. Harmon, there has been a terrible accident. An air train traveling from Paris to St. Petersburg crashed over Belgium."

"That's impossible," I said. "Those things are made to stay aloft no matter what." We had perfected the steam air train to the point where it was impossible to bring them down over land or sea. And even if one should come down, we had invented parachutes and fashioned the gondolas into the shape of boats so that no life would be lost if something happened.

"Sir, according to this message, a German safety brigade air train had been fitted with a narwhal lance and rammed the passenger air train. The German air train was also carrying Gatling guns, and they opened fire on the passengers."

"That's absurd!" I shouted. "Why on earth …?"

"Our people at the Paris and Berlin Harmon factories are still trying to determine why the Kaiser would permit such an atrocity. The latest word is that a rogue officer in the German safety brigade commandeered and armed his air train and dropped leaflets over all the German cities on his route. The cities are now in a state of insurrection, and French parfumier shops and hâute cuisine restaurants are on fire throughout the country. The Kaiser, sir, appears to have lost control of his people."

I knew what the next move would be. Within a few hours, the German safety brigade instigated an absurd plan that my grandfather had long ago intercepted and suppressed. The plan, originally drawn up by an insane German officer named von Schlieffen, called for Germany to attack France by invading Belgium. I had a copy of the plan in my vault.

"Order the French safety brigade to mobilize at once. Tell them to dig trenches on the south bank of the Marne River to halt the invasion until we can gather more forces. Belgium is helpless. They do not have a safety brigade. Notify the British. The French will need reinforcements. We have to stop this madman, whoever he is, before he brings the world to catastrophe."

But it was not to be. The Austrians, on the German cue, mobilized and marched their safety brigade into the kingdom of Serbia, and the Russians marched their troops into unarmed Poland to counter the Austrian attack.

"Godfrey, I want you to go to the vaults. Bring me the plans for the petroleum machines. Bring me the blueprints for the airplane, the tank, the electric light, the dreadnaught, and all the other documents labeled 'For Future Reference Only.'" As I turned, I saw a tear running down Godfrey's cheek. I stepped out onto the balcony and walked toward the incomplete balustrade.

So much had changed so little under the rule of my grandfather and of my father that an alteration in the course of life, and eventually history, was inevitable. My job had been to delay change. I was the one who now stood on the precipice, just as my grandfather and father had stood on the brink. I could look down into the void of death and not be afraid. I could fall and let the world fall with me into an abyss of change and dirt. Or I could let the future finally begin, as it had always intended to evolve. In that moment, I understood what the unfinished railing meant.

As I stood at the balcony door, the first stars were appearing over the eastern horizon, and I thought out loud to Godfrey, "This is the last night of peace we'll know for some time." I drew in a deep breath of the clean air. I knew that the air would soon be fouled with the stench of death and dirt. I thought of all the people who were slipping between clean sheets and holding their partners as they fell asleep together in freshly laundered nightshirts, unaware that by morning the world would be a vastly different place.

THE BIG WHEEL

I OWN A SMALL BURL MAPLE CASKET, three inches square, and it contains a piece of the world's largest cheese. Before it was laid to rest in its reliquary, the tidbit of cheese was dipped in paraffin to preserve it for future generations, a symbol of the beauty and the pride that was Canada, a Canada that measured itself against the world and declared that no other nation on earth could make or cut such a noble figure in cheese.

The underside of the casket is not burl maple but some less noble wood such as birch or poplar, with a dedicatory inscription to Corporal Ewart Willoughby, Royal Canadian Mounted Police, who perished at the hands of an Italian anarchist, Guillermo Modrani, on August 22, 1912 in a failed attempt to assassinate the mammoth cheese of Perth, Ontario. Modrani, a madman from Friuli, resented Canada's challenge in the art of cheesemaking. His actions marked a time when nations were struggling for supremacy in the fine art of fromagery.

Canada rarely shows pride in its greatest accomplishments, but the Great Cheese was an exception. Many fine Canadian achievements such as the electric wheelchair, the green garbage bag, and the caulking gun, are expressions of an intriguing ingenuity that underpins our identity. Yet for all we have done, our greatest works are rarely acknowledged or discussed in public. As a people, Canadians have much more to cheer about than they realize. There is no end to what we can do. There are no limits to what we can conceive when we put our minds to it and see our dreams to their ripened conclusions. Whenever someone in the world cuts the cheese, a moment of reverence is owed to Canada's great cheddar wheel of fortune.

The great cheese was initially conceived, though that might not be a proper word for it, in 1893 and was intend only to age a month or two. Making an enormous cheese was no mean feat and everyone involved demonstrated an uncharacteristic precociousness to bring the fermented curd into the world. Ten master cheesemakers, *fromagers*, gathered the amount of milk ten thousand cows might produce in a single prodigious day of grazing in a verdant *aplage* of Lanark County, and began the arduous task of transforming the curds into a masterful Canadian cheddar. The purpose was to show the world that Canada was, indeed, the cheesiest place on earth. The destination of the great cheese was the Chicago World's Fair.

"What does Canada contribute to the great continuum of culture?" the world would ask, and we, in one unified, proud voice would answer: "Cheese! Let the Italians have their opera. Let the French have their painting, the Germans their music, the Russians their ballet, and the English their sunset-less world. We have cheese!"

"And what do you intend to do with such a gargantuan cheese?" they might ask.

"Why, show it to the world. Wheel out the wheel. Invent everything from the vat in which it was born to the trolley it would ride on to the train freight cars and the barges and ships that would carry it beyond our sleepy, pastoral corner of ice and snow, and let all humanity know that if the Americans could build the Brooklyn Bridge, we could make a cheese defy the laws of nature." No one else had thought of it. We were truly original, and that originality, wherever we are in this vast expanse of no-place, still touches us all.

I am proud to say that my great grandfather, Corporal Ewart Willoughby, was chosen from the ranks of Canada's proud, red serge, Lanark County detachment, to accompany the big cheese as it travelled beyond our borders and into the hearts and minds of an awestruck world. Our enormous wheel of cheddar was a symbol that Canada was not only fit for curdling, but lawful and peace-abiding, on guard, vigilant, and expert at fromagering.

After four months, the cheese masters of Perth, Ontario, were ready to unveil their marvel. The side bracings, watertight and buttressed, were removed from the cheese. The mound began to sag, as if disappointed or ready to apologize for itself – as we Canadians often do – and it was re-braced until it experienced its *affinage* and firmed up, world-wise and manly. It was calculated that the magnificent product weighed 22,000 pounds. To call it a product, however, is to sell the cheese short. It was more than just cheese: It was a work of art. The dairymen, the carpenters, the blacksmiths, and the town council stood in silent awe, admiring their accomplishment. It was a moment when the spirit of the divine entered cheese, a moment of plausibility that suggested cheese could have been served with bread and wine at the Last Supper.

The first crane that attempted to hoist the cheese from the dairy floor onto a specially constructed wagon drawn by twenty-two grey draught horses, bent, then snapped beneath the weight of their accomplishment. A crowd gathered at the dairy door sounded a sad sigh of disappointment and my great-grandfather, standing at the ready to serve the cheese, quickly shut the door of the drying room to avoid any further embarrassment for the cheese. Canadian ingenuity sprang into action, and two hours later, a team of fifteen blacksmiths and eighteen carpenters had constructed a new hoist. The horses groaned as the iron wheels of the wagon crunched on the dairy floor, and the great cheese moved forward. The work of art entered the world at approximately 10:22 p.m. on August 22, 1893, the day of its embarkation, and the band, weary from waiting for its departure, stood by faithfully and struck up "The Maple Leaf Forever" as the cheese left the building. My great grandfather rode at the head of the procession, and the new hoist followed in a wagon so that the cheese could be loaded onto a special railway car for the trip to Toronto's Exhibition. The band followed behind the carpenter's wagon, playing "The Maple Leaf Forever" until, when the wagon rolled downhill toward the Perth Train Station, they grew tired and off-time and fell behind and the procession disintegrated. But it was grand.

It was a handsome cheese by all accounts. There have been many heated discussions about what colour the cheese was, whether it was a hard cheese or soft when it left the dairy. In all accounts, it could have used more time in its *affinage* to harden, for it began life as a soft cheese, perhaps the way babies or nations begin life with a tenderness and gentility that bespeaks life as a process of learning and coming of age.

When the cheese reached Toronto, thousands thronged the hall to see the marvel of the world's largest curd. The cheese had been lowered back onto the twenty-two-horse wagon at Union Station and paraded through the streets of the city until it came to rest in the center of the hall, surrounded by purple ropes to keep the crowds at a safe distance. My great grandfather sat at attention on his horse beside the great cheese and saluted every hour as a local band from the Stanley Barracks played "The Maple Leaf Forever" interspersed with "Abide with Me" and "For He's a Jolly Good Fellow" to hail and celebrate the curded marvel. Then, the floor of the hall collapsed under the weight of the cheese.

My great grandfather, his horse, Prince Albert Edward, the band, the dignitaries, the carpenters, the blacksmiths, the prize-winning dairy farmers who won ribbons but envied the great cheese, and the awestruck crowd fell into the basement together. As men, women and children toppled into the hole, my great grandfather, putting the well-being of the cheese before everything else, blew his brass whistle and shouted, "Women and children and the cheese first!"

The *Mail and Empire* the next day reported Corporal Willoughby's heroics, and how he kept a hungry boy, who had pried open the cheese's wrapping on one edge with his pen knife, from helping himself and diminishing the nation's great achievement. The carpenters and the blacksmiths rushed in to find a way to raise the sunken cheese, and by morning, the cheese had risen from the hole with several local clergymen pronouncing that the resurrection of the great cheese was nothing short of a miracle, commending the men of Perth, Ontario, for both their industry and their quick thinking. These traits of sturdy character, claimed the *Mail and Empire,* would grow into our national traits along with the ambitiousness that cheese-making at its finest level demonstrated. The boy with the pen knife was sent to a reformatory for his mischief.

Toronto celebrated the departure of the cheese which was now ripening in the late summer heat and giving a uniquely equine nose to its presence. The mayor of the city stood on a bunting-decorated platform at Union Station and said he would miss the cheese but that a grateful city would send it off with the best wishes possible, glad to see the last of it as it headed west to its destiny in Chicago where it would show the Americans who was really the big cheese on this continent. The crowd cheered. The draught horses, the carpenters, the blacksmiths, another touring band of Scottish regimentals, and the Lanark County cheesemakers, boarded their train car, and my great grandfather, still mounted on the indomitable Prince Albert Edward, stood on the flatbed freight car, specially designed for the great cheese, and the train pulled out of the station.

My great grandfather, seated on his horse, saluted at every crowded level crossing or hamlet where the people cheered and held up pictures of Queen Victoria and wept with pride at the beauty that was drawing people together in a spirit of national unity, and shouted "Hurrah for the Cheese!" The bagpipe band of Scottish regimentals appeared on the edge of the flatbed freight car to play "The Maple Leaf Forever" at every opportunity until it was pointed out that the breezy movement of the train caused their kilts to flap precariously in the wind and they were replaced in Hamilton by a fife and drum corps from the Salvation Army.

The cheese had just crossed the Detroit River on a specially constructed barge to carry its 22,000 pounds of girded cheddar when my great grandfather's horse began to sneeze severely. Turning toward the cheese that was now on American soil and shaking his harnessed head between achoos, the horse's breathing became laboured. At first my great grandfather thought it was an ague, but on further investigation the horse was suffering from what medicine would now call an allergic reaction to the cheese.

A veterinarian from Detroit examined the horse and pronounced that the horse had developed a chronic nasal distortion from the heady scent of the enormous dairy product that had become vaporous in its *affinage* the longer it travelled in the heat. It had also begun to shed some of its liquid content, and the run-off from the work of art stank more than the cheese itself. The cheese would have to be hosed down before it could be conveyed to Chicago.

In Detroit, my great grandfather wept and stroked Prince Albert Edward's muzzle as he bid farewell to his faithful mount. Prince Albert Edward was sent back to Lanark County where he spent the remainder of his days nibbling grass beneath sugar maple trees beside the Little Mississippi River that bisects the county. My great grandfather wrote to his noble steed at every opportunity, and the correspondence, one-sided as it is, is now in the Lanark County Museum in Perth, Ontario.

That correspondence has been a source of inspiration and information for me throughout my research, and it speaks to the special bond shared between a Corporal of the Royal Canadian Mounted Police and their faithful mounts. I know how much my great grandfather missed Prince Albert Edward, and after the cheese's enormous success at the Chicago World's Fair and its purchase by Mr. Jubal Webb, an enterprising international industrialist who decided to tour the cheese throughout England and Europe, my great grandfather would send his horse pictures of the actual Prince Albert Edward to tack up on the walls of the horse's stalls. These are also preserved in the county archives. The cheese continued to leak.

The Perth dairymen held a meeting with the carpenters and blacksmiths sitting in just in case a mechanical solution was needed. The head dairyman concluded that the poor thing was wetting itself under the stress of being paraded through so many changes of scenery. The solution was to inquire if the Lady's Guild of Detroit would be so kind as to stitch, on short notice, a heavy cloth to cover the cheese and protect it from the sun. On hearing that the cheese was headed to the World's Fair, they obliged enthusiastically, and sewed a quilt that the mayor, the dairymen, the carpenters, and the blacksmiths agreed to display beside the cheese to proclaim the kindness of Detroit, a rare moment in that's city's history. The quilt and the images stitched on it with great deliberation and great haste, were pictures of the American flag. There wasn't a maple leaf to be found on it. All the way to Chicago, those who were accompanying the cheese, my great grandfather included, debated a solution to the stars and stripes that draped the great Canadian accomplishment.

One of the carpenters was an expert in needlecraft, and despite some protestations that the men of Perth were committing an indiscretion of devious advances, the carpenter neatly as he could on a shaking train car, stitched several panels that included beavers, a Union Jack or two, and several stars that were miraculously transformed into our national vegetative device and sewn over the stars. When he pricked his fingers when the carriage bumped, he discovered he could use his own blood, the venerable life-force of a true Canadian, to leave tiny drops on his handicraft that would be explained as the blood of Canadian forefathers who had fallen in defence of Canada whenever it had needed to be defended. One American by-stander, when told of the blood, asked: "When was that?" No one had a suitable, diplomatically acceptable answer. Everyone in the cheese party had agreed they would not mention the War of 1812 for fear that an angry mob might take retaliation on the cheese for the burning of the White House, which was still a very sticky topic between Canadians and Americans in 1893.

Despite the needlework and the weeping cheese, despite the disagreeable smell of the leakage and the allergies of Prince Albert Edward, the cheese arrived in Chicago to a throng of well-wishers, each eager to say they had caught a glimpse of the marvellous cheddar. The crowd pushed forward, and hands reached up to try and touch it as if the great cheese was a magic talisman. One woman claimed she was cured by the curd. Another man who had a stomach ulcer announced that on touching the cheese he no longer felt any pain in his ab-domen. The more word spread of the cheese's arrival at the greatest exhibition ever witnessed by mankind, the more the twenty-two-thousand-pound round became mysterious and majestic. Everyone wanted a piece of the cheese.

The triumph continued in Chicago. President Grover Cleveland made a special trip in his presidential railway car-riage to the windy city to honour the mammoth cheese. "This is positively the biggest cheese I have met, either here or in Wash-ington or in all my political life!" A Marine Band attempted to play "The Maple Leaf Forever" as if it was a Sousa march, then gave up because the rhythm was not jaunty to their liking and broke into the "Star-Spangled Banner." The men from Perth had brought the weight of their achievement to bear upon America and they had conquered! Overcome with happiness and almost sick to their souls on cheap, watery beer, they sold their beloved cheese and caught the next train home to Perth.

The American purchasers were merely acting as agents for an English gentleman of industry, Mr. Jubal Webb, who, on the advice of a former Prime Minister and one of the last living Fathers of Confederation, Sir Charles Tupper, would have the cheese conveyed to England where it would be honoured by the Queen herself! Hurrah! We had not sold ourselves short. We were being protected by the great spirit of the Motherland herself! The old country! At the heart of our empire, our cheese would be measured and measure up against the cheesiest men in the world, men from the birthplace of cheddar, Cheddar, England! What was even more important was that my great grandfather still had employment as the keeper of the great cheese. To mark the transfer of the great cheese from Chicago to Boston, my great grandfather was given a new horse, a proud white mare named Princess Alexandra. My great grandfather wrote home to my great great grandmother that he was beside himself with eagerness and anticipation to mount her and enjoy a long, pleasurable ride. "Perhaps," he said, "he could teach the horse to dance to 'The Maple Leaf Forever.' Imagine, a whole brigade of fine horses, each mounted by a constable of Canada's finest, prancing poetically to the sweet strains of our national hymn."

The Great Cheese of 1893 had now become an international expedition, the Great Cheese Expedition. The marvel was loaded onto a specially designed ship sailed under the Italian flag – for the Italians knew a thing or two about the transportation of cheese – the S. S. Cambozola. My great grandfather and his spanking new horse were also loaded onto the ship (my great grandfather had refused to dismount) and were placed on the outside prow deck of the ship, facing the waves, the wind, the storms, and heart of the empire. He had a rough crossing. As the fo'c'sle dipped with each rise and fall, he and his sturdy steed were washed over by tremendous swells as the sea battered at their faces. Corporal Willoughby would not budge. He was representing Canada. He and Princess Alexandra were redoubtable, stalwart, and credit the force through it all. And when Land's End came into sight, the band of Merchant Seamen struck up a very fine rendition of "The Maple Leaf Forever," adding a few extra grace notes, and my great grandfather saluted as the puffins from the cliffs dipped and rolled in the air overhead. It was a fine arrival.

The arrival of the cheese in London was anti-climactic. It had travelled so far and endured so much, and yet it was not a marvel. It was not exotic because the land of its birth was not exotic. Something needed to be done to herald the great cheese. That is when Sir Charles Tupper, the old war-horse of the Cumberland, one of the last Fathers of Confederation, a knighted Prime Minister, stepped in. In a specially constructed barge, the cheese crossed the channel to tour Europe. It would be accompanied by the remaining members of the Perth party of dairymen, carpenters, and blacksmiths, who were now nothing more than hangers-on to the great cheese. Most of the original party had lost reverence for the giant wheel and had returned to their lives. Tupper, however, inspired us! He not only spoke of the cheese, he spoke to it. In a rousing speech before the actual Prince Albert Edward, he moved the court to tears with an oration that touched on the beauty of Canadian sunsets, the vast unexplored reaches of our mysterious nation, bears, moose, rabbits and pheasants – lots of pheasants. He concluded by telling the Prince's men that in Canada everything was worth shooting except the great cheese. The speech was published in its entirety in *The Times*, and that is where the Italian anarchist, Modrani from Friuli, conceived the plot to assassinate Canada's great cheese.

Granted, in Modrani's defence, it was an age of anarchists. Any self-respecting, impoverished Italian with even an iota of political beliefs was obligated to shoot or shoot at something – a President, a corporate chairman, a banker. Modrani chose to shoot the cheese. It would be a symbolic act, a reassertion on his part that Italia reigned supreme in the fromager's art, and even if he could not kill the cheese, which was his first intention, he would at least make his point. He waited fifteen years, purchased a suitable revolver after six years, scrounged and saved and bought the bullets four years later, and followed the cheese from Berlin (where the Kaiser declared it *der faulig Käse* which some mistook for a term of honour but which means, in words foreshadowing war, "the putrid cheese"), Budapest, Vienna (where it was also called *der faulig Käse* by Franz Josef), Madrid (where a riot over the perfume of the cheese broke out), and finally to Paris. It was in Paris where Modrani lay in waiting.

A friend of Modrani's had stolen the Mona Lisa and hidden it behind the stove in his walk-up apartment, and the two men had spent long evenings admiring their national treasure. "The world has taken so much from us, Guillermo," said the art thief. "Now, you must fulfill your destiny. You must take back Italy's claim to greatness of the ancient *casaro,* the cheesemakers of your ancestors!"

My great grandfather remained steadfast to the cheese. On the day of the attempted assassination by the *formaggio assassino*, the Band of the Guard Republique had just finished playing a very spirited rendition of "The Maple Leaf Forever." My great grandfather was seated on his horse – a new one named Princess Mary who replaced Princess Alexandra who had been retired to a field in Wales – when Modrani stepped forward and levelled his pistol at the great cheese. Princess Mary saw the pistol, too, but remained frozen on her hooves, but my great grandfather leapt from his horse and took down the shooter after the *formaggio assassino* drew a bead on the cheese.

The single bullet pierced my great grandfather's red serge as the Guard Republique pummelled the Italian with their brass instruments, the trombone delivering the worst of the beating.

Corporal Ewart Willoughby lay in the arms of a *boulanger* who had closed his *boulangerie* and his *patisserie* for the day to come and admire the great cheese, and uttered his last words: "Thank God, now that I have saved the cheese, let me die in peace." Those words, so reminiscent of the final pronouncements of General Wolfe when he fell at the Battle of Quebec, made world headlines. People in Quebec felt insulted and there were stern letters to the editors of Canadian newspapers offering sympathy for the Italian anarchist. But throughout southern Ontario, there was not a dry eye. One apocryphal story about Corporal Willoughby's death began to circulate, and it may be true, or it may simply be part the legend of the cheese. When the *boulanger* held the dying Corporal, he looked into the Canadian's eyes and said, "*C'est domage*," to which the Corporal replied with his last breath, "*Mais, non. C'est fromage.*"

Princess Mary knelt on her front legs and bowed her head as the Corporal's eyes fluttered and then closed. A constable walked out into a Lanark County *alpage*, the field where Prince Albert Edward had been set to grass and broke the news of his companion's death to the officer's first and forever faithful mount. Both the *Mail and Empire* and the local Perth papers reported that the poor beast shook his head upon hearing the news and then fell over on his side and expired. Thus, as they had been almost inseparable in life, save for the scent of the cheese, so they became inseparable in death, a Royal Canadian Mounted Police Corporal and his horse.

Corporal Willoughby's body was conveyed to London where, after much discussion, it was decided not to bury him in Westminster Abbey, but in the corner of a quiet country churchyard with a maple leaf carved on his tombstone and the inscription. "Corporal Ewart Willoughby. He loved his country and his cheese." Sir Charles Tupper, who was by now in very advanced years but was still representing Canada, decided that Willoughby's death was not in vain, and that the most prominent members of King Edward's court should, as a form of secular eucharist, partake of the great cheese at a wine and cheese party to be held in the Pall Mall Club in honour of the Canadian's sacrifice. It was a sad day in the Pall Mall Club when the great and the mighty of England gathered and Sir Charles stood before the great cheese and declared, "Gentlemen, we must all, now, cut the cheese together in one trumpeting salute to our fallen man." Everyone shouted, "Here! Here!" and the Band of the Grenadier Guard from Buckingham Palace struck up the tunes that had begun my great grandfather's odyssey with the Perth Giant, "The Maple Leaf Forever," and "For He's a Jolly Good Fellow."

Those present reported to the gazettes that the cheese tasted slightly sour, that its heart was bitter with sorrow, and no number of grapes or Madeira would wash away the aftertaste of grief. The next day, Harley Street, home of London's finest physicians, was almost a ghost town as doctors moved among the terrace houses of Mayfair and the halls of Parliament in Westminster.

I have specially set aside today to remember the Great Cheese of 1893. I open the tiny burl maple casket and peel back the layer of protective paraffin. I will take a nibble of the cheese inside me, avoiding the spot of black mould that grew in one corner of the cube, and I will at last taste the history of this nation. It is salty, slightly sour, bitter, almost distasteful. But we made it, stood on guard for it, watched it age, and then, when the cheese gave itself up in sacrifice after a sacrifice had been made for it, it became legendary, the mythology that nations need to have if they are to do great things. I believe we should revive "The Maple Leaf Forever," as our national anthem and add an extra verse to it to honour the Great Cheese. We have rarely done anything on such a scale or with such purpose and grandeur, though, arguably, there have been many fine accomplishments. But in honour of the cheese, let us hail its shining moment as we sing:

When we made cheese to mark our place
We challenged all the human race
To curdle milk and give it love
Inspired by ah-ah-bove,
We stand with pride to hail the matter
We made the largest cheddar!
Around the globe sing each cheese lover
The Maple Leaf forever!

The only prominent personage who was absent from the gathering in my great grandfather's honour was the Prince of Wales, George, who had a previous appointment with his beard groomer.

Upon George's ascent to the throne, he purchased the remaining portion of the great cheese, all fifteen thousand pounds of it. George knew war was inevitable. Britain had been in an arms race with Germany for over twenty years and needed everything it could throw at its enemies. The cheese had become *ammoniated*. On the king's orders, the cheese was cubed or wedged, depending on how it would be used in battle. The cubes were intended for use in close quarters such as trench wine and cheese parties where the Germans were invited to drop in and partake of the now hostile cheddar. The ploy worked beautifully at the Second Battle of Ypres for about an hour, but when the Germans became dyspeptic and loose, they immediately retreated to their side of No-Man's-Land and shouted curses about the Canadian devils and the ruthlessness of their *der Käse*.

But it was at the Battle of Vimy Ridge where the cheese served with distinction. The Canadians were tunnelling through the limestone hill, hiding an army underground. Above ground, however, they knew the Germans were poorly provisioned, so they would lob wedges of the cheese into the trenches of the famished Huns. The *Landwehr* men devoured cheese, were weakened in unimaginable ways, and soon the Canadians reached their objective. The truth about the weaponization of cheese was quickly buried by the War Office for fear Canada might be charged with war crimes for having tossed its aged and antiquated ambition at the enemy. To do so was a use of dairy products strictly forbidden by the Geneva convention.

I am almost certain that as every brave Canadian soldier tossed his curds at the Jerries he was pronouncing the name of my great grandfather. I have seen letters in the Lanark County Museum Archives describing the moment our boys launched the cheese at the enemy trenches, each brave Canadian fighter holding the image of the of a self-sacrificing Royal Canadian Mounted Policeman, seated on his horse, standing guard for all time. Perhaps they were also recalling an era when the milk of human kindness and a small helping of bacteria stood for love of country.

By 1920, the remaining portions of the great cheese, little more than six eighty-pound bricks, were quietly disposed of at sea in a moving committal to the deep. The long coffin-shaped slabs, draped in a Red Ensign, the flag Canada earned for itself during four tragic years, slid from the planks as the pastor intoned, "We commit this cheese to the deep." The Royal Navy Band of the H.M.S. Stilton played "O Canada," the new anthem of unity that had replaced "The Maple Leaf Forever." The national hymn was followed by a moment of silence before the band broke into "For He's a Jolly Good Fellow" which seemed appropriate as the cheese had taken on a life of its own.

THE SLITHY TOVES

THIS ISN'T SOMETHING I CAN PUT in an academic paper, yet it is the story of how my career in academe was made. It is not something you need to take as fact; little of what I am going to tell you about how my research evolved actually matters now that the real facts about Lewis Carroll are widely known. That said, I was the one who discovered those facts. And what truth about Lewis Carroll did I discover? He was framed.

I understand what Lewis Carroll had to endure. The very *thing* that ruined him made me a target of its destructive force. That *thing* was not scholarly jealousy or even the disputes that embroil graduate students and supervisors in a quagmire of distasteful behaviour. Far from it. What plagued the author of *Through the Looking Glass* and *Alice Wonderland* was the same *thing* that appeared in my childhood garden and haunted me through the early decades of my life. My St. George-like struggle against the beast began one summer day when I was a three.

When the petals of the blooms on the red rose trellis turned grey, my father sweated and delved to discover what was killing the bush. He idled for a moment to investigate the damage, and then plunged his spade into the brown earth. Over and over again, he turned each scoop until he had exposed the rose tree's roots. He stabbed the spade into the grass, wiped his brow, and removing his shirt, hung it on the thorns before going into the cellar to find a box of rose food for the roots. As soon as he was gone, I pulled the heavy tool from the ground and poked the soil with it. I slapped the mud and scraped the bole until small fleshy wounds appeared. Something stirred.

A large yellow worm slithered through the muck, entwining the base of the bush, circling as if swimming in the flower bed. Its body wriggled and writhed. I poked it again and again with the spade's pointed blade, but I didn't have the strength behind my parries to wound the worm. I jabbed it harder and harder hoping to split the thing in two, driven by curiosity to understand what it was.

The yellow and black-striped body surfaced. It sprang up at me, hissing and snarling. It stood on its haunches and shrieked into my face. I began to choke and gasp. The thing's face was that of a woman's contorted into a grimace. Its black painted eye-brows were raised in anger. Its matted, black hair and red lips parted over jagged and rotten teeth.

I dropped the shovel and ran into the house sobbing and screaming.

I stuttered to my mother that *it* had stung me. My mother bent and checked my arms and legs for signs of a stinger's welt.

"Did a wasp sting you? Where did it bite?"

I pointed to my heart and sobbed.

"Nothing has stung you. You are imagining it."

It was real. I woke up screaming for nights afterwards. I saw it. It, whatever it was, lived in my mind. There were no words to describe it. I would see it screaming into my face, its breath worse than the odour of rotting brown marigolds. I knew she was there in the silence of the dark, waiting for me to return to that part of the garden where my father dug out the dead climbing rose.

The thing wanted to steal my breath.

The doctor diagnosed me as asthmatic.

Each time I went into the garden for the remainder of the summer, I sensed it was there somewhere, hiding behind the lilies, lurking in the delphinium, or waiting twined around the base of the mountain ash tree. The Baltimore orioles that sang in the tree's high branches vanished. She, that thing, had driven them away. She was watching me. It was impossible to breathe outside. Lilies wilted before her. I watched them wither and brown as a bugle of earth tubed through the flower beds. The berries on the mountain ash turned black and fell as if drops of poisoned rain.

One morning, I found the orange koi I had named Ramsey floating on his side, his belly torn open, in our ornamental pond near the raspberry patch. His eye reminded me of an eclipse. It stared at a sky it could no longer see.

"It must have been a raccoon," my mother said to console me, but I knew it was the thing beneath the trellis. How could something bring such lovelessness to a garden?

That is when I lost track of eternity. Time came to my childhood garden and the snow fell. The world turned grey. I watched from my window as something slithered beneath the snow, diving in and out of the white drifts as if it were a joy to be among the thorns and dead things. My mother stared out the window at the thing's tracks. "We must have a fox out there, so be careful when you are playing. It might be rabid."

Whatever *it* was, by the following spring I had forgotten *it* existed. Children bury their fears. We moved to a new house, and the garden where there had once been no time became a myth to me and I grew up.

In my final year of high school, I spent spare periods in the library reading the entire eight books of *The Caxton Encyclopaedia of Art*. In the middle of volume L to P, there was a full-colour pull-out of the ceiling of the Sistine Chapel. I borrowed the librarian's magnifying glass and pored over the page. Each panel, each Sibyl and prophet, was inspired by the centre panel in the ceiling that weighed upon the shoulders of each seer. The hand of God reached out to infuse a mortal digit with the splendour of life.

In the panel to the left of The Creation of Man, Michelangelo painted the moment of human tragedy, "The Downfall of Adam and Eve and Their Expulsion from The Garden of Eden." There, wrapped around the Tree of Death, handing the Fruit of Knowledge of Good and Evil to the first couple was the thing I had seen in my backyard.

It was a snake with the head of a woman and the body of an iguana, but Genesis 4 tells us God amputated the arms and limbs of the "*subtil* serpent" as punishment for bringing Sin and Death into the world. God tells the serpent that men will tread it underfoot for having wreaked havoc on mankind. The serpent disappears from the Bible, and I began to understand where it went.

Was I fighting off a harbinger of death in a place dedicated to life and beauty when I poked the thing with the spade? Was I a St. George, slaying yet another dragon?

Michelangelo Buonarotti was not the only painter to have known that thing. Later Renaissance artists painted the same scene. Holbein gives the serpent in the tree flowing locks. Durer paints breasts on the beast. No matter how the motif was treated by the Great Masters, the shock, and the revulsion of what that creature brought to mankind served as a constant reminder that there was always something horrid lurking beneath the topsoil of a garden. I had met that moment in my childhood. It was my own Fall of Man.

The more I stared at the pictures of Adam and Eve and the serpent in the tree, the more I recalled that moment in my garden. The thing had the head of a woman, and its long tail wound around the trunk of the tree as if it would choke life from everything it touched.

I started to question whether my horrific childhood memory had been a psychological mask for something else. I had read articles about abused children. I told myself it was not my parents' fault. I had a good childhood. But when I closed my eyes at night and tried to imagine the future, the thing was there shrieking at me with its black eyes. I told myself my imagination had better things to do. I fell in love with reading and that took my mind off my childhood trauma, whether real or imagined. I went off to university the following September to study literature and see where my imagination, sans thing, would take me.

At the frosh welcome-weekend pyjama party, we were given numbers to pin on our backs and told to go and look for a member of the opposite sex with the same number. It was a means by which the college could maintain its gene pool. I was still very much a virgin, and the idea of meeting someone with whom I might spend my college years cuddled naked in my dorm room was tantalizing. Throughout the evening, I danced with girls who caught my eye, but who did not have my number. I should have gotten their telephone numbers or asked them more about what classes they were in. But I was determined to find "my match."

Not long before midnight, a young woman with blond hair, protruding teeth, and a heavy flannel nightgown came up to me.

"We share the number," she said, removing my number from my back and presenting me with hers. Without talk, she motioned me onto the dance floor. When a slow dance started, she pressed against me and whispered in my ear: "I want you. Let's go to your dorm room now."

The worm turned inside me. I suddenly lost control yet marvelled at the thrill of the experience. She stood between me and my bed and drew the nightgown over her head. Her body was smooth and white, and I wanted to touch it. As I stepped out of my pyjama bottoms I saw her left thigh illuminated by the glow of a light from outside. A lump was moving back and forth beneath her skin.

"I hope this doesn't kill the moment, but is there something wrong with your thigh," I said, and pointed. It was wrong of me to point, but the moving lump inside her leg, like a tongue rolling in the wall of someone's cheek, was putting me off.

She lay back on the bed, tossing her hair to one side, and reaching down, slouching slightly onto her right side, she wriggled out of the lower half of her body, set her legs on the floor beside me, and then pulled the blond wig from her head and spit out her overbite to reveal black teeth. Her yellow and black tail rose up and waved in the air, curling, and beckoning me to come closer like someone gesturing "c'mere with their index finger."

"I thought you had forgotten me," she whispered and began to sneer.

I opened the leaded casement. "'Come to the window, sweet is the night air'," I said.

"'Ah, love, let us be true to one another.' I adore it when a willing young man quotes 'Dover Beach' to me."

She leapt toward me and I caught her. She was just about to wrap her arms around me, her black claws suddenly protruding from the tips of her sham fingers. And that instant I held her, the palms of my hands burned and began to blister. I turned to the window and flung her out.

She thumped off a dumpster below and screamed shrilly as her body hit the ground. Then I picked up her wig, teeth, and her lower half, and tossed them after her into the alley. I closed the window and pulled the drapes shut.

My heart was pounding. I washed and washed my hands, put my clothes back on, and ran into the night toward the crowds of Bloor Street. The all-night student hang-outs looked like safe havens by the time I reached Bathurst Street, and I found a bar with its music thumping and a waitress who was only too willing to serve me as many Jack Daniels as I could buy. I came to my senses several hours later in a doughnut shop, a Korean man standing over me with a carafe in his hand, asking me if I wanted more coffee.

I never felt safe in my dorm room after that night. I obtained a roommate named Ramsey who never seemed to leave the room or the concubines he kept there. I did most of my sleeping in the student common rooms between classes. The night of my first attempt at sex was also my last go at it for the next ten years. The thought of having sex with my childhood nightmare was abhorrent to me.

As the leaves turned orange and red around on the campus, and the sky burst into that brilliance of blue that can only say: "I am dying in the most beautiful way," autumn came to the world of my freshman year. The yellow and purple mums in the planting bowls along the walkways shrivelled and browned. I knew it was her doing. She was lurking in the quads and behind the college walls to suck the life from my world. I stopped giving a damn about worldly things. The only thing I knew I could trust was literature, and I had my passion in Professor Lamoore's class. I heard my new love's voice rolling over and over in my head, its lilting music echoing a power of perpetual spring. "Whan that Aprile with its shoores soote ..." Her name was poetry.

By November when snow was falling in soft, heavy flakes outside a classroom window, I watched as Professor Lamoore leaned against the sill of the window. He was talking nonsense, literally. He spoke about what it meant to craft a new diction and to use it to describe the heroic act of slaying a dreaded beast.

'Twas brillig and the slithy toves
Did gyre and gimble in the wabe:
All mimsy were the borogoves,
And the mome raths outgrabe.

Lamoore was an older, plump man who sometimes tee-
tered as he leaned on a wall or propped himself against a desk
as he lectured. He had taught my mother during her under-
graduate years. His bald head always shone and reflected the
brightness from the ceiling fixtures. With his midland accent,
the rolled r's and hard consonants took on a lively guttural
edge. He leaned over to me as he finished reciting the poem
from memory. "Now what was that?" he asked.

"Gibberish."

"Not quite. It was 'Jabberwocky.'"

The class sat in silence. Some knew the poem and sighed
with a 'let's get this over with' attitude. From under his arm, he
produced a copy of *Through the Looking Glass*. Lewis Carroll's
book had sat on my bedroom shelf during my growing years,
but it was the one volume I could never bring myself to read,
and I could not recall why. Perhaps I was frightened by the
pictures until I forgot it was there.

"The poem is, essentially, a folk ballad in the tradition of
'Lord Randall' or 'Sir Patrick Spens.' We'll talk about the structure and function of the ballad as a poetic form in a few minutes. But there's something unusual about what Carroll does
to the poem a few chapters after it is presented in *Through the
Looking Glass*. A good poet is like a good magician," Lamoore
said as he thumbed his way through the pages of the little book.
"A good magician, a good poet, never explains his tricks or how
they work, unless he gives-in to great temptation and is trying
to prove something. Lewis Carroll must have had a professor or
a *grammarian* lecturer at Oxford not unlike me. In Chapter Six,
Alice meets a big egg named Humpty Dumpty who relishes in

exegesis. Exegesis is the art of explanation. Humpty sits on his wall and professes, and critiques, and insists that everything must mean something. And so, he explains the meaning of 'Jabberwocky' to Alice. Humpty Dumpty recites the first verse of the poem, just as I did, and then he goes on:

"'Well, "slithy" means "lithe and slimy." "Lithe" is the same as active." You see it's like a portmanteau — there are two meanings packed up into one word.'

"'I see it now,' Alice remarked thoughtfully: 'and what are "toves"?'

"'Well, "toves" are something like badgers — they're something like lizards — and they're something like corkscrews.'

"'They must be very curious creatures.'

"'They are that,' said Humpty Dumpty: 'also they make their nests under sundials — also they live on cheese.'

"'And what's to "gyre" and to "gimble"?'

"'To "gyre" is to go round and round like a gyroscope. To "gimble" is to make holes like a gimlet.'

"'And "the wabe" is the grass-plot round a sundial, I suppose?' said Alice, surprised at her own ingenuity.

"'Of course it is . . .'"

I left Professor Lamoore's class that day with a sudden interest in Lewis Carroll. I knew I had met the Slithy Tove and likely so had the author of *Alice in Wonderland*.

Carroll's illustrator, John Tenniel, depicted the tove in the 1871 edition of *Through the Looking Glass* and got it wrong. The badger suggestion, on Lewis Carroll's part, was a purposeful piece of misdirection. Maybe the author meant wolverine but understood that English readers would not be acquainted with a vicious North American creature. Perhaps Carroll wanted to hunt the tove himself without giving away too many clues of what he was looking for. Why? The tove was more lizard-like than badger-like, but its claws and arms, to say nothing of its foul disposition and its cheesy breath, were *suggestive* of a badger.

But what was Carroll really saying in his strange, Victorian, round-about way? What was he trying to tell the world about that thing in the garden that appeared from under the sundial, the thing, like a dragon or serpent he had contended with, the source of agony and struggle he failed to defeat? The more I looked at Carroll's writing and his life, the more I understood the horrors endured by Charles Lutwidge Dodgson – Lewis Carroll's real-life alter ego.

I believed Dodgson was not only someone who had encountered the creature but who had been plagued by it. I became convinced that the tove hated innocence and happiness. The tove spread rumours. The tove whispered in the ears of those who harboured doubts about others, and who wove those doubts into jealousies. The tove poisoned the world. For years I had been living with the nightmare of the slithy tove. And she was there, on campus, watching me. She was waiting to spoil every good thing I tried to do. I vowed I would confront the creature and in a battle of wills, wits, strength, and skill, kill it or die trying.

When I was kicked off the editorial staff of the college paper without any other reason than that I was constantly distracted and looking over my shoulder, I knew it was the tove that had planted the seeds in the brains of my fellow reporters through some nefarious means. She was persistent. When I went into dining hall, no one would sit with me. I would try to converse, but the other students would just look at me and then move their trays. I tried to overcome attacks on my reputation – the sort of college stuff that always happens. I thought that, by being a good person, the kind of person who lends notes and offers to buy classmates a coffee, I could overcome her effects. I thought I had overcome my troubles, but then she struck for real early in my third year.

My roommate, Ramsey, was found dead.

The window was open.

His body was grey and pale as if something had sucked the life out of him.

His hair had turned white just before he died, and his face was aged and lined even though hours before everyone said he was young though slightly overweight. The coroner could not determine cause of death.

I knew it was the tove, but a person can't just go around saying the cause of death was a fictional creature from *Through the Looking Glass*. I told the police I was an insomniac. I had been out all night. I had. I had been putting back coffees in the Korean doughnut shop. The security camera footage from the coffee shop and a variety store where I'd stopped to buy a chocolate bar supported my story. My professors felt sorry for me, and the leniency I received on my final papers helped me to keep my gold medal and win a graduate scholarship overseas.

Lamoore and his wife were proud of me. I was his prodigy. The couple would hold regular teas in their Victorian "house of grace," a gift of free lodging from the college that was a haven for ideas and literary talk. I was always invited to their gatherings. Lamoore and his wife, Gamba, would welcome acclaimed authors or renowned scholars as their guests. Just to sit there and listen to the stories the guests shared was a tremendous privilege. The teas were a part of my education that prepared me for my later work. One day, after I had been accepted on a special scholarship to Oxford, Julia Cassidy was a guest at a Lamoore tea.

Mrs. Cassidy was the wife of a strange but troubled professor whose brilliance and temperament had mixed within him in an unusual way. He was kind and generous with his time, but unorthodox in his classroom demeanour. Word around the campus was that he was headed, so it seemed for years, towards a death by alcoholism until one night Professor Cassidy could not get a drink and he hanged himself. His widow, Julia, had the countenance of a suffering angel and an air of wisdom about her. She was someone who carried an old soul inside. During the course of the tea, Mrs. Cassidy quoted from Rilke's "Duino Elegies."

"He sounds inspiring," I said. "What's his name?"

The words "Rainer Maria Rilke," sang off her tongue through her flowing Irish lilt. "Have you not read Rilke?" she asked with patience in her voice. I shook my head. "We shall have to see to that." She smiled and went back to her dessert.

The next day, as I was packing the few things I could take to Oxford with me, the Porter came to my door with a small package. The outer envelope said simply "Do not open until you are on your way." I abided by the instruction. Halfway across the Atlantic as the dawn was just beginning, I reached into my carry-on and opened the envelope. It was a copy of Rilke's volume of advice to literary types, *Letters to a Young Poet*. I could hear her voice in the inscription: "In your moment of greatest need, Rilke will provide the answer to your question. Be well and journey bravely, Julia Cassidy."

I settled into my room at Christ Church College. The ceiling was slightly vaulted and the stone door frame, fireplace, and leaded windows made me feel monastic. As I lay in my cot the first night, I looked up at the vaulted ceiling where it met the cornice. In the nineteenth-century plasterwork a strange bubble bulged that made me think the pipes were about to burst.

I stacked my chair on top of my desk and reached as high as I could to touch it. If the roof was leaking, I wanted to know if I was going to be deluged in my sleep. The moment my fingers hit the surface of the brittle plaster, the bulge burst and a withered grey corpse I mistook for a large cat fell to the floor with a thud. Someone from a nearby room hollered, "Keep it down in there, you bloody sod!"

Despite the fall, the corpse's sinews held the body together. The skull cracked slightly on impact. I could see the remnants of an upper torso with nothing below the waist but a long series of vertebrae tapering to a point. The skull looked partially human but attached to the sides of the cranium were small horns. The finger bones were tipped with claws. Here was the skeleton of a tove.

I didn't want to touch it with my bare hands. I had seen how toves could suck the life out of a garden, and having flung one out the window of my dorm room and burned my hands, I didn't want those painful blisters again. I put on the heavy leather gloves I had brought for winter, and when I touched the corpse, the palms paled as if the tanning was being drawn out of the dead lambskin. I piled the remains on my desk and stared at the corpse. Here was the proof I needed that the tove existed. But why was it here? Why this room, my room?

In the morning, I went to the Dean's office, not to tell him about my zoological discovery (which I hid in a paper bag under my bed and transferred to a rental locker at Oxford Station later that afternoon), but to ask who had previously lived in my chamber. I was handed a large black ledger. I poured through the names of previous students who had occupied my room until, under an entry for the Michaelmas Term, 1851, I found the name Charles Lutwidge Dodgson. I was living in Lewis Carroll's old digs.

A number of theories began to run through my head. Had the tove harassed Dodgson throughout his life? Had it come to his dorm room just as it had to mine to claim him as a prize? What if the tove had crawled in through a dovecote in the stone eaves, become entangled in the medieval masonry and died there? Had there been other toves that mistook the absence of one of their own for murder? What if they had sought retribution against Dodgson for the disappearance of one of their own?

In studying Carroll's life, I had been puzzled by his missing diaries. There are four missing Lewis Carroll diaries. The absence of these volumes has been used by his detractors to indict him for adultery and even child abuse. The volumes in question date from 1853 to and include the years that Carroll spent completing his studies at Oxford and the years that he spent with the children of a local clergyman, Henry Liddell. Several Carroll supporters argue that he was in love with the eldest Liddell daughter, but spent his time amusing her younger sister, Alice, with his labyrinthine tales of logic and fancy that became *Alice in Wonderland* and *Through the Looking Glass*.

The Liddell home is still standing in Oxford. I researched the name of the current owners, a family named Framwell.

Carol Framwell was quite perky and enthusiastic when I called. "Of course, I am a Lewis Carroll fanatic," she bubbled. "I adore living here, and we bought the home because of the Liddell connection. I shan't be here but do come around on Saturday afternoon. My husband will show you the house."

When I arrived, I was greeted by Richard Framwell who wanted to give me a Cook's tour of the interior.

"I'm not really all that interested in the inside as I am the outside," I said, and he looked disappointed. He was a DIY man and I think he wanted to show off his handiwork. "I want to see the garden."

We wandered around the back and stood in the rain. I had my umbrella up. Richard Framwell is one of those Englishmen who is impervious to water, and he merely tucked his hands in the pockets of his brown oil cloth jacket and remained dry.

"May I ask what specifically it is you're looking for out here?" he asked.

"This is where Lewis Carroll took most of his photographs of the Liddell children if I am correct." Framwell nodded. "What I need to know is the location of the sundial."

"The sundial? As in slithy toves? You aren't secreting any Stilton, are you?" He looked disconcerted and then smiled with the hope that I would catch his allusion. I laughed, and then realized I had made a very unscholarly if not absurd request.

I put my finger up to my lips to motion a hush to him. I did not want the tove to overhear, though I could not tell my host that.

"Do you have trouble growing roses?" I asked in a whisper.

He shook his head, and continued talking in a full voice, ignoring my attempts to keep things in a hush. "I am an ivy man, myself. Holly and ivy. Great Christmas fare. Funny," he continued, "you should ask about the sundial. I found the base of it. We have it in the shed if you'd like to see it. It was there, about ten paces this side of that old oak, though I suppose in Lewis Carroll's day it was exposed to the light far more. I was digging there several years ago and I had a strange experience. The mud started moving beneath it. You don't suspect it was a tove, do you?" He chuckled. He was testing me. I shook my head.

"You don't mind if I poke around, do you? I want to get a sense of the place."

"Be my guest," he said. "I shall put some tea on so please join me when you are thoroughly cold and soaked."

I stood gazing at the spot where the sundial had been.

I could hear the birds chirping and the rain pinging on my umbrella. In the patter and the silence, save for a few distant rumblings of motors, I thought I could hear a conversation. An articulate, polite male voice was speaking softly to a young girl. She was giggling. *"That's enough, Humpty Dumpty interrupted. There are plenty of hard words there."*

"And what are they?" the child asks excitedly.

Suddenly, she screams and points.

A yellow and black worm slithers from beneath the sundial. It rears its head and snarls at her. The young man grabs the child to shield her. He raises his walking stick and strikes the creature from different sides, grasping the stick lower and lower to put more power into each blow.

Snicker, snack.

The thing with the body of a lizard and the head of a woman screams in pain, but despite the man's best efforts to protect the child the worm is around him in an instant and lunges at the girl.

In the melee the man's box camera and tripod are knocked to the ground.

He thrusts his walking stick repeatedly *through and through.* The beast retreats beneath the sundial.

The girl's white dress is torn. He checks to see if the child has been injured. She is sobbing, and he is sobbing, and neither knows what to do next.

"We have to have evidence of this terrible thing!" he cries to the child.

He sets his camera upright and squeezes the shutter lever. The child looks like an urchin. Her dress is a shambles, and in her empty, lifeless eyes there is terror. "Tell no one of this," he says as the garden door of the house opens.

The commotion in the garden has brought the servants and the girl's mother from the house. They have heard what he has just said.

The girl's mother stops, hugs her daughter to comfort her, then stands and looks at the man. There is a look of dismay and horror in the mother's eyes. She strikes the young man who falls weeping to the ground, and picks up the child and carries her to the house.

Through his tears, he tries to make sense of the shouts and accusations being hurled at him by the girl's father. The young man looks up and in the undergrowth of the garden's edge, the tove is sneering at him through the smile of her black teeth. She has won her victory. Charles Lutwidge Dodgson is ruined.

The young man writes in his diary that he can explain. He records the incident moment by moment. He has developed the photograph of the young girl in the garden. In the lower right-hand edge of the image because the captured moment has survived the ravages of time and been labelled "The Beggar Maid" by Lewis Carroll scholars, the bushes are blurred as if something is moving among them. He knows the truth. The girl knows the truth, too. The world refuses to listen.

"Hello, my travelling Canadian friend."

I looked up from my moment of imagination. It was the tove.

She has emerged from the spot where the sundial stood. She brushes the dirt from her forehead. She seems surprised that I am not surprised.

"We meet again," I say. "You seem well-travelled or are you an English tove? Was that you I tossed out the window of my dorm?"

"You broke my heart, you little bastard."

"Only your heart? You got off lucky. Had you a pelvis you might not have been so fortunate," I reply, smiling back at her. I refused to let her get the better of me.

"Had I a pelvis you might not have gotten out of your room that night. I could have given you a night to remember."

"I'm sure of it, but such is life. So, what are you planning to do to me now? You seem to have come a long way to join me in my graduate studies. Bored with Toronto, are you? Bring it on. I'm ready for you."

The tove hissed. "You were born on St. George's Day. You are a sworn enemy of dragons, and toves, and beasts of the netherworld. You think you're very brave, cavorting here with your vorpel sword or an umbrella, but you are nothing."

"And your point is?"

The tove hissed and looked away as if it could not find a rebuttal. "May I ask, what is your name?"

"Agatha."

"Well, Agatha, I've been charting your progress through history. You have a charm for appearing in great works of art – the Ceiling of the Sistine Chapel, paintings by Durer, Cranach, Holbein, and so many other old masters. You must be proud of your species. There's a point of literary symbolism that has always puzzled me, and I hope you don't mind me asking you now that I have you here, simply because I'm curious about such things, but is the serpent in great works of art Satan, or Lilith, or you? And how many of you are there in your species?"

"Lilith was my sister. She was the one who ruined Eden. She was Adam's first wife – did you know that? He threw her away though not from a dorm room window. They didn't have second stories back then. She has been a great fascination to great men. They felt honoured to know her, but they all cast her aside. Then the dreadful Dodgson came along and murdered her. She went to him to seek his love one night, and I never saw her again! Do not patronize me with Darwinian zoological categorizations such as 'species.' I would have ruined that laggard as well, but he just stared at me and started taking notes. A man more interested in finches that rare creatures. Boring sod."

The tove started to turn away then spun around.

"We stayed alive for centuries by sucking the life from living things. There were two of us. Just me and my sister. It's only me now. I haven't seen her in over a hundred and fifty years. That bastard, that man of two names took her. But I showed him. I ruined him by tearing that little girl's dress then stealing his evidence. He could not defend himself, and so the world ate him. It sucked the life from him. He may have been Lewis Carroll, but polite society called him a child molester. And no matter how hard he tried to bottle that life in every word he wrote, the cloud always hung over him. It still hangs over him. He will spend eternity under a cloud. And I put him there! I put him there! And because you follow in his footsteps, you the dragon-slayer, the flimsy knight of swords and spears, I will destroy you, too."

"Yes, but I'm not a child molester. I am a celibate. You did a me a big favour that night. Clear head, healthy loins, I like to say."

She shrieked: "I will destroy you utterly, not just in this life but for all time. You think you're a young man on the rise.

You have not seen what I can do to you. And no matter how hard you may try to put the life of the world into words, you will never succeed because I will be there to pull you down into the shadows where no poetry can protect you."

I determined to stay calm despite my hate for the thing. "Wow. Right. So, exactly what did you do to take his evidence?"

"I stole his diaries! I went to that horridly beautiful little girl as she lay sleeping in her room up there, and I told her just as he had told her, that if she ever revealed the truth I would destroy her and all her family. The frightened little bitch kept her silence, so I destroyed her, too, by making her hold her own words until she finally choked on her own silence. And Dodgson struggled to tell the truth for the rest of his life, and everyone thought it was fantasy."

"I see. I have a proposition for you, Agatha." I looked the tove in the eye as if I were playing poker. "I have a deal for you."

"No deals!"

"Okay, your loss. You'll never get the bones of your sister back."

"You have my sister's bones! Where did you find them? Give them to me."

"Uh uh. That is, unless you give me something in return. Something I need."

"What is that?" hissed the tove.

"The missing diaries of Lewis Carroll, a.k.a. Charles Lutwidge Dodgson. I don't think you're the kind of creature that would steal something, other than the colour from flowers and the life from a man's body or soul, only to throw it away without thinking it might come in handy at some point down the line. Well, this is some point. I think you're a greedy tove at heart. You need trophies. All dragons and slithery things need trophies, shiny things to keep at the bottom of a lake or in your nest or wherever you hang out. You're a collector. A creature like you is probably very clever, perhaps a natural hoarder, a cataloguer *par excellence*. Classification is what drives you. It keeps you functional. It keeps you centred. You'd keep something you take so you can use it later and fawn over it in the meantime like a treasure. Well, Agatha, now is later. If you have them, if you have the diaries, I'll make a trade of the body of your sister for the volumes. If you don't have them, well, kiss Lilith goodbye. If that rattles you, then bring it! I'm ready for you. I've spent my whole life preparing for our final struggle. And remember, bones are easily burned or ground-up, or, worse, put on display in the Museum of Natural History in London."

"Not the Museum of Natural History! Not that damned Darwin house!"

"Alright. Do we have a deal, then? Diaries for bones? And pardon me if I don't shake your hand to seal the bargain." She hmphed and spun round and round, then glared at me.

"Where and when?"

"On Addison's walk behind Magdalen College at three a.m. tomorrow morning. That is where we'll do the hand-over. And remember, no diaries, no tove carcass. And don't plan on pulling any fast ones or Lilith goes to London!" The tove sneered and screamed and burrowed back beneath the spot where the sundial had stood in Lewis Carroll's day.

I got three soccer blokes pissed on multiple pints of Morrell's at a pub halfway down the road to the railway station. I persuaded them to help me roll an empty oil drum all the way to a spot in an area of Oxford known as Mesopotamia where Addison's Walk becomes a patch of wilderness beside the headwaters of the Thames, a river given the ancient name of the Egyptian goddess of the darkness, the Isis. When the chaps rolled off, likely in search of an off-licence, I built a fire in the oil drum and waited.

I stood in the cold, foggy night and watched as the frost etched itself into every crevice and edge of leaf. I gathered some rubbish papers and some kindling sticks and threw them into the flames until I had a nice blaze going. I found a sharp alder rod among the debris and set it aside as my lance, taking my Swiss Army knife out and whittling the end to a very handsome point. I was glad I had brought my heavy leather gloves. I also remembered to bring a bottle of brandy with me to give me strength in the dead of night in case my courage faltered.

Uncorking the bottle, I took a swig and set it open on the ground at my feet. I muttered the words: "And lo, though I walk through the valley of the shadow of death, I will fear no evil, for though art with me." And as I said that phrase, the image of Julia Cassidy popped into my mind. I heard her speak to me in her lilt: "In the moment of your greatest need, Rilke will give you the answer."

What had Rilke said that I was overlooking? I shook it off. I wasn't there to think about Rilke. I had a beast to deal with.

The river whispered in a low shhh as it touched the banks and poured over stones in its flow. At my feet, in a bag retrieved from the railway station locker, were the mortal remains of the great seductress, the subtil serpent that had brought about the fall of Adam and Eve. Agatha approached out of the fog, winding forward on her yellow and black tail. The tove's head was held high, as if in glory. She had an old blue and gold biscuit tin tucked under her arm.

"That's far enough," I said, my back to the lighted oil drum as I raised my alder lance. The flickering flames illuminated the outline of the tove. Her shadow rose up against the woodland. "Put the cookie box down," I instructed her.

"It's a biscuit tin, you stupid colonial."

"Whatever. That's far enough."

"Show me the bones."

I held up the bag.

"Open it!" she screamed.

I opened the bag, reached in, and held up the corpse. The tove gasped.

"Now show me the diaries." She pried open the tin and her claws made a scratching sound like fingernails on a blackboard, and the purple-covered notebooks tumbled to the ground.

"You know, you really are your own worst enemies," I said as I shook the dead thing at her. "I found this thing in the ceiling of my room at Christ Church. It must have gotten stuck and died in there when it came to torment Dodgson. He didn't kill it. It got stuck and died. You've taken your temper out on the world and ruined a man for nothing. You are nothing but rage and hate. So was your sister. What had Eve done other than be like Adam? I can just see Lilith, trapped in the space between the plaster and the vault of his room, exhausted, begging for a mercy that would never be hers for what she had done. And she died because nothing can suck the life out of stones."

The tove lunged toward me in rage. I reached down, grabbed the bottle of brandy, and splashed it in her eyes. She screamed and held her claws up to her face, tearing at her brow.

"I will kill you now!" she shrieked as her vision came back to her. I grabbed the corpse and tossed it in the burning barrel.

"No! No! Our deal! Our deal!" And as Agatha leapt up to bite my face with her black fangs bared, I ducked, and the slithy tove went flying over me into the flaming barrel, hissing, writhing, and clutching at the bones of her sister. I reached down and grabbed the bottle of brandy and emptied it into the fire. The brandy ignited her eyes which became two meteors of wrath. I thrust my lance over and over into the tove's belly.

"*Snicker snack!*" I shouted and watched as blue feathers of brilliant light leapt toward the stars and tindered a green dawn where the river flowed south and east to become Father Thames.

T'was brillig and the slithy toves did gyre and gimble in the wabe. ... said Alice, surprised at her own ingenuity ...

Of course, it is. It's called 'wabe' you know because it goes a long way before it,
and a long way behind it
And a long way beyond it on each side, Alice added.

I watched as the flames consumed the contents of the barrel and the pyre dwindled to ash and embers. As the flames died, I thought I could have made a name for myself with the zoologists, but then again strange creatures that unnerve scientists are usually debunked. The missing diaries were my treasure. When I looked over the lip of the barrel, there was nothing left of the slithy toves.

I had to wait for curfew to pass before I could return to my room. I strolled up and down past Parker's bookstore and paused to look in the window at the latest bestsellers and imagined the book I was about to begin writing there among the Byatts and the McEwens. But what I saw, as the dawn crept silently through the streets of Oxford, was my own reflection against a display of copies of *Through the Looking Glass*. What had I done? I had killed something primeval that had followed me like a shadow through my life, and I was free and so was Lewis Carroll.

When the Porter finally opened the gate, he grumbled something under his breath about blighters being out all night. I didn't catch what he said, and I didn't care. In my room as I lay on my cot, thumbing through the lost diaries of Lewis Carroll, I suddenly realized that I was sitting on one of the greatest literary finds of my era. The secret was now mine, and I would redeem my lost author from his century of purgatory.

May 5, 1862
Went to see the Liddells today. I had so much more of the story of the looking glass world in my mind since I last saw Alice. I wanted

nothing more than to share it with her, to see her face light up with that rare sense of joy in discovery she possesses. Speaking to her in those moments was like prayer. One feels divinity is listening back. But as we were deep in our legend, a terrible thing happened. The creature that has pursued me all my life, the daemon that destroyed my childhood garden, appeared from beneath the sundial and accosted us. It tore Alice's lovely dress and frightened both of us within an inch of our lives. I struck it repeatedly, but it would not be beaten. I tried to photograph the thing, but it slithered away, slimy, and lithe, and active. It was that awful lizard with the head of a woman and the body of a serpent. Mrs. Liddell was the first on the scene. She assumed the worst and screamed and struck me. Mr. Liddell arrived and with a blow grabbed me and cast me to the ground. He bent down as if he were about to strike me again with his fist, but I kept repeating that I was only protecting Alice, shielding her from the awful thing.

I would need to come up with a good story. Where did I find these diaries, I knew I would be asked?

"Oh, well, a slithy tove and I did a deal for the bones of the serpent that brought about the Fall of Man."

Right. Not good.

I understood Dodgson's predicament.

A week later, I was down in London at the Bermondsey Market. I'd spent the night at a friend's place and then took a taxi to the market square just before dawn as the vendors were setting up in the half-light. I felt as if I was back on the battlefield with the tove. There, I found what I was looking for.

On a table crowded with silver and bric-a-brac, I discovered three identically bound Victorian diaries belonging to a lady who loved mice. Coincidence? I call it blind luck. I got a receipt from the dealer with an item description and a date of purchase. In any case, I had my provenance. I'd found them at an antique market.

I would need to bear out their authorship and provenance, but the handwriting and content would support my claim. The British Library Reading Room is a scholar's best friend. I had made my career and slain the enemy of mankind in one fell swoop.

A year later, the proofs for my ground-breaking biography of Lewis Carroll arrived with the morning post as I was cleaning out my digs at the college. I was on my way to Harvard where I had an appointment in the English Department. The Porter was adamant, great breakthrough or not, that I would have to be packed and gone by 10 a.m. for the cleaners and painters to start their business. And there was the matter of the hole in the ceiling. I would have to pay for that. Where would he send the final bill?

That is when I opened my desk drawer and found the copy of *Letters to a Young Poet* by Rainer Maria Rilke hiding behind the paper clips and post-it notes. My eyes fell on Julia Cassidy's inscription and the line: "Be well and journey bravely." But what was the question Rilke was supposed to answer for me?

I flipped through the pages of the large type. There is not all that much writing in Rilke's book, but I tell others that it is worth reading. I had never noticed before, but in the same pen as Mrs. Cassidy's inscription there was a tiny star in the margin that caught my eye.

"How could we forget those ancient myths that stand at the beginning of all races, the myths about dragons that at the last moment are transformed into princesses? Perhaps all the dragons in our lives are princesses who are only waiting to see us act, just once, with beauty and courage. Perhaps everything that frightens us is, in its deepest essence, something helpless that wants our love."

I should have shown the tove love but I realized that something in me was not brave enough to love such a creature.

I am not Rilke. I haven't got the emotional stamina for simple altruism let alone compassion toward a thing that had tormented me all my life. Maybe now I could go forward with my life, meet someone I could fall in love with, marry her, start a family, and plant a garden of my own. I imagined walking into a faculty meeting in Boston in the coming weeks where I would be introduced as the man who saved Lewis Carroll, and afterwards, at a stand-up reception, perhaps over glasses of wine and chunks of gouda, I would meet that person. Love is the one thing that human beings have of their own to give. It is the one thing they have of their own to keep. And it is all we have to protect ourselves against the monsters who reside beneath the sundials and other thresholds of time.

I tucked Rilke and Julia Cassidy's little book in my coat pocket and put the box of page proofs under my arm. I stepped out the door of my digs, suitcase and future well-in hand, and stood looking at the world ahead of me, ready to journey forth to fight more battles. I turned and looked over my shoulder. The orange, yellow, and pink flowers in the Porter's small garden patch beneath his lodge's window were blooming brightly in the morning sun.

THE RIVER TAX

I LOST TRACK OF HOW MANY GREATS AGO IT WAS, but this is the land where one of my greated grandfathers and a greated grandmother built a log house on a parcel of wooded acreage with a stream running along the edge of their claim. They were granted the land on the condition that it be cleared, but that caused the greated grandmother considerable sadness because she loved the darkness of the forest, the voice of the wind through the boughs at night, and the sound of buds opening – yes, in those days a person could hear the buds opening – so that my greated grandfather had to assure her that nothing of the trees would be wasted. They stoked the bread oven with shavings of the bark they adzed off the logs. They turned the tangled roots into stump fences, and the pens were snaked together from the rails they split to square the timbers. Not even the walnut and hazel boles from which he carved pipes on long winter nights went to waste. Everything had a voice. The snow against their windows made a shushing sound and the rain on their cedar-shingled roof drummed softly in the darkness when it fell from spring nights. By listening to what the land wanted to say to them, their existence became a truce with nature. To ease my greated grandmother's concerns about the silence that might befall them should they cease to open their ears, my greated grandfather built their log house about thirty yards from the river where the land crested just enough to protect their home from the rising waters of spring floods.

I was in my fifties when my uncle died and left me the cabin. I call it a cabin because the first floor was open, just as the ancestors had built it. The walls were rough-hewn and chinked with mortar on the inside as well as on the outside, though at some point in the previous two hundred years the outer shell had acquired clapboard. It had been my job, as a teenager, to go to the cabin and paint the exterior for my grandfather who assured me that my labours would help the place to last another hundred or more years. My pleasure, on those dog-breath summer nights was to lie on the screened-in porch my father and uncle had built with my grandfather. Lying there, I would watch the stars move across the night and feel the sway of the metal-fendered glider that was stuffed with horsehair. I would look up through the screening and name, as best I could, each constellation. The stars poured out of the east, each pinpoint of light climbing toward the zenith before it fell or morning chased it into the daylight.

My daughter wasn't sure she wanted to inherit the place. "After all," she would lament, "it's a long drive from the city, and the kids are older now and have jobs. Dave doesn't want to fight the weekend traffic, and it is as far from water as you can be." She had a point. The cabin had seen better days, and so had I. Had it been fifty years ago in the early part of the century when I was young and she was still a child, it would have meant the world to her to wander through the meadows and make daily discoveries among the birds and small creatures that called the land home. Now, it was only me for whom the cabin and the land meant anything.

Having been retired for the past ten years, I had time on my hands. My wife had passed. She never liked the cabin. The wood smoke made her sneeze, and she didn't relish being close to nature even though my uncle had done the courtesy of installing a septic system and an indoor toilet. But as the place aged, I was concerned for whether the old system might be leaching into the river.

I call it a river. It had been a steady flow when I was a child and used to fish for trout in it. But riparian rights had long been ignored by the growth of subdivisions upstream and the need for irrigation between my land and the urban sprawl. The cabin had become an archipelago cut off from the rest of the world by its own history, a place of isolation that was slowly sliding into rural desolation. There was just enough water in the current if I was sitting on the bank to hear it trying to mumble as it passed over the stones that had once been its bed, but no trout. We'd had some dry years, and like the number of greats between me and my forebear's forests, I'd lost count of how time is measured in a place where idyllicism speaks louder than calendars and those who inhabit that place forget how to listen.

I wanted to listen. I thought when the first notice came from the township in the mail that, indeed, I needed to pay more attention to the family seat. I set the notice aside and figured I would get around to it. One spring morning about six months later, I received a call at home from a township man. He introduced himself, chit-chatted about the age of the property, asked about the septic system, and if I had been paying my river tax on the property?

"Well," I said, "it is not exactly waterfront property. We're not talking Muskoka here. What is a river tax?"

Apparently, a river tax is a premium one pays on top of one's land tax for having a river run through the property. When it had been introduced in the Twenties, it was a cash grab for those fortunate enough to have open water for their herds. It was worth paying because the alternative was to pump enough water from a well to keep the cattle in good order. That would have been enormous work. The river tax was the township's way of saying to herdsmen that they had it good. By the Thirties, however, the river tax drove many owners off their land. The township man explained that the money went toward river up-keep and such.

"Haven't I been taking care of my share of the river?" I inquired.

Well, I had and I hadn't. The township was aware that I had been renting out the pastureland about fifty yards back of the cabin to a local dairyman who had not tilled in his slurry as required by the township maintenance laws. I made note that I would have to speak to the renter. I admired the farmer I rented my land to. He was one of the last who had held on to his family farm and kept his inheritance at work while I let mine slide. The lowing of the cattle on a summer night when I slept on the screened veranda was soothing, although occasionally there would be a coyote who would venture through the pasture and set the cows scattering and howling. Cows do sort of howl if they are frightened.

The township man asked if I was still there. My mind had been wandering lately, especially when it was grabbed by a passing memory that needed to play itself out.

"Yes," I said, "I'm still here. I've never heard of a river tax. Should we have been paying it? I mean, it's not much of a river now. It hasn't been for as long a I remember. It is more of a gully that gets damp sometimes. I used to trout fish in there as a boy, but you'd be hard-pressed to find a mud-puppy in there now."

It was the township man's turn to be silent. "What is a mud-puppy?" he asked.

I had to explain that they were larger than salamanders, grey, knob-headed, and kind of strange-looking. They used to hovel among the reeds beneath the willows, but now, even the willows had rotted for lack of water, and had been cut down, for the most-part, by the dairyman because he was afraid one of his cows would rub its behind against the trunk and topple it onto the animal.

"Learn something every day," the township man said. "Well," he said, before turning the subject back to the purpose of his call. "The river tax works like this. You have a stream running through your property. Whether you use the water or not, you're taxed by the township on the length of the stream and how close it runs near your house. It used to be called a 'Mill Tax,' but since the mills in this area aren't run on water, if there are any mills left, which there aren't, you have to pay for how close your house is. Also, if you should suddenly get washed away, it pays for the clean up."

"And that amounts to what per year?"

"Well, you're about thirty yards away, give or take a few feet – I have it in the files because I came by one day when you weren't there and measured, and you're about a dollar twelve a year. You owe about two hundred or so. I know it is tough news, but we brought in the measure back-when to help pay for conservation."

I figured it wasn't much for conservation and for the right to be picturesque, so I decided I would write a cheque and sent it off first thing. I also had a wood lot on property that I maintained for conservation, but he already knew that. One thing happened and then another, and I forgot about the river tax. It didn't seem like a pressing matter, a matter of necessity or life and death.

When I arrived for the summer, a few months of peace and tranquility that I was determined to enjoy, the rains started. Our township, in fact the whole county, had been known as a dry place, but dry places can be deceiving. Prince Edward County, for example, used to be littered with abandoned UEL places because the limestone seams ran dry of ground water and folks couldn't drill wells through the rock. Even if they did, there was little chance of striking water. Now look at it.

They brought in better drilling equipment – hard rock drilling machinery, and the thin, hard-scrabble soil and the limestone base turned out to be the perfect combination for hardy varietals. Who would have known? From scrub grass to vineyards in less than a decade.

But my situation was just the opposite. The rains started to fall that summer. When I say fall, they didn't just rain. It was like someone dropped a lake on us some days. I thought, "This is another one of those wet summers we get every now and then." The meadows were trampled beneath the downpours. I hardly saw any field mice, and those I saw were gnawing at the timbers to get into the cabin. As the rain fell on the shingle roof – the sound of a low patter rather than the snare beats I heard on my tar shingle roof in the city – I imagined the cabin as a kind of drum, a sealed vessel that would see me through any storm nature could muster.

Winter was no better. For insurance purposes, I had to drive up and check the place once a month. During one of the drives up the highway, as a blizzard came out of nowhere, I was beginning to agree with my daughter that keeping the place was a nuisance. I had a snow rake, and in most years, I'd pull the weight of snowfalls off the roof, but that year was different. The snow was deeper. I lit a fire to warm the place up and let the melting do some of the work for me, but as I sat at the harvest table and gradually warmed up with the stove going as well, I could hear the roof beams creaking above me. It was as if the cabin was speaking to me, telling me it was old and that it had a tough time with change. I felt for the place. Growing old is arduous work. Keeping up change is even harder. But it was the world that was changing. Every snowflake was another morsel of entropy. It was accumulating so fast.

Two years of rain happens sometimes. Farmers worry about their crops, about fungus and rot setting into their feed grains, and how their animals suffer when nature is not in balance. I opened the cabin for the season, hoping for the best, but the downpours never let up. After a week or so, I washed some laundry in the sink and had to dry my shorts and socks over the edge of the wood stove. I never like that. Jockey shorts should be soft and airy, not crisp. The books that had been stored on the shelf of the veranda, the old fat, slightly large-type hardcovers that were once published in this country and deemed to have some artistic or intrinsic edifying power, grew rank. I put it on my to-do list to go through them over the course of the summer and toss out the ones that were mouldy beyond redemption. I considered burning them, but that wouldn't be right.

When the rain let up for a few hours one afternoon, the birds sang. A rainbow came out in a parting of the clouds like the proverbial promise of a truce between heaven and earth – mankind's parole for good behaviour. I was curious what the river was like after all the weather, and made my way through the tall, damp grass in my Wellies to stand on the bank of the stream. The creek bed had started to resemble the watercourse of my childhood. The trees had grown lush again. The river was talking to me as it passed over the stones. It had gotten deep in places, and I thought it would be wonderful to toss in a line to see if any trout might be in there. As I stared, sure enough, there were fish. One was fighting the current where the flow passed over a large rock. I hadn't noticed the rock before. It seemed a hazard to navigation, but then I thought, "Who would want to navigate this stream?" But it was now more than a stream.

The local weather forecast the next day warned of severe thunderstorms and the potential for flash-flooding. I laughed. I shouldn't have. By noon, the bank between the house and the flow had washed away. For all the years I had spent at the cabin, I had never realized it was situated at the bend of a stream, and the outer elbow, according to the physics of rivers, is what gets washed away when there is too much water for the channel to handle.

For the first time in my memory, I could hear the river and the rain, but it was the river that bothered me. My greated grandfather had built the cabin close to the river to please his greated wife but it began to worry me that it was too close. The babbling brook and its gentle lap lap over the stones was now almost a rush of an engine, a perpetual motion machine that could not be shut off. As I stared from the kitchen window toward the flow, I noticed, for the first time, the meadow not only sloped toward the stream but was demarcated by a noticeable drop, the sheer cut of an old shore. Familiarity with a place blinds a person to what is there. I not only had a riverbank, I had an old, ghost shore close to the house, and the torrents were reclaiming an ancient watercourse inch by inch as the levels rose.

My first thought was: "What is this going to cost me in river tax?" My second thought was whether the ghost bank would hold. How long had that old shore been hiding in the undergrowth? Would it keep the waters at bay? Would it simply wash away two hundred years of place and purpose and rewrite the story of the property as if we had never been there? Nature never likes permanence except on its own terms.

The next two summers were even wetter and the winters harder than I'd imagined they could be. The spring melt left the riverbanks strewn with a puzzle of debris. The rising waters were taking a toll on the old place and on me. Worry aside, I was wondering if I should simply cut my losses and sell the land. I could use the money. I could go south for the winter and get a new kitchen for the condo I now owned, having sold my house because the upkeep was too much for me. I had never really considered selling the cabin. The adzed beams were still aromatic and held the beautiful scent of the trees they had once been. They must have been cut from hazel stands that once were thick in the area. Each timber was still hard as steel, though the chinking needed regular patching on the inside, and I wondered what was going on beneath the grey clapboard I didn't have the money to repaint every year or two years or three now.

This summer settled me on my choices, or rather they were settled on me. Life imposes outcomes when one dithers. May, June, and July were all wash-outs, as they had been in recent memory.

But then August came.

I woke one morning and the sun was shining. The river was still high, and now awfully close to the cabin. The patch where my aunt had planted her vegetable and herb garden was long gone, probably down stream somewhere with its secrets of seeds and forgotten popsicle sticks on which she wrote the name of each seeded row until the row grew tall enough to proclaim its own identity. I felt as if the cabin and I were fighting a battle – a kind of Lonergan and the ants but with a raging river and with weather that was now too serious to ignore.

The sun felt good. The air warmed.

I decided, that after tarring and patching the shingles, after plugging the holes in the porch where the mice were getting in and mending the screens that had been torn by branches blown from the tree next to the dilapidated shed, an old oak I should have cut down years before, it was time for me to rest. There was a paperback I'd been dying to read. There was a cold beer in the fridge. I put my feet up on the metal-fendered glider and felt a kind of perfection in the place that I had never known, at least not for years, maybe not since my childhood. That's when I fell asleep.

I am not sure how long I was out, but I was out cold. It was a deep sleep, but not dreamless. I dreamed that I was looking up at the sky and asking "why, why," and no one would answer – not the wind, or the sound of the stream, or the leaves that moved in the long-lost willows as the stars flickered through their high and bending boughs. I could see through those high branches. I could see the stars. They were pouring from the Milky Way in a great flood of light. I saw them as I used to see them as a child, when the closest lights were miles away and the darkness was a great river rising out of the east and flowing into the west.

And that's what woke me. The river. The rain had been falling while I slept. The waters had been rising. The world had become a torrent in the lightlessness. It was hammering against the stone foundations of the cabin. I lit a naphthalene lamp and cupped my hands around my eyes to see what was happening. The cabin's kitchen wall on the creek side of the open room disintegrated. The roof fell in.

I looked down at my feet. Two mice ran between my legs for the safety of the porch. As the roof beams of the cabin collapsed, a pair of porcupines raced in after the mice. Wind tore a hole in the porch ceiling and birds flew in – pairs of owls, Canada geese, mourning doves, meadow larks, redwing blackbirds, chickadees, herons, barn swallows, phoebes, blue jays, robins, sparrows. The room had become a frantic aviary of feathers and frightened winged things, including a pair of bats. The screen door broke off its hinges and in came a pair of foxes, a pair of rabbits, voles, barn cats, the old dogs that guarded the dairyman's farm and barked in the night, sheep, a cow and a bull, salamanders, and even two mudpuppies.

The porch broke free from the cabin. I could feel it moving beneath my feet as I held the lantern at the door and watched as the cabin broke apart. "I had a dream whose roof collapsed, letting in the rain," I said to myself. A friend of mine had written that in a poem, and I had forgotten it until that moment. It was absurd that it should come to mind as the porch began to spin, but it seemed the only thing my mind would let me think. I crouched down against the porch wall. The old, mouldy books were scattered across the floor, as the last piece of my solitary retreat bobbed and the animals, some holding on to the metal glider for dear life, stared at me in terror. I must have been looking at them the same way.

We floated and rocked and spun in the current, helpless, and without direction, at the mercy of the river. The water was washing in where the screen door had been, and as a carpet of white water tried to take one of the mice, I shouted "No! They are mine," and grabbed it by the tail and drew it back in. And in the darkness, I asked myself if or when we would hit solid ground, either to break apart or to hold fast to our mooring. I looked around and realized I was missing a pair of ravens that cawed in the meadow every daybreak. They hadn't made it inside the porch, but I prayed they were holding tight to the remains of the roof, and when I looked up at the gash where the rain was pouring in, I saw the black outlines of the pair and was relieved they had not been lost to the storm.

I am still not sure where the voyage will end, but if the birds and beasts and I manage to make it through, at least the creatures will pick up where they left off. I am an old, widowed man, alone and afraid, and I'm not sure if I can speak for the rest of my kind. The owls stare at me. They want an answer I cannot give them. We must wait for it to stop raining, for the waters grow still, or to arrive at our resting place.

If we should be so fortunate, I will ask one of the ravens to fly around and search for signs of life and wait to see if he returns. I will bend down at the open door, reach into the depths that surround us, and cup the water in my hand. I will whisper to the glowing constellations of light that sparkle from the cleared sky on the waves and to the tiny Milky Way shimmering in my palm that I am sorry for not having understood that water is a living thing like those that fly or swim or walk on four or even two legs. I will ask the waves for their forgiveness, for me, my creatures, my ancestors, and the future, and beg absolution for not paying the due all life is owed.

THE KIDS

THERE WAS A RIVER WITH MANY STONES IN IT. Grey stones. And almost as many people as there were stones. We were all crossing the river. It was not deep, and a woman carried me across in her arms.

I looked down. I was afraid she might stumble but she balanced on the slippery rocks, stepping from one to the other. I could see her legs, her dark jeans, and the water white and eddied around her knees. When we reached the other side, tall, thin grass grew like fingers along the shore. There was a sound like a board snapping in half, and the woman who held me slipped in the tangle of undergrowth and fell down.

"Go on," she said.

I waited.

She reached up and put something in my pants pocket. After that, she did not move. She looked up at me. She was holding her side, and she had blood on her hands. She had slipped and fallen on something in the embankment and repeated the words "Go on."

I parted the tall grass with the others. Some had trampled it down for me as they climbed. When we reached the top of the embankment there was a road with white lines painted on it and men with short haircuts and dark blue uniforms who were pointing handguns at everyone who had crossed the river. They ordered the men toward one truck and the women toward another. When the women reached the truck, they still had their children in their arms or by the hands. Some of the older children followed along behind them.

A woman in a khaki uniform with her hair tied back behind her head and rubber gloves on her hands pushed the children away from their mothers. They took the children from the arms of their mothers. The women screamed. I turned and looked for the woman who had carried me on the long journey and she was not there among the others on the road.

I never saw her again.

The children bawled. Some fought back with powerless fists or kicked wildly. We were loaded into a white truck. The windows were blacked out, and we drove away.

The motion of the truck rocked me to sleep. I do not remember where we went, but more people in dark blue uniforms woke me when we arrived at a place beneath tall, bright lights, a place surrounded by barbed wire and a steel fence.

We were ordered to remove our clothes and the people in blue uniform sprayed us with cold water. Before I took off my pants, I found what the woman had put in my pocket just after we crossed the river. It was a gold-coloured coin, not real gold, but it had a face on it. I put the coin in my mouth so no one would see I had it. Then, after the people in blue uniforms had shaken our pants and shirts and slapped our shoes against a wall, we put our clothes back on.

The other children were still crying. One girl had cried so hard she threw up on one of the women in a khaki uniform, and the woman slapped her and swore at her and pushed her back, clothed, into the area where they had hosed us down.

We were taken to a large room and told to lie on black mats. A man handed us silver blankets. We were told to lie down and sleep.

What did I dream that night? I remember low houses painted in bright colours. The sidewalks around them were narrow. The plaster on the front of the houses was cracked and crumbling. Stray dogs watched us in the street as we boarded a bus. "Perro! Perro!" someone shouted. The dogs moved further away but they still watched us.

The place where me and the other children slept that night, and for nights afterward, was a prison that had once been a large store. The men in dark blue walked up and down, staring at us through the fence. "Perro! Perro!" I shouted at them to make them go away. But they didn't. I pulled the silver blanket around my shoulders. I tried to remember the woman who carried me across the river.

Was she a friend? An aunt? Was she my sister or my mother?

The older children, the boys, would grab the smallest children when they went to the washroom. I would try to tell the men in dark blue that the boys had taken someone smaller than me into the room where the walls echoed with the small child's cries. The men would not listen. They would stare at me and say, "Go away, Perro."

That is how I got my name. It means stray dog.

I was only four when they put me in the cage with the other children. The men in uniforms called it "a crib." Since then, when I have stood in front of churches during the Christmas season, I have been told a crib is a box of hay with the baby Jesus in it. Those Jesuses are always smiling. They have haloes. They look up to heaven with their arms spread as if they are receiving the blessing of a higher power or are spreading their arms to say, "I am ready to be crucified." Most of us in the pen were crucified. I lived in a different kind of crib.

The crib, as I learned later, was an abandoned Walmart on the outskirts of an abandoned town. It had once been a good town, people told me. I spent four years of my childhood there. Some children prayed as they lay on their black mats.

Some bit their wrists and did not wake in the morning. Everything I remember about that place was death, and everything I wanted to remember while I was there was a dream of life I slept through.

One of the women in a blue uniform made us go to a room where she taught us words. We repeated them. If we did not repeat them the way she wanted, she would slap us across the backs of our heads. She told us we were criminals. We didn't belong in her country. One girl, a little taller than me, spoke up. She knew how to speak to the woman. "Send us home," she said. The girl was pulled by her hair and taken to a room where I heard her shrieking. Then the woman in dark blue returned, and at the end of the day the girl sat on her black mat, staring straight ahead, one eye swollen and turning black, and the other looking for something or someone in the distance.

A man who said he was the Superintendent appeared and ordered us to be quiet as we sat on our black mats.

"There has been a change in the government," he said. "You are going to be reunited with your parents."

Some of the children, sensing they were hearing good news, cheered. Others who didn't understand sat there, their backs hunched, their hands folded in their laps as they had been taught to do when someone came to speak to us.

The woman who taught us words, who had held up a picture of a man with an orange face and ordered us to say, "God bless the President," called me into her special room. I thought I was going to be beaten up.

"We don't know who your parents are," she said. "We have misplaced your records. Do you know where you are from?"

I told her that I had dreamed of the street with the colourful houses, the cracked plaster walls, the stray dogs, the perros, watching us from a distance. I told her it was a town where the women were tired every day because they sat up all night, afraid the door would open, afraid of gunfire, afraid of the men, the dark perros who came in the night. I thought she was going to beat me the way she had beaten the other children if they said anything, so I sat there and shook my head, shrugged my shoulders. I let her know that I did not know.

She slid a file across her desk. "Is this you?"

In the file there were sheets of paper, some with an American eagle in a circle at the top and some with a strange sun-face designed rounded by a border of squares. Clipped to the upper left-hand corner of the pages was a picture of a boy. His face was blank. His eyes were staring at the floor. He did not look happy. I wanted more than anything to be a boy who smiled, so I shook my head and said, "No."

"His name is Dominicano Juarez. Are you sure you are not this boy?"

I did not know what I looked like.

There were no mirrors in the bathrooms of the cribs. I had not seen my reflection since the day we crossed the river. I had stared over the bank at a frog just before we began our crossing, and I saw a boy in the water whose face moved when my face moved, whose mouth opened and closed with mine, and whose hands reached toward me when I reached into the river. He could have been me, but I had forgotten who I was.

"I am Perro," I said.

She closed the file.

The day I was moved from the crib at Walmart was the day I discovered the world outside the barbed-wire fence had changed. As we drove along a highway in a bus with windows that had not been blacked out, I could see through a small, scratched off portion ruined neighbourhoods, houses burned to shells, abandoned storefronts, and charred cars resting on their wheel rims.

I disobeyed my orders.

There was a young man in a blue uniform who sat at the front of the bus.

We had been told to stay in our seats.

We had been told not to talk to the driver. But I wanted to know what had happened to the towns we passed, so I walked up front and asked the young man. His face was covered in pimples. He looked as if he had not started to shave, but he had a gun in a holster on his hip.

"What happened to these towns?" I asked.

He looked at me as if I were stupid. I thought, for a moment, he was going to shoot me. Then he said, quietly, "They overthrew the President and all hell broke loose. Probably why you spent so long in the tank. People had other things to do. Up north about twenty miles in Austin, a gang of patriots got into one of the compounds and gunned down everyone they took for an alien. You and your pals here were lucky. You were guarded by the dissenters. It came down to the red states versus the blue states, and the red states won."

I had no idea what he was talking about.

"Yep," he said. "The blue states won the day. I'd grown up in a red home, but then I went off to a state university, not one of those Christian places, and I couldn't live with what was happening, so I joined the blue guys. New York and Hollywood types learned how to use guns and good Christian folk like some of my aunts and uncles got the worse of it all. But it's for the best, I guess. No more guns. No more walls. Things went nuts for a while. Really nuts." He turned and looked out the window. "Get back to your seat, you little bugger. Go on. Git." He put his hand on the horn of his revolver.

We spent a day and a night on the bus. There was no washroom, and nothing to eat. All of the kids peed themselves. There was nowhere to go. A couple squatted beneath the seats and crapped on the floor. The bus stank. We stank.

When the bus stopped, a woman in jeans came on board. She was carrying a clipboard. The door opened. She paused on the steps and looked like she was going to puke.

"Welcome to Illinois," she said. "I want everyone to line up, single file, beside the bus."

We waited in the shadow of the yellow bus. The driver and guard stood talking as they leaned against the front bumper. The young guard called over to us, "So long, little buggers." A van came, picked the two men up, and drove away.

Cars pulled up beside the bus and men and women got out. The woman in jeans with the clipboard told them to wait behind a white line that had been painted on the pavement. The woman with the clipboard separated the girls from the boys. One girl had a little brother. As the woman pulled them apart, they screamed and reached for each other. I had to turn my back. I could not stand to watch them sob though I heard their pain.

We were each given a piece of paper with a number on it. I was number 647.

"When I call your number," the woman in jeans said, "you will proceed to the people you are here to meet. These people are now your families. You are ordered to treat them with respect. There will be no talking, no crying."

My number was called, and I walked toward the painted line. My life, for the past several years had been about standing behind lines, waiting to be called to cross a line, being called a criminal because someone I cannot remember stepped out of line. Borders are lines. There are lines everywhere. Those who draw them have no sense of what those who need to cross them endure.

I stood there, and a man and a woman approached me. They left their other children, a boy, and a girl, behind the line. The woman approached but she immediately stepped back and waved her hand in front of her face.

The man said, "You smell like shit."

I couldn't say anything. I had been ordered not to speak. I wanted to tell them about the bus ride, but it would have meant talking.

They headed toward a van. The boy who was with them looked and me and said, "You stink. And you're not like us."

The woman said to me, "Your new name is Jeremy Ward because we're told you don't really have a name. You are only known as Perro."

The little girl, who was younger than me, bent over and barfed.

Another long ride. The van was air conditioned, but because I smelled of shit, the family had to roll down the windows. I had to sit in the back.

The boy turned around in his seat. "We're watching *Frozen,* but you're not allowed to look. The headphones are mine. Shit people don't get headphones. You're shit-coloured too."

Bobby Ward, I was told, was my new stepbrother. He didn't want a stepbrother. Neither did Angela, the girl. I'm not sure why their parents wanted me, either. I heard them talking late that night. The father insisted it was his duty as a human being. The woman said it was all wrong. She said I shouldn't be there. The father said they'd have to make the best of it, they'd have to adjust.

I looked out the window of my bedroom. The father was burning my clothes in a trash can. My coin was in the pocket. I waited until early the next morning. When everyone was asleep, I went to the yard and put my hand inside the can. At the bottom, I found the coin. It had turned black.

My father, Mr. Ward, yelled at me out the back door. "Get out of there, you idiot. Now your hands are black."

He made me stand with my hands under the garden hose until the ashes washed away. He turned off the hose and made me turn my hands over and over.

"They're still black," he said. "They will probably remain that way."

Everything in my life turned black. My memories, over the next several years were black. I blacked out my time at school. My English was not good. We had spoken Spanish to each other in the crib. The English schoolteachers told me I was stupid. I didn't care. It was all part of the blackness.

I was the only kid in the school who was one of the "salvaged." The salvaged, I learned, were the kids who had been taken from their parents when they crossed the Rio Grande. In the process of being taken away from their mothers and fathers the government people lost the kids' identities. Those who were as young as me when we were taken had no memory of who we were. We were just "the kids."

Bobby and I never got along. He played baseball. I said I wanted to join the team, but at the try-out the coach had a word with Father Mr. Ward and I wasn't permitted to play until I got older. The coach told me I needed to learn to catch. The ball hurt my hand when it came to me, and I dropped it.

Bobby said to me on the way home, "You're a shithead."

I didn't say anything. He punched me in the shoulder.

"I said, you're a shithead. Say something."

Father Mr. Ward told us to cut it out or we wouldn't stop at McDonald's on the way home.

Angela was in Grade Five. She avoided me. We didn't speak. If she saw me going to the bathroom, she would lock herself in her room. I heard her whispering to Mother Mrs. Ward that I was dirty, and she didn't want to touch anything I touched. I wasn't allowed to walk around Angela's side of the kitchen table. Mother Mrs. Ward said I was a member of the family and Angela had to take me as I came. Then Angela said her kindergarten teacher had told them that criminals like me were killing America and that they didn't deserve to live. Then she told her mother how much she hated her. Mother Mrs. Ward collapsed on the kitchen floor and cried into her hands. Angela slammed the door of her room behind her and locked it. I didn't say anything.

I kept my silence as long as I could. I didn't say anything at home and I didn't say anything at school. I sort of made a friend. He was Korean, he said. He said his name was Ho.

Ho said, "Let me teach you how to catch and throw."

No one in the school liked me or Ho. At recess we had the area in the back corner of the schoolyard to ourselves. That is when I learned to catch and throw. The next year, I tried out for a baseball team at school. Bobby didn't get picked. I did. I was a pitcher. The teacher who coached us said I threw harder than any kid my age.

"Where do you get that stuff?" the coach asked. "Is all that bottled up inside you somewhere?"

One day Father Mr. Ward was sitting alone in the backyard. It was a weekend and it was summer. I was twelve by then. He was having a beer.

"This isn't for you," he said. "You might get to like it, and it is not to be liked too much."

Then he asked me what I remembered about coming to the States. I shrugged.

"We crossed a river," I said. "I was in the arms of a woman, but she slipped and fell on the bank as we climbed into the country. I'm not sure. Maybe she was shot, maybe she fell on something. She never made it to the road. The rest is, well, I don't remember."

"Or want to remember?" he asked.

"I don't care."

He said, "You should. Maybe you have family somewhere. Maybe they are wondering what became of you."

I shrugged again. Then, I reached into my pocket and pulled out the coin. I held it in my hand and stared at it. "This was what I wanted from the ashes of my clothes. The clothes smelled like shit. The coin didn't."

He reached over, and I let him hold it in his hand. He squinted, rubbing it with his fingers to see if the blackness would disappear like someone who was waking up and rubbing the night from their eyes. "Honduras," he said. "This is a 100 lempira. You're from Honduras?"

I shook my head yes, then no, then yes again.

"Not certain, are you," he said. "I should see if anyone in Honduras is looking for you."

"They haven't looked for me," I said.

"Maybe you don't know they are. You haven't exactly been easy to find. I mean, you got here. They told us you went by Perro, the name for a wild dog. That could be anyone's name, anyone's word. Then we called you Jeremy. I'd say you're hiding in plain sight, but no one can see you. You've become invisible."

It must have been two weeks later. It was late at night. I had come home from baseball practice and Father Mr. Ward and Mother Mrs. Ward were sitting at the kitchen table and said, "Jeremy, come here. We've got something for you."

They were holding a letter from the International Red Cross. Someone had paper clipped a xeroxed photo to the corner of it. The photo was of a little boy. He was not smiling. He stared into the camera. He was not looking at the world. He was looking beyond it.

"Jeremy," said Father Mr. Ward, "do you ever remember anyone ever calling you Dominicano Juarez?"

I didn't know.

Mother Mrs. Ward held up the letter. "We think that's who you are. We think that's why you called yourself Perro. Dominicano means 'dog of God,' like the Dominican monks. That may be how you got your nickname 'wild dog,' Perro. It says in the letter you have a grandmother in the town of Cedros which is just north of the capital. She met an aid worker and gave them your name and this picture."

"I'm not sure if I am that boy or not," I said. "My life has been a long sleep. Everything in that sleep has been a dream. I have been called everything and nothing at the same time.

I am no one, except Jeremy Ward, Perro, shithead, stink face, criminal. Now you tell me I have another name, a real name, and a real family somewhere. I don't know what to believe."

"We've been in touch with your grandmother," Father Mr. Ward said. "I am not sure if you want to hear the story or not."

I shrugged. All my life I survived because my shoulders never got tired of trying to touch me ears, and all my life they never managed. That's why I shrug. I need to hear what I need to hear, but my shoulders never block out the sound even though I wish they would."

"Your father and mother," Father Mr. Ward said, "were murdered by a death squad. They had saved enough to buy a small piece of land to work, and the big landowners didn't want anyone moving in on them. Your grandmother, who moved into town with your uncle, was threatened as well, but she refused to leave. It was your aunt, Marita, who decided you would not have a life unless she fled with you. The last anyone heard from you or Marita was in a town near the Mexican border. She told your grandmother that she had paid all her money to get across the river, and they would be crossing the next day in the afternoon. No one heard from you or Marita again."

I sat silently. I did not know what to say. If it were true for me, could it be true for the others? There were thousands of us. We were not misplaced. We had our names, our lives, our families, purposely stolen from us. It was part of some great plan to make America into something it never was, something that betrayed the ideas America was supposed to represent. Someone had to stand in the way. Someone had to be blamed. So, they blamed us. They blamed the kids. Some people called us dreamers. But do they know what we were dreaming? We weren't dreaming of who we wanted to be, but just of who we might have been.

I do not remember much of my Spanish. That language has died in me, but I am trying to learn it and take it back because it is in me and it is mine. I have spoken to the old woman on the other end of the phone.

She weeps. She says my name over and over.

I tell her I am not God's dog. *I am Perro. I am Perro.*

I try to remember a dream I had in the crib of the detention center. It is a dream of an old woman who smells of blossoms. Her flesh rolls over her elbows and is warm to the touch when she holds me in her arms and says the names for things she has laid out on a table where she prepares a meal.

She sets me down on the floor as she stands at the table and pats round dough between her hands then rolls it with a dowel. I look up at her, and with flour on her palms she rubs my head so my hair turns white like an old man's. I kneel and cling to her leg. I am the dog who refuses to leave her side.

SAVING SELAH

I PUT DOWN THE RECEIVER. Had Selah been saved or not? I would never know for certain. That afternoon, the U.S.S. Forestall pulled up along the coast not far from the capital. The defenceless city was bombed, mainly the oil depots and the refinery. There was American film footage on the evening news of bombs exploding over the tangle of tiny houses and the knots of small streets in the Moslem quarter. Within days, Selah's country had ceased to be newsworthy, as is the case with all news. It only lasts as long as it lasts.

I was working on an Asian assignment for NKP, on loan to them from the CBC. The Japanese were wonderful to me. They gave me a go-anywhere pass on JAL and all its associated airlines, and when I wasn't covering an event – a bombing, a trade agreement, or a new industrial initiative, I was encouraged to enjoy myself and see as much of Asia as I could. The CBC and the BBC, in a joint venture, asked me to interview Selah Palagong and his wife Naomi and to do a radio documentary, something I could cut together quickly, and then enjoy the beautiful beaches on the country's coasts, before heading back to Tokyo for a Monday morning meeting. I met the couple, asked the questions, and then something that I don't usually permit myself to do happened: I became friends with them.

One question has stayed in my mind from that interview. I don't know why I asked it. It was a minor issue at the time, though minor issues of today often become the headline of the future. "The Moslem population here, they are growing, how shall we say, uneasy with the state of things. You once mentioned that your father, who you never knew, was an Islamic revolutionary. How do you feel about extremists?"

"Extremists only believe what they believe because they have chosen to believe it. I know that is circuitous logic. A Moslem has every right to his faith, as I have to mine. A Moslem will defend what he believes in as I defend what I believe. I do not fear them. I honour them because they have convictions a world where so many great human capacities – faith, courage, honour … those Faulkner things – are so easily cast aside. It takes courage to believe in what you believe."

A group of us returned two years later on a tour sponsored, of course, by our generous funding agencies, and our reception made us feel like rock stars. Selah stood up in front of a packed auditorium and introduced me as his friend, fellow journalist, and cultural activist, Dave Benton of the Canadian Broadcasting Corporation. I could not help but like the guy. The look on his face was genuine. He was as proud to be my friend as I was to have him as mine. Life in his nation was good and often, on those winter days when it snows sideways for hours and hours, I wished I lived on that beautiful hillside. Selah's nation had become a veritable Shangri-La. But life for Selah had not always been the paradise I thought it was.

By the time Selah Palagong was born, his Moslem father had deserted his family to serve in the revolution. His mother, in a rage at the idea that her husband could simply betray his family and walk away for nothing but a wild idea that had little hope of succeeding, picked up the children one night and knocked at the vestry door of St. Simon's Church a half mile away from their village in the small coastal city of Kalamalatan where a groggy priest opened the door and took them in.

After several months of refuge in the old rooms that had once been a noviciate behind the main church, an area walled off from the rest of the world where Kavari and her daughter could only hear the shouts in the streets of the Islamic revolutionaries pounding at the church door and firing off their weapons, she sat down with the priest and was received into the church. Her first act as a Roman Catholic was to have her son christened. Kavari became Catherine, Anar became Anne, and the infant boy's name was changed from Khalid, as his father had wished, to Selah.

"What does it mean, Father, this name Selah?" she asked as the priest drew the chrism across the sleeping child's forehead and repeated "Selah, in the name of the Father, the Son, and the Holy Spirit."

The priest smiled after sealing the bond within the child and handed the baby back to Catherine. "It is an exclamation. It means, 'here it is,' or so we are told. I do not take naming lightly, so I spent a great deal of time at the seminary searching out the meaning of the mysterious word. It also means 'to measure and weigh in balance' because the poets of the Psalms wanted to think that those who heard the beautiful wisdom of God paused long enough to consider it and make it their own. You could say is means more than 'pay attention.' It could be 'think about it,' 'consider,' and 'exercise good mind.'"

The revolution failed – the military invaded the Moslem quarter. There were reports of atrocities. The priest decided to move Catherine and her family to a safer place. Although he hadn't the heart to tell her, there had been reports that Saleem, her husband, had been in a cadre that had attempted to seize the market square one day when the sun was at its height. They thought they could succeed, Allah be praised, in slaughtering the shoppers to demoralize the town. Instead, the shoppers turned out to be paramilitary. Every stall was a fortified position. The revolutionaries rushed through the aisles with their guns blazing and were mowed down.

The survivors of the attackers were taken to an old cricket ground where the infield still bore the scar of a gravelled pitch – a last reminder of a forgotten empire. The men of Saleem's cell vanished. No records. No marked graves. The military decided they did not deserve an iota of information. The priest hoped that Catherine would pray for her lost husband, but her determination to reject him was so evident that he did not share the news with her. Better she did not know, he decided. God would reveal himself in good time.

The coastal road north to the Christian dominated city of Esdran was heavily guarded. Checkpoints popped up every two miles. Beside some, there were corpses lining the shoulder. The priest obtained transit papers for Catherine and her children. A man in a collar, on a mission of mercy, passed through the checkpoints easily. "Father forgive me for the lies I told to get you here," he said to Catherine when they arrived in Esdran. He pointed to the plastic rosary she held in her hands, folded in her lap. "The presence of the Lord did not hurt our cause."

A family named Cruz took them in. The priest explained, "His name means cross. He is Joseph of the Cross. That is a good name for a man who says he awaits our Saviour. He is *your* saviour."

The Cruz family had a small shed at the back of their garden that had once been the house's kitchen when the Cruz's were a powerful merchant family in the city. Catherine was employed for food and shelter as a maid and cook in the Cruz household. The balconies that demarcated the generations shadowed the courtyard that Catherine swept each morning just after dawn.

Times change. The powerful mercantile Cruzes had re-
ceded into history. A shipload of goods from England, on
which a Cruz patriarch of the time had invested heavily, was
sunk en route to Esdran by a rogue German cruiser, the *Emden*.
As is the case with many powerful families throughout the
world, a single event had triggered a sad decline in the family's fortunes. José Cruz was now a tailor, and on the side he
mended shoes.

José claimed he could transform a man from head to foot
in a matter of hours. José's father had taken to the sartorial
trade when bolts of heavy British wool piled up in the family
warehouse during the Second World War. The wool, he explained, had nowhere to go. It could not turn back and it could
not head on. So, it sat there, wrapped in heavy layers of brown
packing paper, taped, and sealed against the attrition of insects,
and hidden in the cool darkness of a long, sleep. The stacks
of bolts, José would tell those who entered the warehouse, reminded him of the empire. "It is in darkness now, but someday
its fortunes will revive and our representatives in Durham will
want to do business with us again."

During the war, the shoe trade was José's biggest business.
Leather kept better in the dark than wool. Aussies on their way
to the Malay jungles would discover a sole was coming loose
on their boot, a hat band snapped, a heel had lost a nail, or a
holster was coming unseamed. José did well in leather while
that phase of his commercial life lasted. There was little call for
wool in the tropics, but always with an eye to future business,
José saw that worsted could be traded for other types of cloth,
and once the war ended a bespoke suit of jute cut just as fine
a figure in the post-war world as a Saville Row pin stripe and
was far more suited to life in the sun.

As Selah grew up, he would sit in the cool front corner
of José's shop. The old men would gather there to discuss the
hardships of the country. Selah could see out the window and

down the street as carters unloaded their goods and shoppers came and went. When word got around the foreign community, especially the oil men who came from Amsterdam and London, that there was an old tailor who made a good suit from good material, business picked up. Selah not only heard the dickering over cut and price, but he also heard the exchanges between his world and the outside world.

After school one day when he was seventeen, an ex-pat Pole walked into Cruz's Tailors and ordered a double-breasted suit. "A Pole?" José asked.

"I was in broadcasting before the war. Then I fled Poland. I landed in London and did propaganda work on the BBC. I got work in Shepherd's Bush and got to know a number of the producers and newsmen. I practiced my English, and can you hear it – just a touch of an accent – to sound just a little bit foreign. That's why they assigned me to the Overseas Service. I am here to tell the world about the lovely things in your lovely country if they are lovely enough to talk about."

José smiled as he measured the man's inseam, and looking up from his crouch asked, "And when will that be?" in perfectly unaccented public-school English.

"I will come by more often," the Pole said. "You seem like a man who has a lot to know, and this is a cool, friendly place to spend a hot afternoon."

That is how Selah got into broadcasting. He was told to keep his eyes open, his mouth shut, and to handle the feeds of judiciously tentative two-minute reports the Pole fed back to London.

The studio where Selah handled the Pole's feeds was hot and airless. "I can go into the jungle or an extremist mosque, but I can't handle that damned glass booth." Selah sat through late nights with Tadeusz at the lone table in the bureau. The Pole had found the bar at the Overseas Club but had returned to the office having overheard something he should not have.

"Two Americans. I can't say more than that. Something is going down, but now is not the right time to report it. The Americans are always up to something. Did you know before the war I worked in Poland for a remarkable man? His name was Maximilian Kolbe. He was a priest. He wasn't a Communist or a Fascist. He was a man without sides. That's dangerous, especially when you are brilliant. Being brilliant and dangerous is no one's business. No one's. And Kolbe? He was amazing. He had a newspaper going, and radio station. He even broke into television. The first television station in Poland! No one, of course, had a television set to watch what he was doing, but he was doing it, nonetheless. And his message? Simple. He said the Nazis weren't telling the truth. They were making up stuff. And were they? Of course. You see, Selah, real journalism, the kind of stuff you and I are doing, is the antithesis of propaganda. Propaganda wants people to believe things; journalism wants people to know things and understand them. We journalists don't care whether something glorifies the people in charge. That's not our job. Our job is to make sure everyone knows what is being glorified and why. And tonight, I think things in glory land are going to change. Can't say yet, but when Americans show up in the Overseas Club and a general shows up it means someone, somewhere, perhaps on the other side of the world, wants a different set of medals in charge of things."

"What became of your journalist priest?"

"Max? When the Germans crossed the border, he kept broadcasting. He'd built a wall around his broadcast centre. He said it was his version of an abbey. I thought it looked more like a fort. He kept broadcasting. I don't know how the information was getting in but it was getting out. It was like a candle burning down to its last wax. There was the light and gradually the light went out. The Germans stormed the place. They made him stay long enough to see everything blown up. You know what he is reported to have said? 'You can't blow up ideas.' Ideas. The very thought of ideas. They make me sad and yet happy to be what I am. I'm an idea. You're an idea. Yes, the Nazis killed Max. They killed him in a concentration camp. He took the place of some man who had ten children when someone escaped from the camp and ten needed to be punished for it. He kept those ten men alive in a filthy, airless cell for a month. When the Nazis came back to see if they were all dead, they were singing an Ave. An Ave! So, the bastards pulled him aside. 'We're going to finish you. We don't care about the others, but you have been trouble to us because you are about ideas.' So they shot bleach into his arm with a hypodermic. He didn't die. They started to club him to death with the butt ends of their rifles. He didn't die. 'I am an idea,' he kept saying. So, they shot him. They put more bullets in him than it takes to win a battle. But did they kill the idea? No. Because someone was listening. Someone was reporting. Someone saw what happened and passed on the facts others. Eventually, a couple of years later the story reached me in London and it was I who read it on the BBC World Service to the people of my country."

"So, why are you here and not in your country with your ideas?"

"That's a whole other story. Men in grey. Men in green. Men in red. Men in black. Too many shirts. Here, the shirts are just one colour – no colour – and that suits me fine because ideas don't have colour. You can see through them."

The next day, as Tadeusz had predicted, three tanks and a soldier on a loudspeaker mounted on a troop carrier announced that the city was under marshal law and that orders were to be obeyed. One woman decided she had stayed too long at her sister's house and dared cross the street, only a few yards, after curfew. She was shot. Selah saw it out the window of José's shop which was now shuttered except for a tiny wedge of light that filtered in between the sheet metal and the stone wall. That is where the truth lies in extreme times, Selah thought to himself in a moment of poetry, as he sat in the shop front, the room overheated from having been closed up all day. Truth lives between metal and stone. He had wanted to write a poem about it, but both José and Tadeusz, who had taken refuge with the Cruz family while his bureau was sacked and his transmitters smashed, warned him that poetry in the face of stone and metal was a fool's gesture. Better to stick with the facts when they are ready to be spread than to dabble in something that could be misconstrued as a weak-hearted lie.

That night, however, Tadeusz made his way through the streets with Selah by his side. He had heard that the offices of Radio Luxembourg had not been attacked, and with a report in-hand and ready to let the English-speaking world know what was happening in the aftermath of the coup in Esdran and other cities in the country, the short two-minute news item was sent. Tadeusz was succinct. He stated that a group of generals had seized power in the capital and had declared marshal law. He reported that the capital was under lock-down and that travel was strictly prohibited. He also noted that large oil tankers had sailed past Esdran the day before, presumably bound for the capital port where vast oil reserves had accumulated when the previous government had shut down exports in defiance of international trade agreements. At the end of the report, he said his name, the location he was reporting from, and the name of the BBC World Service. That was his last report.

On the way home, Tadeusz and Selah saw a huddle of men ahead in the road. They were carrying guns. Tadeusz turned to Selah and told him to walk very carefully down a small alley they were passing and not to look back. Tadeusz took off his panama hat and his jute suit jacket and handed them to Selah. "There's money in the pocket, son, take it and be safe getting home." Then the Pole walked forward. Selah wanted to turn and look, but as the man's shadow disappeared off the alley wall, he knew that making a slow, quiet, passage home through the maze of streets was the only thing he could do.

Several months passed. Life in Esdran gradually became safer, though the presence of the military, soldiers stationed at street corners with rifles rested on their shoulders and their new, American-style helmets tilted back to the base of their necks, became a common sight. The Overseas Club remained closed. It had become a regional HQ of the new regime. No one came into the tailor shop. José fretted they would die from starvation when Selah produced some of the money he had found in Tadeusz's jacket. There was no word from the Pole. He had merely vanished in the night.

One morning there was a banging on the shutters of the shop. The steel sounded like trumpets. José cautiously opened the front door. "What do you want?" he said to the soldiers. "We are good people. We are obeying the curfew."

"Do you fix boots, old man?"

"Yes. But I cannot open because of the curfew." Six soldiers stood waiting outside.

"We hereby authorize you on the authority of the regional commandant to open your business and repair the boots these men have been wearing. They were purchased by the previous regime and are shoddy. They need work. Open up now."

So, José opened his shop. As he stood at his cobbler's bench, watching the men admire the samples of cloth and the mannequins in double-breasted wool suits, he felt a breeze blow in through the front windows and he felt relieved. Selah stood beside him, handing him his awls and hammers as José tapped and threaded and tightened the stitching before passing the boots back to Selah to be polished. By the time the guards left, José had sold five suits, a dinner jacket, two pairs of wool trousers, and a pair of restored brown loafers an Australian had forgotten to collect during the war. Other shops on the street, seeing José's establishment open for business again, raised their shutters, and gradually men and women flowed into the streets, tired, emaciated, and ready to do business again. That is how the American years began in Esdran.

Selah returned to the BBC bureau office. The place was a shamble, but in the midst of the killing and the chaos and the weeks of silence and curfew, someone had still managed to deliver the mail. There was a stamp with Her Majesty's profile on it, a young-looking woman who had become a ghost in cameo since Selah had last seen a British letter. Opening it, the letter inquired at the whereabouts of Tadeusz Prokevski, and asked if any local efforts were underway to locate him as the British Consulate in Kalamalatan had exhausted all means of determining Mr. Prokevski's whereabouts and condition. In the meantime, the message noted, the Service was in need of a reporter on the scene, and if one was available the individual should immediately contact an overseas telephone number that was written in the body of the letter.

Selah paused for a moment. The thought of spending his life dedicated to ideas seemed the noblest calling of all. Tadeusz had taught him that. He had no way of finding ideas, yet ideas seemed to come to him, and perhaps that would be a good thing in the journalism business. "It is a tricky life," Tadeusz had told him during one of their late-night chats in the bureau while they sat and waited for confirmation that an item had gone through to London in good order. Tricky? Perhaps. But even being a tailor, José had told him repeatedly, was a tricky business. Everything was tricky. Sleeves. Soles. Lapels, especially. The customer had to be satisfied. Who were the customers for ideas? The purpose of his life unfolded before him as Selah looked at a map of the world that had not been torn down from the wall. The map was divided into time zones. When there was night there was also day someplace else, and by night or day, people would listen to a voice out of the blue sky or the starry darkness because they wanted to know what was happening in the world. Selah picked up the telephone and called the number. A few weeks later, after the American senators had come and gone, and after moderate freedom of the press had been guaranteed with the new constitution, Selah, journalist for the BBC World Service, reporting from Esdran, opened the boxes containing the new transmission devices and an over-the-shoulder reel-to-reel tape recorder and microphone. The bureau was ready to report again. Ideas lived to fight another day.

The first order of business for Selah was to determine what had happened to Tadeusz. He recalled that the favourite place of mass executions was open spaces. He stared at a map of Esdran and found, on the outskirts, an old polo ground not far from the newly re-opened Overseas Club, that had been renamed the National Club in honour of the coup d'état.

With the new resources forwarded from London, Selah hired a driver, a Christian named Paolo whose background was a mixture of local, Portuguese – a hold over from several prior colonial regimes – and English, though his English left much to be desired, and local parentage. Selah wanted it that way. He wanted someone who knew the roads and back alleys, but not the complete depth of what might be discussed with an interview subject in the back of the car. Following Tadeusz's disappearance, Selah was finding it harder and harder to trust anyone.

The first stop Paolo was asked to make was at the old polo grounds. The grass had grown waist-high, and the old stands sat crumbling in the morning sun. The royal box, that had never been visited by the royalty it was intended to seat, was the first place Selah went to survey what was rumoured to have been a killing ground during the coup, and he thought to himself "this must be what kings see." Just below the tufts and plumes of the overgrowth, Selah could make out what appeared to be an arm that was still pointed to the sky. The bastards had not even thought to return to clean up their butchery. Wading into the grass, he was not ten feet from the field's perimeter when he stepped on a skull.

Selah looked into the empty eye sockets of what had been a person only months before. He leaned over and retched up his breakfast. Another and another lay beneath every step. He wracked his brains to remember details of Tadeusz, what he may have been wearing. The corpses were still clothed. As he approached the centre of the field, he recalled the two-tone loafers that José had sold Tadeusz and that Tadeusz had been wearing the night they had parted at the alley's mouth. It was then the smell struck him.

The stench reached into his entrails and he felt as if they were about to be ripped out. And just as he was about to faint, he looked down and the man, the bones at his feet, were wearing the two-tone shoes. Selah bent down. Between the buttons of the man's shirt was a medallion of a Madonna, a Polish religious medal that he saw Tadeusz once tuck back in his shirt, self-consciously, while he sat in José's shop. "A little piece of my lost homeland," he had said, smiling. "The Black Madonna." Selah reached down and pulled the chain from the body's neck only to watch the head snap back and roll to one side.

That night, Selah sat by himself in the bureau and recorded his first report. In the two small minutes that the network allotted him, and with only a faint hope that the item would make it to air with all the noise of the world drowning him out with its morass of affairs and tragedies, Selah reported the death of BBC World Service Correspondent Tadeusz Prokevski. He described the weedy patch of ground, the sound of buzzing insects hovering over the bodies, the fact that no one had made any public mention of the deaths of the foreign journalists – for many had gone missing that night – or the sudden absence of the local correspondents. He left the item, against network policy, with a rhetorical question: "Who will acknowledge this atrocity?" He signed off with: "This is Selah Palagong of the BBC World Service reporting from Esdran."

The next morning, Selah was summoned to the offices of the Minister of Public Information in the capital. As Paolo drove silently through the checkpoints and the roadside fields where the stalks of sugar cane stood sentry in the rising sun, he and Selah were silent. They pulled up in front of the Ministry. "If I don't come out after half and hour, Paolo, you are to leave without me, and make many turns and U-turns as you leave the capital in case you are being followed."

"But sir …"

"Do as I say please, it is for your own safety."

Selah was seated for an hour in an outer office. Inside, he could hear shouting. One voice was speaking his language and the other was speaking in English. There was a long silence and the door opened. The Minister of Public Information motioned him inside and pointed to a chair in front of a large desk surrounded by two flags of the nation. Another man, a North American in a seersucker suit, sat in the other chair in front of the desk. The minister, a colonel with ribbons and gold braid on his green uniform, took his seat opposite the two men.

"Mr. Palagong, thank you for coming today. This is Mr. Jenkins of CBS. Like you, he has been here to report on the problems that have taken place with the recent change in our government. Your broadcast on the BBC last evening has caused considerable attention that we wish to address."

"I think what the colonel is saying, young man, is that you've raised a storm with your report. Do you have any evidence that foreign journalists were murdered?"

Selah sat motionless. He did not know what to say until Tadeusz's words echoed through his mind. "Ideas are important." He reached into his pocket and pulled out the Black Madonna medal he had taken the day before from the corpse in the Polo Grounds.

"Here is your proof," he said, holding up the medal and letting it dangle in the air. The virgin and child seemed to spin as if moved by the wind. He then put it back in his pocket. "I have the religious medal, a Polish memento of his faith, from Tadeusz Prokevski. I removed it from his body yesterday at the killing place. There were numerous bodies there. I don't know how many of them were foreign journalists, but I know that at least one of them was Mr. Prokevski. He wore this medal as a testament to his faith and to his work with the holy martyr Father Maximilian Kolbe. If you wish to suppress the proof of the massacre, if you wish to silence the truth, you will have to kill me to take the medal from me. What I witnessed is the truth and I reported what I saw because I am a good journalist."

The other two men threw knowing glances to each other and nodded. "Would you excuse us for a moment," the Colonel said and pointed to the door." Selah stood up. His heart was pounding. He imagined the moment he stepped into the outer office he would be seized and dragged away. He looked out the window onto the street where Paolo had been waiting. The car was gone. "Good man," he thought. "He will survive at least another day."

With the inner office door closed behind him, Selah heard the two men conversing in muffled voices, and then the sound of a telephone being dialled and more muffled conversation. Selah sat in the waiting room chair. Nothing happened. He could hear traffic in the street outside, and then the sound of trucks and shouting, followed by gunshots across the road in the capital building. He looked out the window. Soldiers were rushing up the steps. The guards at the pillared entrance were gunned down and fell forward in their own blood, their bodies sprawled on the steps.

The outer office door flung open. Selah jumped to his feet because he thought they were soldiers. It was an American camera crew. The inner office doors parted and he could see the colonel standing up, donning his braided cap, as the American reporter took a microphone from his sound man.

"Are we rolling?" the reporter asked. "Good. I am with Colonel Pradagonang who has just seized power in the second coup in weeks here." The colonel buckled a sabre belt around his waist and strode forward. He turned to the camera, drew his sword, and paused. "This is a great day for our nation. The much-needed reforms that will save our people from poverty can finally be enacted now that I am President." He walked toward Selah and put his arm on his shoulder. "I hope you have your little tape recorder with you. You are an honest reporter, a man of the truth, and you are the new Director of our national radio. You will be escorted by Mr. Jenkins and his crew who will document your new role as the conscience that will guarantee the freedom of our nation." And with that, the Colonel calmly walked across the street to the government house, climbed the steps, and began his fifteen-year reign as the undisputed leader of his nation. It was all caught on film, and would, most certainly, make the televisions of America by the weekend.

As he took his seat in a leather chair in the Director's office of the national broadcast headquarters, Jenkins put his feet up on the edge of Selah's new desk. Selah was numb.

"You're one lucky sunnuvabitch, I can say that for you. You were in the right place at the right time. I've known the Colonel for some years now. I followed him as a jungle fighter when he was busy seeking out an imaginary Jap invasion force in the hills. There were no Japs. They never got close to this god-forsaken place, but that didn't stop him from hunting them. And he cut quite a figure doing it." Jenkins reached into his pocket and drew out a cigar. "Smoke?"

"No, thank you. Mr. Jenkins, you appear to be a cliché American, right down to the cigar. May I ask, simply from one reporter to another, what is in this for you? You are obviously not merely a reporter for an American network. I cannot imagine you selling soap or cars or cola. Your camera crew was waiting for the shots to be fired. You knew that something was going to happen."

"That's perceptive of you, son, but none of your god-damned business. I'm here. You're here. You're not dead. In fact, you've been given a plum job."

"I can see that. I'm obviously not seated here for interrogation. Why was I given this job and approximately how long will it last before I'm taken off to the nearest polo grounds for lead poisoning?"

The American threw back his head and laughed. "You're here as long as he's here, and he's here as long as we're here, and we need a free press or this whole reform business and our plans won't work. Go ahead. Don't stare at me in disbelief. I want you to keep track. I want reporters crawling all over the place. I want every iota of rotten truth hidden in this country to be exposed, reported on, revealed. The whole truth and nothing but the truth, or so God help you." He winked at Selah and drew a long puff on his cigar and exhaled before waving his hand in the air to clear a path for his exit. "Son, you are just what we need here."

"You still haven't told me why I am here and what this whole business is about."

"See you at the National Club. Drop by and have dinner with me when you're back in Esdran to collect your things. Maybe I can talk you into some good old single malt and you'll see the sense in all this. Remember, the whole truth and nothing but the truth. I want investigative journalism at its finest."

As soon as Jenkins left, Selah put his head in his hands and began to weep.

Not long after the colonel's nearly bloodless coup d'état, Selah met a beautiful journalist, Naomi Dakanagong who had been training in Canada at the *Globe and Mail*. The open door that was now presented to her to return to her country and work as an investigative reporter – partly to right the wrongs that had been inflicted on her family and that had caused them to flee shortly after the Second World War, and partly to indulge her nose for exposé journalism – was too much of an attraction to turn down. After several months of stellar reporting, the young leader of the broadcast team presented her with an elegant assignment: marry him. And she did.

Together, the nation's new power couple purchased a house on a hilltop overlooking the capital. It was an old colonial home with a spreading terrace off the dining room. At night they would stand on the terrace and look down on the lights of the capital and quietly whisper to each other the stories of blood and terror that had shaped their lives. The air on the hillside was full of ghosts in the darkness, and the lights of the city below, even in what seemed an ideal and benign time for the couple, only served to remind them both of what they had lost and could lose in the high stakes game of show and tell that entwined them both.

But in every letter we exchanged, I sensed a growing anxiety in Selah, and while the Colonel grew older with each passing year, the oil money that rolled in with the departure of each super tanker seemed to cement the old soldier's place at the helm of the nation. Despite the newfound wealth, most of which was leaving the country because the old Colonel had refused to enact nationalist policies, the poverty rate climbed and social unrest, trouble in paradise, started to spread. Old men, especially old leaders, have two things to fear as they age: inevitable death and those that would hasten their demise.

Bombs started going off among the shops. Selah was worried for José and called him everyday. "I am a shoemaker who will live forever," the old man laughed. Selah hadn't been back to Esdran in three years. His last visit had been for the funeral of his sister who had died from cancer. Selah blamed the fact that her house was in the path of the oil smoke from the refinery that had gone up beside the beach where they had played as children. Anne's death had made Selah feel mortal. It had shaken in him some of the bravado that had been the hallmark of his captaincy at the network. The network had begun to receive threats, but Selah was assured by visiting foreign broadcasters that crackpots are a dime a dozen everywhere. The bombs did not help allay his fears.

That is when the Moslem clerics started to disappear, mysteriously by night, and their disappearances were followed the next day by angry marches through the streets. The shopkeepers kept their shutters half closed just in case they needed to shut their gates in a hurry. The half-closed steel barriers looked like the eyes of a tired man. And when the shutters were completely closed, slogans in Arabic would appear spray painted across the metal shutters in the night. The Colonel ordered a curfew after eight p.m. Shots were heard nightly in the streets. The patrols did not ask questions.

But even with the violence and the turmoil in the Moslem quarter, life continued as it always had. The Colonel announced that he would have one more election – he had had six over the fifteen years of his regime and had won every time, each vote monitored by international observers and the main party that stood against him, in the British tradition, calling itself "the loyal opposition." Life was business and everyone accepted it as that. The press was free, and the network ran the documentaries that Selah and Naomi had become so adept at producing.

They had proven, beyond a shadow of a doubt, that the junta that had taken the life of one Polish journalist and umpteen other international reporters was Soviet backed. They had proven, beyond the shadow of a doubt, that the turmoil in the Moslem quarter was caused by Jihadi forces based in Pakistan and that real Moslems, true Moslems, condemned the violence and the unlawful acts of rage as being totally against the beliefs of good Moslems and good human beings.

Everything was life as it should be until the morning Selah and Naomi woke to the cries of their children and the sound of gunfire rising from the city below. Naomi picked up the telephone to tell the school that the children would not be in today only to discover that the line was dead. Selah told his family and his servants to stay put, to lock the doors, pull the drapes, and if anyone came to the door not to answer it.

"What is happening is not good. It is probably a coup d'état. None of us are home today if anyone calls or comes to the door."

Paolo would be bringing Selah's car around at the usual time in a mere fifteen minutes and he would go into the broadcast centre and collect what information he could. As the car pulled up, Selah saw that Paolo had been shot. Selah and Naomi ran to the car, grabbed Paolo, and, bending low in case there might be more bullets, helped the driver into the living room where they laid him on the couch and raised his legs.

One of the servants shouted that she would go for a doctor, but Paolo called her back. "You will be killed," he said, and winced at the burning sensation at the base of his neck. "The militants are everywhere. The city is being seized. The station has gone off the air. I think the militants have taken control of the radio and government house."

Naomi, trying to keep her cool, knitted her brows and said, "They can't be everywhere. That's impossible. There aren't enough of them. They can't take the city let alone the country."

Selah turned on the radio and heard only static. Then, out of the chaos of broken sound, he heard the sound of a Mullah calling the faithful to prayer, a call that echoed daily through the Moslem quarter but that the rest of the city ignored as a matter of getting on with their days. The call was followed by blaring marching music and the sound of a voice in Arabic.

"What are they saying? What are they saying?" Selah shouted. One of the servants spoke up.

"I know a bit of the language. They are saying they have taken over the nation. The Colonel is dead. The army have been trapped in their barracks, and if they do not co-operate, they will be shot. No ships are permitted to leave the harbour. All travel is banned. God be praised. That's all they've said. They're just repeating it now."

Selah sank into the closest chair. He stared straight ahead. "My God," he said, and crossed himself. He reached beneath his shirt and took hold of Tadeusz's Black Virgin medal and tightened his fist around it. "We are in grave danger." The music blared from the radio. More frantic marching bands. "Turn that fucking racket off!" Selah shouted. "I've got to think."

An explosion shook the hillside. The children and the maids screamed. Selah and Naomi leapt off their chairs to the floor. One of the French doors to the patio cracked wide open. Selah ran out to the patio to see what had happened. Had it been the oil depot? The government house? He scanned the horizon of the capital. The militants had blown up the army barracks.

He came inside. "The barracks." Naomi gasped and put her hand to her mouth. One of the maids wept inconsolably. Her husband was a sergeant. As the tears flowed from the children and the maid, and Paolo shook and cried softly with the pain, Selah and Naomi sat in silence. He looked over at Paolo. "I can't just let him sit there and die." And with that Selah left the house. He scrambled over the patio parapet and eased his way down the hillside. He crouched low in the scrub growth and made his way from tree to tree. He realized his white shirt might give him away, so he took it off, rolled it in a ball, and stuffed it under a fallen log among a horde of ants.

He waited and then darted across each of the winding hillside roads, hoping that no one would see him as he crossed each gap. He finally reached Dr. Devakutty's house and made his way through the shrubs in the front flower bed and knocked on the window glass. The doctor appeared at the window. "Palagong, what are you doing in my flowers?"

"The city has fallen to the militants."

"I was curious about the gunfire. Another coup?"

"No, the Islamists have seized the core. The explosion a few minutes ago was the army barracks going up. I suspect we are defenceless, and to make matters worse, my driver was shot on the way here. Can you come with me? He's bleeding heavily." The doctor grabbed his bag, threw some syringes and bottles into a paper bag, and together he and Selah started the climb up the hill. Selah stopped momentarily to catch his breath and saw his shirt swarming with ants. "That was my shirt," he told the doctor.

The doctor looked at his own white shirt. "I'm not taking mine off and giving it to the ants if that is what you are thinking." By the time the two reached the top of the terrace and pulled themselves over the parapet, Paolo was dead.

The phone started working again and rang. Selah, confused and shocked to tears stood over Paolo's body. One of the maids answered it, as she was trained to do. Selah looked up, horrified. She extended the receiver toward him. "It is for you, Mr. Palagong. They say it is someone important in the new government."

"We are going to kill you. You are an enemy of Islam. Your father was Islam, no? You turned against your faith. You will be killed." The person on the other end hung up. The calls were repeated every hour.

"Who was that?" Selah shouted at the maid. The woman broke into tears again. "Who was it? Who was it?"

Naomi intervened. "Stop it, you are frightening the children!"

"You were the one who translated the radio broadcast," he shouted at the maid. "Who the fuck was it?" The woman did not answer. "Get out. Get out now and don't come back. You're fired. You hear. Fired! And tell all your friends in the quarter that they can't just seize a country, Moslem majority or not."

The day passed. Darkness settled over the hillside. The house began to fill with ghosts. Selah wondered who the ghosts were, whether they were shades of the old colonial days, lost souls of the coups that had unsettled what the British had left behind, stunned spirits from the barracks looking for their paths beyond the turmoil, or merely the echo of a man who knew the roads of his country well and drove someone to places where the truth could be discovered.

I was getting ready for work when my phone rang. My story for the day was going to be about the overthrow of Selah's country by an Islamic fundamentalist movement.

"Dave, this is Selah. I'm not sure how long I can talk or who might be listening, but I have received death threats every hour since the morning. You know what has happened here, don't you?"

"Yes," I said, not knowing what else to say. "Is everyone okay there?"

"No. Paolo is dead. I recall you were fond of him and gave him gifts every time you left. We need to get out of here and as quickly as possible."

"How should I contact you?"

"I don't know. I'll let you know. I'm sorry. I'm exhausted. Everything here seems to have gone to hell and in just a matter of a few hours. I remember us having a conversation about tragedy in light of the journalists who were murdered during the coup years ago. Well, this is Aristotle's reversal. Everything has fallen apart. Can I beg your assistance?" I was just about to agree whole-heartedly when the line went dead. That was not a good sign.

I went into the newsroom at the CBC and strode up to the assignment editor.

"What have we got on that Islamist coup?"

"Not much I'm afraid."

I immediately called Susanne Whittington at Words Without Frontiers. They are an international organization that "extracts" authors and journalists from situations that are untenable. "Have you heard about what's going on with Selah Palagong? Can we save him?" I explained that he had called me as I was leaving for work and told her what I knew. She agreed to call the members of the emergency council and get back to me.

I called again the next day? "Was there any word from the council?"

"We're trying to meet."

"Aw, c'mon. For fucks-sake. The guy is in danger. Hell knows what's happened to him between then and now."

"Have you tried calling him back?"

"Yes, and all I get is 'Your call cannot be connected as dialled. Please try again later.'"

"There's nothing going in or out of the country. You'll just have to be patient."

"Susanne, the guy is in danger. He may already be dead, as far as I can tell." I gave her Selah's number and I related his background to her so she'd have something to put before the emergency council. A few hours later I was asked to sit in on a conference call, not with Selah, but with some very influential people – a former Governor General, the head of a large publishing firm, and a writer who had won an international short fiction prize. We discussed what we could do and what we couldn't do. We couldn't call him directly. We couldn't fax him – this was before email became what it is now. We couldn't write him any special delivery letters or any letters, for that matter. We couldn't send him a package. I felt as if we were leaving Selah in the dark to die.

"We have contacts on the ground," Susanne said. "We can communicate with him, but it will have to be delicately. The wire services just announced that the American consulate in Esdran and the embassy in the capital have been sacked. The ambassador, the consul, the non-national staff all escaped by helicopter. There is word that the nationals who were working for the Americans have been shot. Dave, I know you are anxious for Selah, and we can probably figure out a way to get him out, but it will take time, and if he lands here in Canada he will have to come alone. His wife and children will have to go to another location or he won't receive refugee status."

"That's absurd," I said in protest.

The former Governor General cleared his throat. "I'm afraid the red tape kicks in the moment we try to get him out. I know it is a mess, but we can only do what we can only do." I asked the council to keep me posted. I heard nothing for another two weeks. I watched the wire services. There were scant reports from Selah's country. Knowing nothing is the worst situation. It is a vacuum where one is left to guess. Finally, Susanne called me. "I spoke with Selah several days ago, and he said he had figured out a way to get his wife and children and himself out of the country. I tried calling him today and reached his home but they knew nothing. There was a second number in Esdran and an old man answered. He said Selah had disappeared. I'm sorry. That's all I know. I have to go now. There's another meeting waiting for me."

I once asked Selah as we sat on his patio why he believed Tadeusz. "I mean, Tadeusz was working propaganda. The now sainted Maximilian Kolbe was a propagandist, albeit for the cause of freedom of speech and belief." I recall that Selah smiled.

"There is no such thing as absolute truth, but there is the truth one feels in one's heart, the truth that cannot be denied, that speaks to our ability to embrace ideas the way we embrace those we love. I chose, and Tadeusz chose to speak for what he believed, his side, his perspective, because it was his and his alone, and no one told him what to believe. I bet on myself, Dave. I bet on what I can determine given as many facts as I can discover. Yes, I'm wrong sometimes, more times than I care to admit. But it is my wrong. It is a wrong that I arrived at not merely with my mind but with my heart. It is the wrong of one's own ideas, and that for me is the freedom I defend every day with my broadcasts."

Ten years changes a country. When I returned to seek out any trace of Selah Palagong, to find his body in the polo grounds of that portion of the world that slips so easily from the evening news no matter how hard we try to keep it at the forefront and no matter how tough our questions are when we are confronted by events, the whole place had changed. The hard-liners were gone. Revolutions eat themselves eventually. The house at the hilltop was boarded up. The capital had become a dirty backwater. The oil was almost gone, and Selah's nation was little more than a broken dream. I found nothing in the capital that convinced me Selah was there, so I hired a driver – he reminded me a little bit of Paolo – and headed up the coast to Esdran.

During my short story trip, Selah and I had gone up the coast. We had gone to visit his childhood home. "You need to meet José," he said. "You will like him."

At that point, José must have been in his mid-nineties, and although he had some years on him, he looked far younger and his handshake was firm as he gripped my hand. I met him while he sat at his cobbler's bench. His supply of wool had long run out or been eaten by moths and insects or had merely gone out of fashion like everything else from the age in which it had been spun.

As I approached the old tailor shop, I saw the shutter was up and I thought it a good sign. It was as I remembered it.

Through all the change and turmoil, there was José hammering away on his cobbler's bench. I approached through the open front and stood watching him for a few minutes. I said hello, but he didn't hear me. Then he looked up and a smile rose like dawn across his face. "My friend! My friend!" he shouted and stood up. I moved toward him to grab his arm and he waved me off. "I'm still good at standing." He shouted something back to the house and I saw a woman hurry across the courtyard. We moved to the window seat where Selah used to spend the afternoons of his youth, and José motioned me to sit down as he pulled up a battered chair.

Shortly, the young woman from the courtyard returned with a tray of tea and some sweets, and José told me about Selah.

Selah and his family had made it through the checkpoints because he had decided to escape the capital on a Friday at midday when the guards were at Jumu'ah. José contacted a local fisherman who had a boat – one of the few that was permitted to enter and leave the harbour in the days after the revolution. The fisherman's wife was a Moslem and her brother was the harbour master – José wasn't sure of the details and waved them off with the palm of his hand.

Early the next morning, as a heavy fog sat on the bay and the boats bobbed on the surface as if they had resigned themselves to their fates, Selah and his family were at the dock with José. The people in Canada could not find a way to locate Naomi and the boys in the same place as Selah, and Selah refused to be separated from them.

"His love for his wife and children was greater than his love of life. He could not leave them behind. For him, it would have been wrong. He put them in the boat, and I thought he was going to get away – they did. They're in Mumbai now along with so many other refugees from this place. They're still not permitted to return. Just as the boat was leaving its mooring, Selah leapt out. Naomi screamed and I asked him what he was thinking and he shouted at the fisherman to go on. He knew he had to stay. The children were bawling their eyes out. Naomi could not bear to look. He stood there, not waving but just watching as they disappeared in the fog. Then he turned to me and took the medal from his neck. 'Someone who defends ideas will come in search of me,' he said as he closed my palm around it."

José reached into his shirt pocket and held out the medal. "He was aware of all your efforts, Dave, he told me that if I ever saw you to thank you for what you tried to do. He said that ideas had to be defended no matter what, and that no question is ever completely answered – it is father of the next question. Please take the medal. I'm an old man now. I shall go on mending shoes, maybe until the last day before eternity comes. You must have what Selah treasured and then pass it on to the next person who goes in search of the truth."

"Do you know what happened to Selah?"

"No, he walked off into the thick fog and I have not heard from him since. There were rumours several years ago, that someone in the hills had been doing broadcasts on an old shortwave the Aussies left behind, but no one has a short-wave radio anymore – they were banned by the Revolutionary Council – and if it was Selah, no one can say for sure. You know where the abandoned stadiums and the lost polo grounds are, and I know you will search them until you find what you are looking for. If I am still here when you are certain of the answer to the question you carry with you, please come by, and tell me, and I shall put a new shine on your shoes for you."

AT DAWN

WE BEGAN BEFORE DAWN as the day I had feared for years arrived, the day every one of them would have to be killed, and I realized death doesn't smell like other things, especially nothing living except for chickens. When we had to put down both barns the air was worse than death, and darkness fell ...

People used to say they could smell our farm from a mile up the road. The scent carried on hot summer nights when everyone who drove up and down our concession had their windows rolled open so the breeze could blow in and mess their hair. When they crested the rise, the aroma would attack them, make them gag, and sting their eyes so that they'd stop and shout at us if we were working on the free-run area near the road. They'd holler we had no business putting that kind of belligerence in the atmosphere and that we were a hazard to public health.

I didn't have the heart to tell them that the vegetables and strawberries they consumed grew in the stuff that caused the stench or that the creatures who created the guano produced their eggs for breakfast or their breasts and drumsticks for dinner. If I told them that and started rolling up my sleeves, they'd drive away in a cloud of dust because most people are chicken.

I didn't tell them I couldn't take the smell either, the way it lingered and hung over our property and stayed in my nose even when I went away. It couldn't be washed off. It couldn't be driven away. It was a fact of life that came with what we did. They should have been grateful we filtered the air from the barns before we released it. It would have been ten times worse if we hadn't.

When winter came, we had to keep the doors of the two large sheds shut because poultry and December don't mix well. Cold air kills.

No matter what the season, people need their scrambled eggs or their hot evening meal. To the average person, a chicken is a sign of plenty. Politicians campaigned on the platform of a chicken in every pot. No matter where a person goes in the world – Africa, South America, Europe, Asia, from the poshest restaurants to the poorest villages – there is always chicken on the menu. Even people who refuse to eat the flesh of another creature will crack an egg in a pan without giving their sunny-side-up a second thought. The poultry business is one of the few truly universal forms of livelihood along with funeral parlours and brothels. You'd think people would realize all three possess their own dimensions of feculent aromas.

Feculent. I learned that word one summer when the ventilation system in the west barn broke down. If the ventilation system fails, we're in trouble. If we hadn't gotten it up and running in a day, the pullets asphyxiate themselves on the overheated vapours from their own waste. In the winter, they don't succumb to their guano but are so sensitive to cold their hearts stop if the barn dips below forty degrees Fahrenheit. The feathers on a chicken are a lousy reminder that the dinosaurs went extinct the moment something upset the perfect balance of their climate. Those ancient reptiles had feathers, too. If chickens had been intended to survive in the cold they would have hatched with fur.

It is a wonder we have so many chickens in our barns. The moment I step in the door all I see is a sea of white heads pecking away in the perpetual daylight of the pullet rows. They never seem to rest. I often wondered if they ever rested, and if I turned out the light on them, would they dream? As Hamlet would say, 'Aye, there's the rub.' And what would a chicken dream if it did fall asleep?

When they are slaughtered, they must know fear. I know what that fear is because I felt it, deep down in me, right to the core of my soul, the night Ma and I rushed Dad to the emergency room at the hospital and we just sat by ourselves in an empty room lined with rows of chairs, a perpetual light burning above us in the windowless enclosure, wondering if he was going to make it.

And when he didn't, when I held my sobbing mother in my arms as her heart broke. I looked at the rows of chairs and they reminded me of our barns, of the portholes through which our hens poked their heads to peck and eat and drink and lay and survive without realizing they weren't leading a life as much as they were aimed at sustaining someone else's existence, fixated on what they were doing because the others were doing the same thing, and none of them had any idea that there might be another life they could lead. I would rather be anything in this world than a chicken.

In our hatchling shed where we have to keep the heat up high, we lose over seventy percent of all the new arrivals. Those have to be the worst odds an animal can face. Chickens are susceptible to a sneeze. That's why we have to feed them antibiotics. Among livestock, they are the invalids of the food industry. They exist only when all the conditions for their survival are met, and there are so many variables to the business I've wondered if a bad thought wouldn't be just as lethal to them as a failed heater or an errant virus.

All things are delicate in their own way.

Chickens possess a kind of marvelousness that leaves me fascinated. My grandmother used to chop the feet off a dead hen she was preparing dinner and show me how one pull on a cord in the back of the leg could make the claws grab and pick up a pencil.

I would turn the foot over in my hand, examine its scales, the pinkish hue of the claws, and wonder why the bird had evolved not only to possess the means of holding on to a tree branch but bear the weapons with which it could fight back against the world. The birds I knew, the pale descendants of ancient wild chickens that once populated the high branches and open-air, were so docile. I think they were afraid for their lives so they surrendered willingly to us. We bred the beauty out of them when we redesigned them to be food, and part of that beauty resides in the intricacy and craft that goes into a chicken.

The eyes of a rooster, for example, are finely filigreed in a yellow membrane at the edges of the lids as if someone crocheted a fine band of lace around their field of vision so the bird has something better to look at than a bleak life spent in a shed or a barn. But what moves me more than anything about the thousands and thousands of birds I've raised and that I either killed or sent away to die is that they do not accept death, at least not physiologically. Something in them fights back when they encounter their finality.

Before he moved on, my older brother taught me how to butcher a bird for the pot, saying, "Winner winner, chicken dinner," like a carnival huckster – which he became. He got fed up with the poultry business and declared all such winged creatures to be terminally stupid. I can't say I agree with him, but to make his point he showed me how to kill a chicken both humanely and inhumanely.

In industrial abattoirs, chickens are grabbed by their ankles, hung upside down, and dipped in a bath through which a high voltage current flows for a millisecond. That short shock doesn't kill them. It only stuns them, so that when their throats are slit supposedly they don't know what is happening to them. The idea is that to be insensate is to be immune to suffering and horror, at least to the point where death is not death but a state of extreme confusion. Is that humane?

The humane way my brother showed me was to corner a chicken in a place from which it could not escape, an actual corner for instance, and after the chicken raised its talons at him and fought back and flailed in a cloud of feathers, he'd grab the bird's body under one arm as if he was playing the bagpipes and snap its head with the other hand. The twist could be a problem because a chicken can turn its head almost three hundred degrees. If the rotation weren't beyond the point where the neck snapped, the bird would suffer even more. That method of butchering was sickening to watch because the neck made a terrible cracking sound.

The next time he caught a bird, an old, motley rooster that I knew would be tough and sinewy when served, he grabbed it, stroked its neck gently to calm it as it blinked, and tilted its cockscomb from side to side as if it was trying to make sense of the situation, drew his fingers through its long, plumed tail, reminding me how nice it looked, and then stretched the bird on an old stump we kept in a corner of the rooster shed, a solid piece of an old oak trunk we used as a butcher's block, grabbed a cleaver off the bench beside the stump, and severed the animal from its head with one swift blow.

I threw up.

The rooster's wings flapped madly. My brother held it up by its feet as the thing tried to fly. Its body decided it could live without its head. The head lay in the sawdust shavings on the shed floor. The body attempted to set off in search of a better life without its brain. The neck and the wings splattered blood everywhere. When the flapping stopped, the body became limp. My brother sank the cleaver point into the stump, tilted the carcass upside down, and exclaimed, "That, little bro, is what you'd pay money to see in a horror show."

As I tried to wipe my mouth clean, I sputtered that what he'd done was worse than anything I'd read about in history books. Beheading was the way traitors and unwanted royal wives were executed. I pictured Charles I stepping onto the balcony of Whitehall Palace one cold morning, his torso attired in three white shirts so he'd be warm and the public wouldn't see him shiver and think he had pangs of cowardice. I imagined Mary Queen of Scots. I'd seen her pearls in a travelling museum show in the city. One of her ladies-in-waiting had retrieved them from the pool of blood. She had refused to remove them for her executioner. Some were tinged brown. And the French Revolution – I didn't even want to go there. I'd just finished reading Dickens' *A Tale of Two Cities*.

The thought of losing one's head is one of the most horrible ideas human beings have concocted, yet that form of death always carried a sense of nobility. The headsman wasn't for common criminals. A person had to be someone important to die that way. I stared at the rooster's head in the sawdust shavings on the slaughter area floor, nudged it with my toes as it blinked, and realized it was wearing a crown, maybe a fool's coxcomb, but a crown nonetheless.

My brother pointed to the block. "That chunk of tree has meaning for us," he said. "It's a piece of the last tree our great-great-grandfather pulled from the soil of our farm when he pioneered here, and he kept it knowing we would see what he'd done to the forests and earth. Everything dies, buddy boy. Everything dies so that something else has a chance to live. You're here because of all the birds we've put into other people's mouths. Remember that. We didn't want to raise chickens for a living. A chicken farm is always the farm of last resort, a kind of consolation agriculture for those who couldn't manage other types of crops, sane crops, crops you can pick from a tree branch or pull from the earth and shove right into your mouth. The old guy started by farming wheat, but when the West opened up, the market for grain from hereabouts fizzled. He wanted to plant an orchard but figured the trees would take too long to bear fruit. Everyone else was growing hay or vegetables, so he became a chicken man. And there you have it. That's the story of why we're here."

He held up the carcass by its feet. It was still bleeding. My brother had blood splattered on his face and his work smock. It was even on me. He began by pulling the major feathers from the tail, and then switched on a plucking vacuum – we were one of the few poultry farms in the area with such a suction device and therefore could sell the birds to local restaurants and butcher shops as "Fresh Killed."

With the feathers gone, he slit the bird along its stomach and with his right hand in a heavy rubber glove pulled out the entrails. He held up a few organs – the liver being choicest among them – but tossed them aside.

"We used to have a call for those. People made their own paté, but now it's just as easy to buy it in the jelly block from a meat counter. It's all spiced and seasoned, ready to spread on bread or crackers. It doesn't look like it came from any living creature. That's what we do to food. We disguise it, make it into something it never was. People couldn't tolerate it otherwise."

He handed me the naked bird.

"Take it in to Mom. It'll be on the table tonight."

The carcass was still warm.

When a person goes into a store to buy a chicken for dinner, the meat is chilled. It feels like it is dead. It doesn't resemble a chicken to the eye or the touch. It isn't a chicken. It is meat that needs to be cooked. In grocery stores there are rotisseries where the chickens revolve around a glowing element in a kind of Ferris wheel in a box, and when they come out, sometimes covered in barbecue sauce but more often than not just roasted with a bit of butter rubbed on their skins to create that crispy quality, they are put under a heat lamp in a display case, each in its little plastic boat as if they are survivors of a maritime disaster waiting to be plucked from the sea in their survival pods.

Hens have it much easier, though that statement needs to be qualified. They eventually meet the same fate when their usefulness for a purpose other than meat has been exhausted. Their lives are a monotonous purgatory spent in a barn where the lights are kept on twenty-four hours a day. A week in such a place would kill a human being. But hens are strong creatures either because they don't take in their surroundings or because they choose not to care, though choosing not to care would give them credit for being more intelligent than they probably are.

Brains come with a cost because those creatures that have them not only suffer, they know what suffering is. I don't know if it is better to be aware or not be aware. I am certain that pigs – there's a pig farm down the road and the hog man's daughter and I were considered a couple – know the score and feel for one another. If I pass them in a truck on the highway as they are travelling to the slaughterhouse, I can't look at them. I can't meet their gaze. When I see a load of chickens stacked on each other I don't feel the same sense of despair. Maybe I'm immune to their fears or maybe they just don't know any better.

In the long sheds, the poultry barns that people complain about because they catch of whiff of the guano we shovel out several times a day – and in the summer we conserve electricity by lowering the air conditioning in the evening and opening the shed doors for ventilation – the hens are lined up drumstick to drumstick, their heads locked in place and poking through 'neckings' as we call them, so they can eat what we put in front of them and lay their eggs.

They'd trample their own produce and break the white shells as they drop if we didn't have a system where the hens drop their loads on a small conveyor belt that brings the eggs into the washing chamber where the shells are scrubbed and graded for size. Sometimes, if we're not busy, we candle the eggs ourselves to make sure there are no blood spots inside them.

We do our best to keep the hens from the roosters, but there's a kind of immaculate conception thing that happens on chicken farms and heaven knows how some of the pullets get impregnated. Maybe the Lord looks down on the hens in their white feathers, their heads framed by a veil of metal, and their beaks bobbing up and down as they eat or drink, and says, "Maybe this will save you. Maybe you can be the chicken who lays the golden egg," or some such rot. I always imagined these things but never told my brother.

He would have laughed at me.

Or perhaps he did think these things, perhaps thought them too often, and maybe when he lay down on a sunny day in the backyard hammock and looked up at the sky when he should have been busy with me and Dad in the barn, he saw a billowing white cloud cluck across the sky and wanted to follow it.

On an August morning, just as the sun was rising and the roosters were doing their chanticleer 'I can sing louder than you' routine from their shed without even being able to see the sun outside and maybe sensing dawn with some sort of weird chicken sixth sense, I called up the stairs to tell my brother Mom had breakfast on the table and there was no reply. I entered his room. He'd torn open his pillow and emptied the contents around his room as if he'd had a pillow fight or wrestled with an angel and lost.

Granted, it was goose down, not chicken feathers. They haven't made chicken feather pillows since before the First World War, but the entire room was covered in feathers, and opening his door merely raised them into the air so they floated like dandelion fluff or milkweed seeds. The sun was coming in through his drapes and each feather reminded me of a tiny angel, perhaps the spirit of a former bird who had looked me in the eye during its terrible, purgatorial life, and declared that it had a soul even though I fought the urge to acknowledge such tripe.

I knew my brother had to leave.

He'd stopped eating.

He couldn't put a bite in his mouth, whether it was from a chicken pie or a breaded fast food cutlet.

I think he understood too much about what we were doing. He was twenty-five, had outgrown the rebellious teenager thing. He'd watched a heavy metal rocker bite the head off a chicken during a concert at the local fairgrounds and on the way home as I sat in the back seat necking with the hog man's daughter he turned to me and said, "I can't take it anymore."

My Dad said it was because my brother had seen too much of the world.

In Portugal, my brother must have suffered something close to a nervous breakdown.

He told me about having lunch one day in a sidewalk café in Lisbon.

"That country is really beautiful. I ordered the sardines because a man I met, a Portuguese guy, said that sardines and chicken were their national dishes. I should have had the chicken. When they brought out the plate of fish, the heads, eyes, and all, were still on them. They'd been roasted so their skins were black, but their eyes were still shining and staring at me. I paid the check and left. Thank God for the cheese, bread, beer, and olives or I would have starved. And the oranges are brilliant. After I'd finally gotten enough to eat, I was walking aimlessly around the streets of the Alfama where the light cuts like a knife between buildings, especially late in the afternoon, and on the shadowed side of a street there was a shop that sold souvenirs. I was looking for something for Mom. I chose some bird tiles because the birds didn't look like chickens, but as I went to the far side of the narrow store there was a whole wall of these hand-painted black chickens. I asked the clerk what they were, why they had all those roosters. He understood me."

" '*Ah, sim! Sim!*' he said, meaning *yes*. Those black roosters with their red combs, brightly painted, are called *barcelos*. They're supposed to be the national symbol of Portugal. I asked why on earth they would choose to have a chicken as their national bird. I mean, Americans have an eagle – vigilant, warlike, dangerous – and Canadians have their loons and geese. But the Portuguese chose a chicken, a *barcelos*. You know what he said?

"'The *barcelos* represent honesty, integrity, trust, and honor.'

"I bought the biggest honking one on the shelf for Dad, the one he keeps on the kitchen table. I mean, what's a chicken? And as I walked around the streets until I was dog tired and sat down and had a glass of wine in a *barzinho*, I watched all the people passing by, their eyes fixed on the ground as if they were searching for something they'd dropped as they hurried from shop to shop, and I realized they saw the world in an entirely different way, in a way that said life was about patience and perseverance. And I could see it everywhere, even the sidewalks. The sidewalks aren't cement slabs like the ones in our town. They're mosaics composed of millions of small, perfect, pale stone cubes laid together in a mortar of sand. Think of it. Think of the people who create the sidewalks of Lisbon, laying cube after cube. And I thought of home, our farm, and our poultry."

After he told me that story, I knew my brother wasn't going to stick around the farm. He had reached the point at which one has to stop raising animals for slaughter, that point when the farmer looks at his herd or his flock or his brood and understands each creature not merely as something he raises to make money but as beings, physical and, yes, spiritual that are as brim with vitality and the inexplicable desire to keep existing. to fight for with every breath.

And I knew once he'd gone inside the head of a rooster or a hen he would have to leave the work he'd been raised to do since he was a small boy. My brother reached that point where he not only understood his flock, but where he saw each bird, each pullet with its neck tethered to the feeding system, each rooster fighting for its space against its fellow kingbirds, and he saw them as symbols of nobility and life.

Maybe that's why he and Dad painted the giant roundel with a red and black cockerel on it, surrounded by maple leaves, and hung it on the face of the west wall of the barn-like a barn star. The west barn is what someone sees as they come over the crest of the road toward us. They highlighted the Portuguese bird with the words *O Por Bem Barcelos* as the farm's motto: *All to the good for Chickens*. It was my brother's tribute to the life he left behind, its traditions handed down over three generations, and to the birds that lived to die.

People often pulled into our laneway and asked if we were Portuguese. They seemed disappointed when I told them we weren't, that the roundel on the barn was purely a fanciful decoration my brother and father had dreamed up as a kind of blessing or benediction on the brood. That's what the agriculture inspector was looking at two days ago when I walked out of the barn and found him staring at the roundel. He asked me what the motto meant and whether it was Latin. He said he didn't know Latin or any other foreign languages except for a smattering of high school French.

"Well," he said handing me a summons printed on official Ministry of Agriculture stationery with the department's federal logo at the top and the red and white flag beside the branch's name, "for the good of all the other chickens within a five hundred mile radius, you're going to have to close down your operations, exterminate your stock, and make sure every last feather is either carried away or ploughed under."

I stared at the paper. I couldn't believe I was being ordered to destroy my brood, hens, roosters, chicks. Even the eggs had to go. I'd heard that avian flu might be coming to our county but figured the antibiotics we fed the stock would stop all that. I was wrong. I tried to explain the antibiotics.

"No," he said, shaking his head, "that won't stop it. It has spread and we tested the hens you sent to the processing plant and traced them back here. Most of your chickens are infected or will be infected in a day or so. I'm sorry to give you the bad news."

"I don't have a bulldozer. Am I on the hook for the extermination and the disposal? I'm not sure we have land enough for a mass grave."

He guaranteed me that part of the bill would be covered by the province and the federal government. He said the exterminators would put a tent over both barns and a small covering on the rooster shed and the egg sorting building.

"When it's all covered over, we pump in the gas. It won't take long. We'll provide a hazmat crew. Part of the bill is on you and I hope you have insurance to cover this sort of thing."

My father had let it lapse.

I knew the local inspector. He was a cousin of the hog man's and even though I'd broken up with the girl my license had been renewed twice yearly. I thought everything was in good order.

The extermination crew arrived the next morning at about three a.m. I think they startled the roosters from their sleep.

The men were dressed in white coveralls, their heads helmeted with only plastic portals revealing the masks and respirators over their mouths and noses and eyes that signalled there were human beings inside the suit.

I was going to lose the farm. I would have to take my Mom out of the home and put her in the care of the county. This was defeat, not just for the birds but for everything that had been my life.

One of the men left the door open to the rooster shed and a Rhode Island red flew out and perched himself on the crest of our house. There weren't supposed to be any escapees.

In the darkness, with the buildings covered and sealed and my chickens inside and anticipating only another day of the constant monotony of their lives, the valves on the gas canisters were opened. I could hear clucking from inside the barns, then squawking as a kind of madness must have broken out among the flock. I knew they were suffering but there was nothing I could do to save them.

The inspector who had shown up with a coffee in one hand and clipboard in the other pointed to the red atop my roof.

"That's going to be a problem. Got a shotgun?"

"I don't want to put a hole in my roof," I said. "I have a gun, an old hunting rifle of my father's, but I don't think he ever shot one of his chickens. We never had any fugitives, at least not until now. The birds seemed to like it here for as long as they were fed and useful to us."

The government man was talking into a hand-held two-way when I noticed the barns had gone silent.

At that moment, just as the dawn was approaching and the sun's bald and glowing head rose above the far end of our property, the rooster began to crow. It crowed three times, stopping between each burst of ignited energy and sound, and looked down at me as if to say, "So this is what it comes to."

The hazmat men opened the barn doors and began to carry out the limp birds by their legs, tossing their white bodies into dumpsters, and I wanted to cry but instead, and I'm not sure what possessed me, I looked up at the *barcelos*, the living cockerel to whom my farm had been dedicated, and saluted.

The rooster flapped its wings and stretched its neck as if it were about to crow again when a shot broke the dawn and the sun appeared to stand still in awe for a moment before the day could begin.

CHACONNE

W E MET WHEN WE WERE PAN-HANDLING the same corner, and rather than tell me to get lost or me tell him to fuck off, he told me his story. "Why was he working the cows for change?"

He replied he was just trying to get some change so he could buy a cup of coffee and a subway token so he could jump in front of a train.

"But why not stick around to tell someone your story? I got ears. You gotta have some story."

That made him listen, and the more he listened, the more he told me. He was not the sort of man to hide behind the masks everyone wears. He knew what the masks meant and how to wear them and he'd tell you what they meant. James Bennett was a natural-born teacher and he taught me how to survive the end of the world.

He'd been a scholar of Italian Renaissance literature at the university and had risen to the top of his profession, establishing himself as an authority in the field of *commedia dell'arte*. He was admired by his students as a *bon vivant* whose bawdy sense of humour was attributed to the *Arlequino* he had absorbed by osmosis from his research.

Several strokes were against him from the start. He was a non-Italian teaching in an Italian department, and his passions led him to believe he could conduct his life as if he were a Tuscan *cavalieri*. He told me he'd made a clown of himself. I knew what he was talking about. "We're all clowns," but I added, "we have to listen to our own beat even if it is not the one the world wants to hear."

The passion that did him in was a graduate student who bore a striking resemblance to the Mona Lisa, though her eyes were not as soft and gentle as La Giaconda's nor did her dark hair fall with the grace and beauty that enticed thieves and emperors to risk everything for her. When I passed Ms. Giaconda on the sidewalk, she looked right through me. She was Italian by birth, sophisticated, and beautiful in a sculpted way. Something about her beauty, her white marble complexion, spoke of coldness, with an element of the reptilic about her. I find that a turn-off. One look at her and I could have told him she was dangerous. Bennett was certain he was in love with her and she was in love with him. But in reality – and there is always a *but* behind every reality – nothing was farther from the truth.

And though Lizina Albero had become the centre of his world, an offering of forbidden fruit in the academic garden, he saw the house of cards he had built collapse. It was grand theatre, a scenario worthy of a frame but not a painter. What had it all been for? Lizina was just another student with a pleasant smile when she needed to smile and shrewdness when she needed to serve her own ends.

In April of 2012, Lizina brought the matter of her affair with James Bennett to the attention of the university's Sexual Harassment Officer. By the autumn of 2012, Jim had lost his sense of humour. He also lost his wife, his job, his home, and most of his mind. Take away a man's world, leave him with only his naked silences, and he will fill the void with babble and the trash of false dreams.

In short order, he was brought before a tribunal of his peers and dismissed from the university. His lawyer, an old school friend, did not even show up to defend him. When Bennett went home, Lizina had already spoken to his wife and the locks on the front door had been changed. On the night of his defeat, the 20th of October, Bennett tried to check in to a downtown hotel only to be told that his credit cards had been cancelled and he had nowhere to go. He wandered the streets all night and at dawn sat down on a bench at Bloor and Spadina, loosened his black and white tie with clown faces that someone had given him years before as a joke, and wept beside the tumbled oversized black marble dominos stacked at the corner.

He should have seen it coming. He knew the jealousies of his department. His so-called friend and colleague, Gabriel Sole, had long wanted to eclipse him, while giving him the friendly sort of advice one gets from a bartender or a priest in the intimacy of confession while both dish out stuff to roll the head. Bennett came to realize that Sole was his Iago. Sole coveted Bennett's research on *commedia* and clowns. Dashing and dark, Sole was *Scaramouche*, the fiery lover, the dark presence who in faculty meetings knew how to humiliate Bennett subtly and reduce the stupid Anglo to a simpering *Arlequino*.

When Bennett walked along Bloor Street towards Bathurst early on the drizzly morning of October 21st, he saw Lizina and Gabriel, arm in arm, kissing outside of a coffee shop, sharing an aubade of lovers parting at dawn, a veritable Romeo and Juliet who might as well have been debating ornithology in their birthday suits as standing there balancing lattes and briefcases with their free hands. Jim knew his betrayal had been a farce from beginning to end. Good luck to Gabe, Jim told himself. Life is a comedy where everyone is a clown. Each man in his time plays many parts until the party is over and with the judgment knell of midnight the truth is unmasked. But in that moment of absolute humiliation, he no longer felt as if he were *Arlequino*, but the dupe of the drama, *Il Dottore*, the impotent professor, or worse, a hobbling *Pantalone* who would never recover the vigour that had once driven him in his hubris. That was the beginning of the bad part for Jim.

After one night in the Fred Victor Mission when someone stole his Paul Smith socks, he decided he would use his negotiable skills and get a job, a fresh start. But as the days of November wore on, the problem of "no-fixed-address" became an impediment. The morning we met, he'd asked me as we stood huddled with some other guys outside a coffee and doughnuts place on Bloor Street what other accommodations might be available. He'd had a terrible night among the coughing, agitated bodies spread on cots. Wasn't there somewhere else to go?

"Seaton House. It is the filing cabinet for the unwanted men of Toronto. It is dangerous. Someone will steal your shoes. That is a level of unkindness one step beyond stealing your socks. And winter is coming on. If you thought the Freddy Vic smelled, wait 'til you get a whiff down there in the S.O.B."

He didn't get my drift.

"S.O.B.," I explained to him "was the name for the area around Seaton House, an abbreviation used by taxi drivers for Seaton, Ontario, and Berkeley Streets. It is an acronym for a place you don't want to go. There's a room upstairs, monitored day and night, where the methadone addicts – the guys coming off heroin who are touch and go – lie under white sheets like snowdrifts who have melted into themselves. I once looked in through the window of that darkened room. The dude at the window, the watcher, told me to come and have a look. The bodies were arranged in tidy rows in the dim light. One or two of the sleepers had their knees crooked, but the rest were just these shapes who were adrift in their own perished dreams, each his own personal Franklin Expedition. And from a distance, as I looked in, the room was an arctic landscape of men suffering from their own desires.

"You don't want to go there," I told him. "You don't want to go there."

Jim can be a resourceful guy, so, he found us a basement room in Kensington Market, an 'apartment' below a butcher's shop that smelled of a gas leak and damp rot, with two cots, a hot plate, and a chair we could take turns sitting in. We dubbed it Plato's Cave. He'd run into an old gym buddy of his who loaned him a couple of hundred bucks. I thought it was heaven after the street. Jim thought it was hell, but I said, "Hey, you must have a reasonable grasp of Dante, right? So, what's your problem?"

"Hell is a narrative, a place where people are trapped in their own stories, and I am living in it now," he said. "I am living my story and it won't end."

"But, I responded, there was a way out and up, right?"

Jim finally asked me how I knew so much about Dante. I think he was being sarcastic. I told him even a PhD candidate in Math with an engineering degree had read his Dante and Tasso, too, and that shut him up. *Jerusalem Delivered.* Could be. Had been. Dante got out alive. Tweegie and Bennett delivered.

Our first night in the cave, he asked me about my last name which I hadn't told him and I said, "Yeah, Mike Tweegie, and don't say anything about me seeing a puddy-tat."

"Great," he said, "here I am living in hell with a caged mathematician who has a fear of cats, and nothing adds up."

But I assured him that it did. Even when the numbers sailed away from me on the horizon of my mind's eye and the alphabet of equations began to resemble hydro lines, I knew it would lead somewhere. I'd been bad once. I'd written all over the wall of the York Club, so much so, they had to send in masons to turn each brick around. Now I'd met him.

That first night, I heard him weeping in his cot, so I climbed in with him and we just held each other. It was good to hold another human being again. I tried comfort him. "Hey," I said, "we should put a sign on the door, a nice professional-looking brass plate. *Bennett and Tweegie, Spelunkers and Mountaineers.* I'm your Virgil."

He began to talk more and more now – constantly, in fact – about the world ending, that everything in his life was a sign of life's demise and that the Mayans were right. It was all going to disappear in a puff of smoke or the thud of a dark invisible comet just as the sun was coming up on Friday, December 21st, the solstice of 12/12, and that if there was something he could do to stop it, something that would make his miserable life worthwhile, something he could die believing in, he would seize it and make the world his own again. Damn, he wanted to save the world. I liked that. He especially went on with his date rant after we'd pass a former graduate student on the street during our evening wanderings.

Wanderings aren't a bad thing to pass the time. Vagabonds, the original clowns, did this as both a hobby and living. Remember Hamlet's players and their king? The nineteenth-century poets, Bliss Carman and Richard Hovey, made pointless walking into a popular poetic theme, a motif that was taken up by W.H. Davies and even Samuel Beckett. I'm sounding like a literary critic, eh? Jim and I were ambulatory Vladimirs and Estragons, waiting for something to happen, and wandering broke the monotony of the wait. I once wandered, non-stop for three weeks, just up and down the Bayview Extension, through the labyrinths of Rosedale and the rat's maze of Cabbagetown and into those great little places to hide where the other street people seldom hang. Now, I had a companion to wander with. Every now and then Jim would say something slightly upsetting, and I'd think of Rumi in his cave and how he murdered his only friend in the world, but I didn't figure Jim for being homicidal. I mean, a man who grieves the loss of Paul Smith socks isn't exactly homicidal in my books.

During one of our November evening wanderings along Yorkville, Jim ducked into a classical music store. He knew the owner and the shop had been one of his favourite haunts. He said he'd dropped a lot of money there and they'd let him browse so we'd be warm for a few hours. There was music playing. Something early Baroque.

As we stood in the CD store, I was suddenly struck with a horrific pain at the centre of my soul. It began with the low bass notes in the opening bars repeating and repeating on the store's stereo. I thought a monster was coming to eat me. The low moaning notes were overlaid with the weeping of a violin, a voice struggling to make sense of a great tragedy, a heart consoled with trivial explanations and afterthoughts that somehow didn't matter in the great scheme of things.

"This music mads me!" I screamed and put my hands over my ears.

Jim looked startled and embarrassed as I writhed on the floor. The sad, tragic violin notes were like a knife slicing through everything that had been my life. I wept. The clerks came running and gathered around. One asked if she should call an ambulance. Another wondered if I was epileptic. Jim told them all to stand back and give me air.

He knelt and whispered in my ear. "That is Vitali. It is his 'Chaconne pour Violon,'" he said in a gentle voice. "Would you like me to ask them to turn it off?" But when I pulled my hands from my ears, I suddenly felt a clarity that I hadn't known in years, a sense that the world I had given up for dead around me was alive and brilliant and as ordered as a Fibonacci sequence, its miracles blossoming in my blood. I remembered reading what Toni Morrison had once said about a young woman named Marie Cardenal and how she had been changed by hearing a Louis Armstrong trumpet solo. I was now part of that experience of transformation. The gathering helped me up from the floor.

"What is a chaconne?" I asked. "I need more. I need more."

Jim begged the indulgence of the store owner. She brewed a pot of coffee and the three of us spent the evening listening to chaconnes and ciacconna, passacaglia, and grounds. Bach, Bertali, Busconi, Pachelbel's "F Minor Chaconne for Organ" – one of the most beautiful pieces of music I have ever heard – all passed through the night and into my heart.

Numbers and equations started coming back to me with a tremendous alacrity. I suddenly felt as if my life and its disorganization was not a cess pit of madness or a disorder but simply a song, a melody, a limited human expression in its brevity where a voice in the music longs for a lost or inaccessible order. I had once thought that mathematics could do that for me, but in the infinite universe of numbers and possible questions and probable and palatable solutions, I heard the voice inside me dwindle and grow silent as if it could say nothing more. Now, I felt I could speak again, effortlessly, limitlessly because to say something, anything, is to add a few grace notes to the beautiful cacophony that is the human experience.

Jim was quiet, withdrawn, and pensive. He sat there with his chin on his fist and his elbow propped on his knee like Rodin's Thinker. We started talking about the chaconne as a lost form of music that was constantly struggling to be reborn in every age. The chaconne had been the music one dared not play in the seventeenth century, yet it was the music everyone wanted to hear, and was to its own era what the blues has been to ours. As a dance, it was popular into the eighteenth century. That's when Vitali's sad violin lament was written. He transformed the chaconne in all its blues brilliance into the soulful *crie de coeur* that Vitali – a name that echoes the word for life – harnessed in his "Chaconne pour Violon." That is what had driven me to the floor. The chaconne was forgotten through the nineteenth century until in the early twentieth Busoni reinvented Bach's horny-rhythmed little dance as a piano masterpiece. Heck, now that I think of it, I realize that Bruno Mars' "The Way You Are" is a chaconne. The tune overlays a repetitive bass line. Bob Dylan, Johnny Cash – they are the *chaconnieri* of the world we know and take for granted.

Jim had been thumbing through a music reference book that the clerks kept behind the cash register of the CD store so they could appear knowledgeable if anyone sprang a pop quiz on them.

"Here it is," he said, holding up the book. "The chaconne was Mayan in its origins and had come to the Old World via the survivors of Cortez' expedition who destroyed Aztec civilization and converted Mexico to the sexless ways of Christianity."

I pictured Bernal Diaz and a group of Aztec captives in a small coastal *bodega* on his return to Spain. The Aztecs huddled in a corner like guys from the street. They played their beloved music for the last time before being seized by the Inquisition and having it tortured out of their bodies. They knew the world would end four times and begin again, each time destroyed by one of the elements, the last of the destructions by fire. They were the survivors of the fiery death of Tenochtitlan and lived to sing the requiem of all they lost. The chaconne spread through the streets of Europe where the musicians of the *commedia* took it up as their banner of bawd. Masked, the players thrust out their loins to both men and women alike, inspiring the comedies of Shakespeare and the etchings of the French master Jacques Callot. It was a music that matched the lives, passions, and professions of outcasts and street walkers – the *pasar calle* whose rhythmic struts became the signature of the *passacaglia*. And even as those Aztec *chaconnieri* burned at the stake for refusing to abandon their rhythm, they shouted their hymn to life. The last sound from their lips was the song of a phoenix rising from the ashes.

A group of Italian travellers heard a chaconne in the smelly, smoky confines of a vagabond taverna – the kind of inn

Cervantes knew and captured in *Don Quixote* – and they could not get the music's lustiness out of their heads. They hummed it to the point of madness, a vitality that spoke of real life rather than heavenly reward. They carried it home with them to the scandalous courts of Italy and Naples and the world of Caravaggio and The Seven Mercies. A linguist later told me that the *chaconne* and its Italian derivation *ciacconna* may have come from a Mayan word for a medicinal plant known as the *cinchona*, an evergreen that in the dead of December blossoms in Central and South America at the solstice like the Glastonbury Thorn. The flowers of the *cinchona* contained large doses of quinine to cure a dying child or an enfeebled old man from the scourging sleep of malaria. The chaconne was the music of life in the midst of death.

Just after midnight Jim stood up and went to the window. "I know now what it is we must do to save the world," he said. "We must make an offering of synchronicity to the sky." Jim turned from the window. "We must make the world dance."

I had been cured by a chaconne. I was ready to begin again. Jim saw the cure in a different way. The world needed to begin again and in a new way. As we walked back to our stinking cave, and cars disappeared one by one from the traffic of the foggy night on Bloor Street, Jim told me his plan.

He knew street musicians who busked near Yonge and Bloor. One guy, an almost blind beggar who sold pencils and whose body was twisted from birth, played an empty white shortening bucket he had salvaged from a garbage pile in the heart of Chinatown. He would provide the beat, a pulse that could speak precisely through the indifference of a street corner and reach directly into the nervous system of a passer-by. Another was an elderly drifter from Louisiana who had long ago given up his dream of jamming in a jazz band. He would carry the core bass melody, that repetition of four notes in the "ground" or bass line. Jim and I would build our own instruments out of whatever we could find – he told me he had played the cello before his demise and that if he could find the wood and wire he would construct his own version of a *viola da gamba*.

I was told to duct tape together as many narrow-necked bottles as I could, containers of different shapes that would serve as a chamber organ, the instrument of choice for cha-conne composers such as Schmelzer and Biber whose music brought the *ciacconna* to its apotheosis during the 1640s in the lascivious courts of the Vatican cardinals. I found what I needed in the back of an LCBO. Having crafted our instru-ments, we would gather on the sixth hour of the twenty-first day of the year and play the world back into existence with a song to worship the rising sun, return of light to the world. The bass line would be the steady pulse of the turning planet. The beat would be the presence of time. And our variations on the narrowly defined theme of three or four notes would be the voice of humanity crying with a synchronicity and vitality needed to restart time from its dead, singular, zero point.

Hollywood, the pint-sized the percussionist, Zeke the axe, me as Pipes on the "organ," and Jim on his viola da gamblin' as Zeke called it because that's all you have left after you've played your last hand, gathered on the corner of Bloor and Avenue Road as the dawn was breaking on the morning of the 21st, the day rising of the winter solstice when the world would shed its darkness and its history. And if the planet survived past the sixth hour or the twelfth day of the twelfth month of the twelfth year – the spirit of harmony in all things – would be everlasting, reaffirmed and renewed in a world without end.

Jim had convinced them of his plan, though he had not told them of its complete details. The two new guys wanted to know where they were going to play. Jim had spent the last of his money on the gig. He pointed upwards to the top of the Park Hyatt.

"The music," he said, "will carry over the sleeping university from the rooftop terrace of the bar and wake the world either to its fate or its salvation."

He had chosen as the signature piece for the eternal moment Bertali's "Ciacconna." Zeke wasn't sure it made much sense or music, for that matter, though he said he was still drunk and didn't know what he was doing and didn't really give a damn as long as he could play.

Hollywood said he was game because this was his moment to shine, and though Zeke was still the worse of it he went along with the gamble. "I guess it's warmer in jail than out here and I ain't one to stand out in the cold if my friends are going inside." And so, he came in with us. We were a quartet.

We marched unnoticed through the lobby of the hotel and took the elevator to the Rooftop Lounge.

"Just like Carnegie Hall," exclaimed Hollywood as the elevator climbed. "Next stop Hollywood!"

Security never stirred. I looked at Jim in the mirrored and polished brass box. His face was glowing. With one tremendous shove, Jim burst open the portal to the lounge and then flung wide the French doors to the parapet terrace. Zeke stopped at the bar and slipped a bottle of Jack Daniels into his pocket.

We began to play at approximately 6:03. Sunrise.

We weren't that bad considering we had only practiced for an hour or so the day before.

We opened with a very moving version of Pachelbel's "F Minor Chaconne" or what sounded as if it could be that piece. The music wafted over the intersection, over the top of the Museum and its giant, obtrusive crystal addition, and across the sleeping campus where not a student was stirring.

By the time that piece was over I knew the odds were against us. The light was rising along Bloor and over the top of the condo behind the Church of the Redeemer and soon it would break through the portal of the bell arch on that church and the intersection below would light up with the rest of the city, a golden glow shining brighter than an ancient idol on the empty streets with no one there to worship it.

And just as we were about to break into the Bertali, Jim leapt up on a tabletop beside the balustrade, stripped off his clothes, and shouted to the dawn to proclaim his belief to the sleeping city.

"Let there be synchronicity!" he shouted. "And if the world is not to end this day, let us all be reborn as new brothers and sisters in the human comedy! Let us play the world back to life and bring heaven and earth together once again for the everlasting joy of humanity!"

"Here! Here!" shouted Zeke. And we began to play.

Hollywood's beat thumped like the works of a clock, and Zeke's four notes repeated over and over in a steady defiance to time and change with an irresistible constancy to which he hollered "Hallelujah!"

Jim put his make-shift *viola da gamba* under his arm and pressing it against his naked breast stroked the music from it as if it was his lover. And I blew on those bottles, my neck turning this way and that to capture the beat and the majesty of the melody. And by God we were magnificent.

The sun broke through the arch of the bell tower of the Church of the Redeemer, and I heard the shadow of its summons echo through the streets and off the glass walls that were lit with the golden light of a new dawn as if it were chiming the hour of redemption. And as we laid down our variations on the theme over top of those four simple notes, the music drifting sure as a damp morning breeze toward the lake and the infinite heavens above as the security men arrived to wrestle our instruments from us. Yet, in the mayhem of that final struggle, 6:12 a.m. on December 21st, 2012 passed, and the world was reborn, everlasting, with all the love and suffering it had always known.

As the police loaded us into the squad cars, I looked over at Jim and he was beaming.

"I am a new man today," he said. "Thank you, Tweegie, for your love and devotion."

"What will you do with your new life?" I asked him. I had an inkling of what I would do with mine once we did our time for break and enter.

"I have taken a new name," he said. "I am Giaccomo Bennetti. I am master of the *commedia dell'arte*, and I shall carry the message of the human comedy into the streets of this city, where the rebirth we have witnessed here today will live among the people forever."

And when I saw him again, four years later as the blossoms broke like laughter on the slant bank of old Taddle Creek outside Hart House, he was wearing a mask from the *commedia*, the face of *Il Dottore*, the experienced man whose knowledge has gone amiss. He was tacking up a poster advertising for players who wanted to take the people's art and voice into the busy streets and crowded downtown avenues of Toronto to delight those who hunger to know what lies behind all the masked faces they pass without a second thought, and to teach what it is to love the world as one would a wild and hopeless dream.

ACKNOWLEDGEMENTS

"Cantique de Jean Racine, "The Slithy Toves," "Tilting," and "Chaconne" appeared in the *CVC Anthologies* published by Exile Editions. The stories were also shortlisted for the Carter V. Cooper Prizes.

"Balcony Scene" appeared in *The Write Launch* (US).

"Saving Selah" appeared in *Griffel* (US).

"Magnetic Dogs" appeared in *Rumble Fish* (US).

""Leipszthou" appeared in *The Spectatorial*.

"The River Tax" appeared in the anthology *Water* edited by Nina Munteanu.

"At Dawn" appeared in *Variety Pack* (US).

"The Kids" appeared in *The Puritan*, was runner-up for the Thomas Morton Fiction Prize, and was shortlisted for the Tom Gallon Trust Fiction Prize (UK) given by the Society of Authors.

"Dragon Blood" was longlisted for the 2021 Carter V. Cooper Prize.

Thank you to the Ontario Arts Council and the Recommender Grant Program. The support was greatly appreciated.

The author wishes to thank Benjamin Ghan, Michael O'Connor, Michael Callaghan, Exile Editions, Nina Munteanu, Colin Carberry, Veronica Garces Flores, Antonia Facciponte, Marty Gervais, and the Archives of the Canadian Imperial Bank of Commerce in Toronto for their advice, assistance, and feedback. A very special thank you to Michael Mirolla, the editor of this book, Rafael Chimicatti, Connie Guzzo-McParland, Margo Lapierre, and Anna van Valkenburg of Guernica Editions for their support and belief in these stories. And thank you to Dr. Carolyn Meyer, Margaret Meyer, Katie Meyer, Kerry Johnston, and the author's writing companion Daisy Meyer.

AUTHOR BIO

BRUCE MEYER is author of more than seventy books of poetry, short stories, flash fiction, and literary non-fiction. His stories have won or been shortlisted for such prizes as the Carter V. Cooper Prize for Short Fiction, the Thomas Morton Prize for Fiction, the Tom Gallon Trust Prize for Fiction, the Fish Short Story Prize, among others. His broadcasts on The Great Books with Michael Enright of CBC Radio One remain the network's bestselling spoken-word audio series. He has been Visiting Writer/Writer-in-Residence at Dobie House in the University of Texas at Austin, and the University of Southern Mississippi at Hattiesburg. He is professor of Communications and Liberal Studies at Georgian College in Barrie, Ontario, and has taught at Victoria College in the University of Toronto, Laurentian University, the University of Windsor, Skidmore College, Humber College, and Seneca College. He was the inaugural Poet Laureate of the City of Barrie from 2010 to 2014. His most recent collections of short fiction are *A Feast of Brief Hopes* (Guernica Editions, 2018), *Down in the Ground* (Guernica Editions, 2020), *The Hours: Stories from a Pandemic* (Ace of Swords Publishing, 2021), and *Toast Soldiers* (Crow's Nest Books, 2021). He lives in Barrie with his wife, retired CBC journalist and researcher Kerry Johnston, the daughter Katie Meyer, and his pal Daisy Meyer.